People of Akiane

Book One

Pegasus Colony

By Phyllis Moore

Myth Ridǝr
Publishǝrs

Novels are a ride into another world.

Published by Myth Rider Publishers

Library of Congress Control Number 2014917877

Moore, Phyllis

Pegasus Colony / by Phyllis Moore — 1ˢᵗ U.S. ed.

Summary: After 300 years of nonattendance, Lieutenant Jessica M. Hewitt is ordered to establish relations with Earth's first galactic colony and convince the people they are still an Earth colony.

ISBN 978-0-9907091-0-7
1. Science Fiction — Fiction. 2. Soft Science Fiction — Fiction. 4. Pegasus Colony — Fiction.

First U.S.A. Edition 2014
Typeset by Cheryl Barr
Printed in U.S.A. by Rapit Printing & Promotional Products
300 books

Myth Rider Publishers
MythRiderPublishers.com
infor@mythriderpublishers

Acknowledgments

It is said that writing is a lonely profession. That is somewhat true. There are many lonely hours of writing and rewriting, but without the help of friends, family, fellow authors, and professional help, books would never come into existence.

I'm not going to give every name that has had an influence on the writing of *Pegasus Colony*, but I will name those close to the end who encourage me not to give up.

Coworkers: Andy Dreissig, Bill Codere, and Justin Campbell

Fellow authors: Cassandra Amesley, Ronald Peterson and John Palmer

Special thanks to North Star Press of St. Cloud, MN. Without their encouragement my manuscript might never have been completed.

And Patricia Morris worked with me in the last rewrite of my manuscript, editing of the story and helped smoothed out the rough edges.

Thanks to all,
Phyllis Moore

CAPTAIN'S LOG

WSC EAGLE
Captain Richard Fontner
Year 2144, November 1

Folded space is a success. We have traveled faster than light. It only took twelve years to travel twenty-seven light-years to the planet Akiane within the Pegasus Constellation.

The star of this system shines bright. Five planets orbit it, including our destination planet, Akiane.

We have been in orbit around Akiane for nine days, running tests and sending out probes.

One probe orbits this system's star and has been recording the star's activity. The solar flares are amazing. We have witnessed some astonishing coronal mass ejections, larger than anything Earth's sun can produce. Eruptions from the huge star has set off a series of plasma waves 25 million meters in height, traveling millions of kilometers across the physical surface of the star.

Specific details are in the science officer's logs.

One probe orbits the planet Akiane. Several were sent to the surface of the planet to gather information about the soil, snow, ice, and open ocean water. Except for the equator and areas around active volcanoes, some of which are near water, the oceans are covered with six meters of ice.

The planet was quiet when we first arrived, but now as a giant gas planet approaches, many volcanoes are suddenly active.

We continually attempt to stream data back to World Space Coalition, though the communications officers say the enormous sun flares are interfering with our transmissions. The magnetic charge is too high for our transmissions to get through to WSC.

Science can cure the common cold, but not override electrical interference of plasma flares. We may have to retransmit everything again after the star has quieted.

Akiane and one gas planet the size of Saturn orbits their star elliptically. Every eleven years their orbits cross. We have arrived in time to study the phenomenon. Those back at WSC will be delighted with this new information to study.

Captain Fontner's Office

The captain's office door unceremoniously flew open.

"Captain!" the first mate called.

"Computer, stop and close." The holographic computer screen disappeared. "Yes, Commander?"

"We've lost control." The commander's usual calm demeanor had crumbled. She slouched in the doorway. Worry lines etched her young face. Her hands trembled.

The captain tensed. "Lost control of what?" he asked.

"All of it, Sir." Her voice shook. "Everything. We've lost the ship."

Captain Fontner stared at her. "How is that possible?" he asked weakly.

"I ..." Before she could answer, the ship swayed.

Like an old eighteenth century windjammer, the *Eagle* gently creaked and groaned.

The commander looked up and around searching for the source of the noise. "A space ship doesn't make those kinds of noises," she said. Tears of fear rolled down her cheeks.

"Commander, control yourself," the captain said.

The creaks and groans became louder.

She was right. Something was wrong; whatever was happening, it wasn't normal. Captain Fontner's head pounded with anxiety.

The ship tilted.

The first mate lost her footing and disappeared behind the wall. Captain Fontner gripped the armrests of his chair.

The ship tilted in the opposite direction. The commander slid past the doorway.

Eagle seemed to twist in awkward angles then dropped several meters.

Fontner hit the ceiling. When *Eagle* righted herself, Fontner dropped belly first onto his desk with a "Humph."

He first heard the impenetrable glass in the bridge observatory window crack. Then the window in his office did the same.

He thought of his wife and children. He would not get to say good-bye.

In the next instant, everything flipped upside down.

Screams of fear came from the bridge as people were tossed about like rag dolls.

The captain's shoulder dislocated as he slammed back into the ceiling. *Eagle* tilted to one side. Fontner slid toward the window in his office. Bits of glass disappeared as they were sucked out. Oxygen whistled as it escaped into space.

The window twisted. He knew it was illogical, but Fontner felt his blood start to boil as the vacuum of space invaded his office.

WSC Eagle exploded.

Chapter 1

Lieutenant Jessica Hewitt
The New Assignment

THREE HUNDRED sixteen years after Falcon, Eagle and Hawk launched ... the year was 2447.

I was never supposed to set foot on Akiane, nor did I want to. I mean, why would I? It was an ice planet, so cold that in winter a thick sheet of ice covered the salty ocean.

I'm not sure why I joined the space program, moved to World Space Coalition's moon base or why I volunteered for the Akiane Project.

World Space Coalition was a partnership of the world's nations that combined their financial resources and their scientists to explore and study space, and establish off-world colonies.

WSC built its headquarters on Earth's moon so no one country could lay claim to it. After they colonized Mars and Europa, they wanted to expand beyond Earth's solar system. The first galactic colony was to be in the Pegasus Constellation on the planet Akiane.

The colonists were to land and establish the colony in the year 2144, but WSC lost contact with the colony. After repeated tries, it was thought everyone had died and because WSC didn't want to risk any more lives, the project was abandoned.

A little over 297 years later, in the year 2429, to the astonishment of Earth, WSC and it's colonies, it was discovered that not only had the colonists survived, but they had procreated.

WSC was excited to reclaim its colony and provide any assistance needed to its people. It took three years to prepare *WSC Britannia* and her crew for the journey.

I wanted to escape my life on Earth. I wanted to get away from overbearing media and my dad's obsessive fans.

With all the excitement of reestablishing Earth's first galactic colony, I thought I'd be lost in the shuffle. And I was … at first. I should have stayed on the base.

What I wanted was a hole to crawl into and to be forgotten so I could forget my life, forget me, forget what happened to Dad.

I signed on to the mission to get even farther away from everything — Earth, family, myself. Six years, five months to reach Akiane, seven days layover, then six years, five months for the return trip. By the time I returned to Earth, everything would be different. I'd start my life over and this time, I'd get it right.

Somehow I became the focus of media attention throughout the entire world. My name would be firmly set in history. I'm still not sure how it happened.

At the time, I was Ensign Jessica M. Hewitt, Communications Tech. My assignment was to sit at the radio in Command Center on the Transport Ship *WSC Britannia* and wait for messages from World Space Coalition, which I would relay to Captain Norris. I'd then relay his reply back. In fiction, working in command is exciting; in reality, it's brain numbing.

My other job was to listen for space anomalies. Space is silent. No, not silent; it's dead. My job was to listen in case there was something out there, in case *something* happened.

Nothing happened. Ever.

Then something did happen that changed everything.

While at my station, in 2447, August 27, I received the first of five messages from the colony on Akiane.

The first message read:

We have no need of your presence. We are not your colony.

Captain Norris apologized, but stated, "We were already on our way." His orders did not allow him to turn around and return to Earth.

Each message over the next two years was increasingly more forceful in its demands that we turn back, which made Captain Norris all the more determined to continue on.

Then the messages stopped. I thought the colony had resigned to our coming.

Exactly four years, eight months, one day, and fifteen hours after leaving Earth, Captain Norris called me into his office. He sat straight-backed, with his forearms resting on the desk. He didn't look happy.

I could think of nothing I'd done wrong that would have so soured his mood.

"What did you say to those people on Akiane?" His voice was calm, but challenging. He stared at me over his hawk-like nose.

I had no idea what he was talking about. "Excuse me, Sir?"

He didn't offer me a chair or say, "At ease." I stood, arms at my side, feet together, and head held high, looking straight ahead at the blank wall behind him.

"You received several communications from the colony on Akiane. Is that correct?" he asked.

"Yes, Sir, I did. Five messages in all, Sir," I said, still not sure where he was headed.

"With whom did you communicate?" He was obviously irritated. Clearly, I *had* done something wrong.

"I don't know, Sir. They sent text. I spoke to no one, Sir."

"You must have spoken to someone, Ensign. Made a friend with *someone*," he insisted.

"Friend, Sir? I don't understand. Did I offend someone, Sir?"

He rose and rested his hands on the desk so his face was directly in my line of sight. His stormy gray eyes locked onto mine. "If you were unhappy at your post, you should have come to me instead of trying to go over my head, Ensign." He said each word clearly and distinctly.

I couldn't ask him directly what the problem was. There were rules and a pecking order, and at that moment, I was the one being pecked. I bit my tongue and waited for him to get to the point.

"Someone from Akiane has requested you. By name."

I blinked. What? "Me, Sir?" I gulped. "I can't imagine why, Sir."

His hairy brows furled. "I have relayed all messages from the colony and the request for your presence to WSC. They have made their decision." He paused.

"But I never received such a message." If I had, I would have refused the request.

"Some one spoke to the on-duty tech while you were off duty." He made it sound like I was to blame. He straightened to his full height, while he glared.

"Sir?" I weakly asked.

"Seems someone on Akiane likes you."

"Sir?" I could think of nothing else to say.

"They want a negotiator. You've been requested by name. WSC has agreed."

"Negotiator? Me? Negotiate what?" I was so surprised, I forgot myself. I relaxed my stance.

He glared.

I snapped to attention.

"Sir," I finished.

He continued. "Since you've read most of the communications from Akiane, you are already aware that the colonists don't want us on their little planet," Captain Norris stated. "They insist the planet belongs to them." He snorted as if their feelings were not a consideration. "World Space Coalition claims all natural resources and scientific finds, as well as the planet and the inhabitants, as its property. WSC did, after all, plan the project, train the crew, and pay for the original expedition, as well as this one."

He focused his full attention on me as though I'd created the problem entirely by myself. "The colonists won't even discuss it with me. I've tried. It seems they want *you* to open the dialogue."

What? Open a dialogue? I barely knew how to carry a normal conversation.

"Once you're on Akiane, you'll have seven Earth-Standard days, the length of our layover, to accomplish your mission," he barked.

What mission? I wanted to scream.

"Your mission is to convince them they are Earth's colony," he said as if he heard my thoughts.

"And if I don't finish in the allotted time, Sir?"

"Then you will stay on Akiane until you do complete your mission, and only then will you return on the next ship."

"But, Sir, the next transport is two years behind us!" I didn't want to stay on Akiane for two whole years.

"Correct!" he replied with a little too much enthusiasm. "So don't fail."

Captain Norris shifted his stance.

"You've been promoted. Pack your things. You will spend the rest of the trip living with the civilians. They will help you with your studies of Akiane, so you will be properly prepared when you arrive."

"Sir?" I was confused. I couldn't think clearly.

"Your station on the bridge has been assigned to another," he said.

He was exiling me.

I'd done nothing wrong. "Sir, permission to speak."

"No."

I couldn't even defend myself.

He sat down and leaned back in his chair, placed one hand on the armrest and the other on his knee. "There is one good thing to come from all of this."

Good? I wanted to yell at him, *What possible good?* Instead I said, "Sir?"

"You'll be famous. Every person on Earth will know your name."

My knees turned to jelly. I thought they'd give out. I became light-headed. I almost lost my balance.

My father was a well-known, and well-loved, author. His death was headline news, which brought my life, alongside his, into intense media interest. Practically everywhere I went, someone either took my photograph or asked questions about me and Dad. Okay, so the entire world wasn't interested, just his fans. It's just that there were so many of them. I hated it.

My family was just as bad, five aunts and uncles, all married, thirty-five first cousins, all of which wanted to console me and felt they needed to repeatedly check in on me to see how I was dealing with Dad's death. They drove me crazy.

I joined Space Force mainly because the paparazzi and fans are not allowed on the moon, and family contact was limited. I hoped that the twelve years and ten months journey to and from another planet would be long enough for everyone to move on and forget about me.

The captain's words, "Every person on Earth will know your name," vibrated in my head.

I'd become Earth's representative to their long-lost sisters and brothers on Akiane. Now the entire world would want to know everything about me. I would become a worldwide household name. So much for anonymity.

"You'll be responsible for the reunion of two worlds," the captain said.

I lowered my head to look at him. "Why me, Sir? What if I fail?"

He grimaced. "Then you will be responsible for Earth's first galactic military takeover. The Akiane Project is an effort to rejoin two worlds. If those people are unwilling to accept their status as colonists, then they will be taken by force," he said.

No pressure there.

Like any other empire builder, WSC was not about to give up its colony. You'd think Earth's history regarding imperialism would have taught the bureaucrats something. I guess not.

"For the rest of our journey, your new orders are to study and learn all you can about Akiane and its people."

I tried to process what he was saying. For the next thirteen months and nine days, I was to study a planet and its people. I'd have no other responsibilities.

I'd thought communications was boring. Now I'd truly know what a dreary existence was.

Damn protocol. "But, Sir, why me?" I desperately asked. "Surely, there must be someone, almost anyone, who is better qualified. I don't know how to deal with people from another planet, much less negotiate peace." Then as an afterthought I said, "Sir."

"Your name is on the orders," he said, settling the matter, and for him it did. "Once you're on Akiane, someone will contact you."

To say I was surprised at my promotion was more than an understatement. This was not one that I wanted nor was it one I could refuse. Once I'd signed the contract, my life belonged to Space Force. If they gave me an assignment, I had no choice but to obey. There was nothing I could do to get out of it. Nothing I could say to change my orders.

The captain picked an envelope off his desk and handed to me.

I opened it and pulled out a single piece of paper. On the top of the page, bold letters said: "Lieutenant Jessica M. Hewitt." Everything else was a blur.

CAPTAIN'S LOG

WSC Falcon
Captain Faris Assetti
On approach to Akiane
Year 2144, November 1

> *We had just arrived in Akiane's star system, when we saw the explosion.*

> *Eighty good men and women were lost on* Eagle. *There was nothing we could do to save any of them.*

On the bridge

Falcon's crew stood or sat in stunned silence.

"What just happened?" Assetti quietly asked.

No one moved.

"Ensign!" she demanded.

Ensign Kawn jumped. He shook his head, pulled his eyes from the window, and concentrated on the screen before him. His hand slowly raised then seemed to drift to the console.

"Ensign?" Assetti yelled.

"Yes, Captain. I…" His limp fingers pushed buttons. "It's the gas planet, Mum. Both planets are in an elliptical orbit. Their paths cross every eleven years."

"Yes, Ensign Kawn, this we already know."

Kawn bowed his head. He pushed a few more buttons then said, "Together the planets create a gravitational pull. The force pulled *Eagle* apart."

"Thank you," Assetti said.

"Mum?"

"Ensign?"

"We have picked up all data *Eagle* was streaming to WSC."

"Save it. We'll deal with it later."

Chapter 2

Adumie
One Last Inspection

ART RENDERINGS told of feelings, fears, and hopes; of life and death, hunters killing tupilak, fishers bringing in nets full of fish, Kahair's rising, and the Storm's destruction. The colorfully painted walls of this family unit had been a testimony to those who had once lived here. It had been a place to come and remember the existence of those now dead. All 127 of them.

Adumie placed a hand on the freshly painted white wall. He picked this room because it was the most isolated. *No, that wasn't the real reason,* he admitted to himself.

He picked this room because Petra had lived here. He'd hoped that by having the walls painted and the scenes erased, she'd cease to haunt his memories. Already, he regretted his decision.

The walls of this family unit had once been filled with scribbles by the youngest occupants, clumsy stick figures drawn by older children, and elegant renderings by adults. All of it, even Petra's sketches, had been painted over, and were gone forever.

Each family unit had their own living quarters, and each family told their history on their walls from the first colonists to the present.

At one time the Community was filled with healthy family units. When the main buildings became too crowded, meetings were held to determine how the Community would expand.

Petra's family unit was the first to build a room outside of the main buildings. They chose a space between two exit tunnels and enclosed it in to make it habitable. It was such a success that other families eagerly considered construction on their new quarters. Petra's family was planning their next expansion so they would have more room to grow.

Then the sickness overtook them.

Slowly over the next years, dread descended and construction stopped as the sickness spread. Whole family units were wiped out, including Petra's.

After 21 years, Petra's face and memories were as fresh to Adumie as though she still lived.

He sighed. Walking around the sterile room, he determined it ready for the Invaders from Earth to inhabit. Those of World Space Coalition claimed all of Akiane, including its people, as its property. They were not interested in Petra or her drawing; they came to dominate. Occupying this room was just the beginning.

Several times a message had been sent demanding the ship *Britannia* return to Earth. Each time the captain refused. Finally Jecidia spoke to someone requesting a priest.

Arrogant Earth Invaders ordered rooms for working and for living. What kind of work did they intend to do? They had no right.

Adumie would not give them two family rooms. He would not erase the memory of another family to appease the Intruders. This one unit would be enough. A wall had been erected to divide the room in half. They would work on one side of the wall and sleep on the other side.

Petra's family had already installed an *ashag* for the growing of food. There was also kitchen off to the side. Good. Adumie did not want Intruders wandering Endurance. This one space contained all that was needed for them to live. There was no reason for them to leave this area.

Scuffling feet caused Adumie to turn just in time to see the back of Nu Venia's head dart around the corner; Cameron was near. Those two were rarely apart. It was difficult to tell who was raising whom.

When Cameron did appeared, it was Jecidia who walked at his side. No doubt Nu Venia lingered outside, out of sight, just as Adumie preferred it.

Jecidia had shriveled in size. Why had he come all this way? Walking was no easy task for him. His long black braids were just starting to streak with white strands. Light gray blotches were beginning to appear on his cheeks. Eventually, his skin would turn ashen, signaling that death was near.

In contrast, Cameron stood tall and straight, his skin free of blotches, his braids lava black. *If God was truly just, Cameron would be ill, not Jecidia*, Adumie thought.

"World Space Coalition just contacted us." Cameron's piercing voice bounced off the empty walls. "They have entered our star system. They are within days of landing."

Cameron looked forward to their arrival just as much as Adumie dreaded their coming.

Jecidia moved around the room like a chovis snuffling corners. He placed a hand on one of the walls. His body sagged at the realization that the renderings were forever lost. After a

20

moment of silence, he turned from the wall to examine the rest of the area.

He looked through the far door to view the beds. He crossed the room to the *ashag* then peeked in the kitchen. Slowly he came to stand with Adumie and Cameron.

"Has one considered the sharing of meat?" Jecidia asked.

"Meat?" Adumie asked, irritated.

"Yes, if we eat meat, it is only logical they do also. We are not so dissimilar as that," Cameron said, as if Adumie was a child and should know such things.

"We are different! And when they learn how different, World Space Coalition will again be abandoning us," Adumie declared.

"But if they can help us…"

With a wave of his hand, Adumie cut Cameron off. That one needed to learn respect for leadership and not be so contrary.

"World Space Coalition comes to claim our world as their property, to claim *us* as their property! They have no concern as to how we persevered for all this time," Adumie angrily declared. "We built Endurance without their help. Endurance is ours. It belongs to us. They have no right to demand ownership. They abandoned us! Those of Earth do not come to help. Nor are they sent by God."

"Then why come now," Cameron demanded, "if not being sent by God?"

There was no explanation for the Intruders coming. Adumie only knew it was too late. "This conversation is of no use. There is already agreement to speak to the ship's priest," Adumie said, "but that one is from Earth. Much is not expected."

"God is the same throughout the universe," Jecidia said, reverently.

21

"The ship's priest must also speak for God, just as our priests do," Cameron agreed.

Cameron was young and naïve; Jecidia had become old. Both had hope. Adumie knew better.

"Are we to hunt for them? How far must our servitude extend?" Adumie snorted. "Let them hunt their own meat."

Cameron was concerned for their comfort; would welcome them, give them a place to live, food to eat, beg their help.

Adumie would have them build their own habitat on the far side of Akiane.

"Will they have knowledge to hunt tupilak?" Cameron asked in protest.

Adumie said nothing.

Cameron insisted. "The tupilak could easily kill them."

If only the tupilak would kill all of them, Adumie thought. He grunted.

"If one wishes them to live separate from us, it would be unwise to allow them to roam where they please," Jecidia spoke softly.

It was difficult to ignore Jecidia's words of wisdom. He was right. Adumie did not want Intruders walking about Akiane, observing what they were not meant to see.

"We will hunt for them," Adumie conceded, with a low growl. "Shall we also cook the meat for them?"

"Will those of Earth go to the waters to receive tupilak?" Jecidia asked.

"No," Adumie said, a little too quickly. "Keep them from open water. Hang the meat. The fur is ours."

Nodding, Jecidia said, "Hooks will be installed and meat will be hanging before they arrive."

"Are you satisfied now, Cameron?" Adumie asked.

"It is not a matter of my being satisfied," Cameron said. "It is a matter of what is right, Adumie."

"Cameron, if things were right, we would not be dying, and those from Earth would not be invading us. Why will you not see the inevitable?"

"Why are you resigned to it? Where is your hope?"

"Hope?" Adumie spat the word in frustration. "Cameron, we are a dying people." *Petra is already dead*! he wanted to shout.

"One's hope is in God's love. God will provide for us. We will not die," Cameron retorted. "We must pray those of Earth are here to help us."

"Prayer." Adumie almost spat that word too. "Have you been praying?" He knew the answer. Cameron always prayed. "And how have your prayers been answered?"

"Sometimes in God's immeasurable wisdom, response comes in unforeseen ways," Cameron declared.

Adumie used to believe. Now he ached with the bitterness of knowing unanswered prayers. He was High Priest. He was to the one who spoke God's Word to the Community. Yet when he prayed, God did not answer. He had begged. He had sought with all his heart. Instead of a promise of hope, he received disappointment, and loss of faith.

"Sometimes God's response is, 'No,' because He has larger plans," Adumie said bitterly.

"What larger plan?" Cameron asked. "Does God speak to you of such a plan?"

"He is calling us to Himself. We are a people meant to die." Long ago, Adumie had concluded this was the only explanation for God's silence. *What other reason could there be for so many deaths?*

Cameron seemed genuinely shocked at this revelation. "Why would God call us to die? What is God's reasoning for such an unloving act?"

There was only one logical explanation for their deaths at this time, Adumie knew. "God is protecting us from the worse fate that those of Earth bring." How could he explain to one who refused to understand? "God has decided," Adumie said gruffly. "Those of Earth cannot change divine destiny, nor can you."

Chapter 3

Rona Montgomery
First Glimpse

GRINNING LIKE a possum eating a sweet potato, Rona Montgomery still couldn't believe it. She was a small town girl from rural Georgia. Two of her sisters took over their parents' hydro farm, a 30 acre building six stories tall. They could keep one tomato plant alive and producing fruit for years. To her sisters' disappointment, for they wanted her as a partner, Rona wasn't interested in the molecular structure of produce. She was more interested in the molecular structure of human beings.

She was chosen from thousands of applicants to study the DNA of people who had been isolated from the rest of humanity for 318 years.

All her life, she'd worked hard and as the highest ranked in her college class, she graduated summa cum laude.

As an intern at an Atlanta based genetic company, she was first to arrive and last to leave. Once her internship was up, the company offered her a job, head of her own project. She turned it down, moved to WSC Moon Base for a chance to be a part of the Akiane Project.

Since she was ten, she'd been awestruck by how two parents contributed their genes in the creation of an entirely new individual; a science that she later learned was called transformation genetics.

Through the generations, minute changes, or mutations, provided a natural evolutionary shift in human development. The broadest example was how the human race had divided into indigenous groups such as Asian, Western European, African, Middle Eastern, and many tribal people. The world population might not be as visually distinctive as it once was, but indigenous DNA markers had not changed.

Rona joined the expedition for the opportunity to study population genetics in the people of Akiane, who had been isolated from the rest of the human race, without any fresh genetic input. She wanted to learn how much their DNA had changed from their Earth cousins, if at all.

A generation is determined by the common birthing age of a woman in her culture. In past centuries, when there were still third-world countries, where child mortality was high, the common age for girls to become mothers was in their early teens. Now the normal age on Earth was thirty. If it were the same on Akiane, only eleven or twelve generations had passed. Not a long time for evolution or for any major mutation differences.

It also fascinated Rona that 99 to 95% of DNA was exactly the same between any two human individuals, and yet, from that small amount of difference, there was no end to physical variations. As she looked around the *WSC Britannia's* Eatery, she noted how each person in the room was unique. That was what she would study, that minute difference between Earth inhabitants and her cousins on Akiane.

Rona was honored by her position and as nervous as a goldfish swimming in an aquarium being s by a house cat. She had accepted the responsibilities of a major project, one that would be carefully watched and scrutinized by the entire scientific geneticist community. It was important that she not fail.

Her thoughts were interrupted by the ship's vibration. As if the space transport was an airplane caught in wind turbulence, the ship slipped out of folded space with an intense shake. It only lasted for a few seconds, but the effect was similar to her home being shook by winds from a violent hurricane.

A hologram of the captain appeared in the middle of the Eatery cafeteria, as it did throughout the entire ship. The captain's image did not appear in private rooms, only his voice filtered in, but in the Eatery, he suddenly appeared to be standing amidst them.

The image turned as if he were looking at everyone. "This is Captain Norris. We have just entered Kahair's planetary system." He paused for effect. "We're here, folks."

The room erupted with applause.

Rona and Jess were just finishing their breakfasts. Jess was the only one in the room who remained silent. She sat straight-backed as if at attention. Jess always dressed in her blue Space Force uniform, even when off duty. One would think she didn't have any other clothes, but since they were roommates, Rona knew better.

Chow Lu came running into the cafeteria with her chin-length black hair bouncing about her face. Her hot pink jeans accented her youthful nature. She plopped down in the seat next to Rona.

Lu was Rona's project partner. Together, they would unravel scientific finds regarding Akiane's human genome.

Lu had finished her master's degree at thirteen, applied for the Akiane Project, and was accepted. She'd completed her first PhD in Genetics, within a year while training for the project.

While on the ship, she and Rona worked on their PhDs in Microbiology together.

Lu was now twenty years old. And even though she was as talented as everyone else on the scientific teams, she was oddly awestruck by the brilliance of those around her, which often caused her to stutter when she was nervous.

Her childlike enthusiasm was exceptionally high this day. "We're here," she squealed. "I can't believe it! After six and a half years of traveling though space, we've finally arrived."

It would have been disappointing to sit through this exciting event with Jess and her sour mood. Rona was glad Lu had joined them. Now she could better enjoy the moment and shed her usual level-headedness.

Jess took a sip from her third cup of hot herbal tea. It wasn't calming her nerves. She gripped the mug with both hands as if it kept her from jumping up and running away.

But her sour mood wasn't going to dampen the moment. "Takes the cake, doesn't it?" Rona sat up straight and strained her neck, pushed her long black locks behind her ears to get a better view out the observatory window.

Three large windows wrapped around the room, giving a close up view of one slice of the Pegasus Constellation.

"Which one do you think is Akiane?" Lu asked loudly over the chatter in the crowded room. She adjusted her chair so it sat at an angle to the table and she could fully face the window.

It wouldn't be long before she repositioned herself. Lu was always on the move.

Seven planets orbited the star Kahair, but from this distance, they could only see two of the planets.

"I think it's the smallest dot, closest to the star." Jess knew which planet it was. She had just spent the last year and a half studying Akiane, but she enjoyed teasing Lu and thought her a bit naïve despite her intelligence.

Lu frowned. "Jessica, Akiane would melt and dry up if it were that close to its star."

"Oh," Jess said, "then it must be the largest of Kahair's seven planets. That one there." She pointed to the pale, a virtual baseball-size sphere.

"Jessica," said Lu. "Why would you think that? You know full well which one it is." She looked dismayed that Jess could be so wrong about which planet Akiane was.

"Jess," Rona gently rebuked.

Then Lu got it. "You're joking." She dropped her head in embarrassment. "Why do you always do that?"

"Because you're so easy, Lu," Jess said.

"You must think me simple."

Jess shrugged. "Not simple, just fun to tease."

Lu had been thirteen when she left home. She'd spent her entire teen years either on WSC or on *Britannia*. She hadn't experienced the world like Jess had, so yes, she was a bit naive. She often took everything literally.

In may ways she still held on to her child like innocence. Everything to her was new and exciting. Sometimes that enthusiasm got on Jess' nerves. That's when Jess would tease her not so much for fun but to calm Lu down.

"So how are my favorite women?" Jorg Krause slipped into the seat next to Jess. He wrapped an arm around her shoulders and squeezed. "Hey, Jessie." He grinned, exposing his dimples.

At seeing him, Jess brightened for just a moment, as if she'd forgotten her troubles. But almost as quickly, that which haunted her rolled back in and the smile faded.

Rona had the feeling Jess held a dark secret that ate at her, but when Rona tried to pry it our of her, she just clamed up.

Jorg greeted everyone as if they were his best friend whom he hadn't seen in at least a week. On the *Britannia,* with limited spaces where civilians could freely roam, it was easy to run into the same person five or six times day. Still, Jorg greeted each one in the same manner, with genuine affection.

Reaching across the table, he gripped Lu's hand and held it with both of his. "How are you doing, Lu?"

"Better than fantastic." The tip of her tongue popped out then quickly slipped back in as she squealed again. "We're actually here!"

Jorg chuckled. He never made fun of her youthfulness. Instead, he was enchanted by it.

He released Lu's hand to hold Rona's in the same manner. "How are you, Rona?"

"As excited as a bee in a spring flower patch." Rona squeezed his hands and looked deeply into his eyes, hoping he'd get the hint. He didn't.

Rona liked Jorg, a lot. Not just because he was 2 meters tall, with blond hair, and brown eyes. He was brilliant and genuinely cared about people. Instead of talking only about himself, he wanted to know about the other person. He was comfortable to be around and easy to talk to, unlike so many others.

But he never noticed Rona's interest. Even though she was almost as tall as he was, with long black hair, blemish-free velvety brown skin, midnight eyes, was also easy to talk to, brilliant, and his mental match.

For a while Rona thought they were two peas in a pod. They were good friends, just not as close as she would have liked.

"Where have you been?" she asked.

Jorg released her hands and turned his attention to the window. "Running."

"Without us?" Jess asked.

He shrugged as he casually leaned back in his chair and rested one arm on the back of her chair. "Can't a man run on his own?"

Jess leaned forward to clear his arm, but she didn't move out of the reach of his fingers as they played with the material of her sleeve.

"You just wanted to run without us slowing you down. Well, I guess Rona and I will have to run without you," she said.

Jorg laughed. "I guess that will show me."

Jess gave him a smirky little smile. It didn't matter if he'd run without them, when Jess and Rona went for their run, he'd be there with them. Or rather, he'd be there with Jess.

She refused to believe Jorg cared about her, and insisted that he was just being nice, like he was to everyone. Yes, he made everyone feel special, but Rona knew only Jess was truly special to him.

He jokingly asked, "Did I miss anything?"

"Oh Jorg, you rarely miss much. Don't worry, we haven't orbited yet," Jess informed him. "We can't even see the planet yet."

"Good, I'd hate to have come all this way and miss the big event."

"There." Lu pointed across the room to the cafeteria window. "I can see Akiane."

"Where?" Jorg asked.

"Squint," Jess said with a hint of sarcasm.

He leaned closer to the window and into Jess. She didn't move.

"Oh, yeah." Jorg squinted his eyes until they were thin slits. "I see it."

"No you can't," Jess said.

He couldn't. No one could. Akiane was still an indistinguishable speck against a starry backdrop.

In a demure tone, he said, "But, Jessie, I can."

She looked at him then swung the back of her hand in his direction.

He ducked pretending she hit him, when in fact she had no intention of touching him. He flashed a big smile at her, deepening his dimples, and wrinkling his freckled nose.

Jess shook her head.

Times like this, Rona wondered what Jorg saw in Jess. She could be so serious and him so playful.

Rona fidgeted a little as she stared out of the cafeteria window. This had been a long trip. She felt like a bear waking from too long of a hibernation. She was ready to wake up herself and leave the cave, or in this case, exit the ship. Like everyone else, she was eager to set foot on the alien planet and get to work.

Except, of course Jess, who just wanted to go home.

When she and Rona had first sat down for breakfast, the Eatery was almost empty, but after the captain's announcement, the room quickly filled.

The Eatery consisted of three levels of tables and chairs; each level descended from the bar area, to the observatory window. The bar stools and every chair in the room was filled. Like a flock of birds settling in, people sat on the edge of each level and along the window's frame. All were patiently waiting for their destination to come into view.

A white ball suddenly popped into view. The room again vibrated with cheering, clapping of hands and laughter.

"There it is," Lu squealed, ecstatically. "This time I *can* see it." She could barely contain herself as she bounced in her chair like a jumping bean.

"Yep," Jorg confirmed, loudly.

Kahair bathed the planet with its light.

"Akiane sparkles like a giant crystal snowball," Lu observed.

"It looks cold," Jess said, her mood darkening.

"Well, Akiane is encased in meters of ice and snow." Jorg laughed.

"Yes, I know. I've been studying all about it. Can't wait to see it up close," she said in her usual cynical tone.

Jess had grown up in northern Minnesota and despised cold weather. When she talked about her teen years, which she rarely did, she spoke of blizzards and days being confined in her small cabin.

When she was thirteen, she was lost just outside her home in a blizzard. If her father hadn't found her, she would have died within minutes.

Now her orders were sending her to a place where the cold made Minnesota's winters seem like spring in the Bahamas. The fact that she'd be living in a warm, cozy habitat hadn't eased her mood.

"Think they're as excited as we are?" Lu asked.

"Who?" Jess asked.

"The colonists." Lu sounded as though they were headed for a family reunion.

"I have it on good authority that they don't want us to land on their planet," Jess said. "That's why I'm being dispatched to the colony, remember? To talk them into welcoming us."

"They've been separated from us for 318 years," Lu said. "Why would they not welcome us?"

"Because, according to them, we abandoned them 318 years ago," Jess said.

With a puppy dog look, Lu turned her dark eyes toward Jess. "They weren't abandoned, Jessica. WSC lost communications and thought everyone had died."

"Nevertheless, that's how they see it," Jess said.

"Jessica, WSC sent three robotic ships so they could return to Earth, but they didn't," Lu persisted. "They didn't even send word they were still alive."

"I can't speak to that, Lu. I only know what they think," Jess said.

"But all of Earth is excited."

"I'm not the one who needs convincing, Lu. I'm just telling you how they see it," Jess said. "I received their requests that we turn back. They don't want us here."

Rona hoped Jess was wrong. If not, it could make her research very difficult.

Chapter 4

Lieutenant Jessica Hewitt
Shuttle Ride

THE *BRITANNIA* had four individual shuttles. Her crew had already brought the scientific equipment, personal luggage and cooking utensils to everyone's respective offices, living quarters and kitchen. They had also dropped off a small solar powered, hovercraft for the geological teams, and an aquatic craft for the oceanographer team.

Each shuttle carried 20 people, and it would take six trips to bring all 103 of us to the planet. I was in the third shuttle.

Not one scientist sat quietly in his or her seat. As soon as we entered Akiane's atmosphere, they all crowded behind the pilot to look out the window. They could have seen just as well from their seats, but they were too excited to sit.

I sat alone. I was always alone. Set apart. Different.

"Jessie, don't sit back there," Jorg called to me. "Come up here."

I felt inadequate next to the scientists. That was the real reason I rarely participated in their leisure time. They were brilliant. Each had multiple PhDs. I couldn't keep up with most of the technical terms of their conversations. They were confident of who they were and what they wanted out of life, and were a constant remember of my lack of confidence and the lack of a direction for my life.

With a reluctant sign, I stood and slipped through the group to stand at Jorg's side. I tried not to think about my inadequacies, and looked out the window instead.

As we flew toward the surface, I had to admit it was an amazing view of an alien world.

Salt water freezes at a lower temperature than fresh water. This planet was cold enough to freeze almost all of Akiane's salty oceans.

They named their star Kahair, Arabic for "good." I presumed the *good* was for when the star brought light and warmth. Kahair was a larger and brighter star than Earth's Sun, and could sustain life at a greater distance.

Akiane was in an elliptical orbit, which took eleven years to circle its star. The orbit managed to stay within Kahair's Goldilocks Zone, the distance from the star that is neither too hot nor too cold to sustain life. Akiane moved just far enough for the ocean surface to freeze, but not kill all life. Now it was moving closer so temperatures were rising.

Coincidentally, spring came at the best time for Earth to send a transport.

Soon, the oceans would thaw and the land, what little there was of it, would emerge from its winter cover. Jorg said it would bloom like the Alaskan tundra with trees, bushes, and flowering plants.

According to him, trees would only have a few years to grow before they died during the harsh weather. They never get the chance to grow to their full height and would be considered dwarf trees.

With Kahair to our backs, the frozen world below sparkled, glimmered, and shimmered. We saw a world devoid of personality with no wild animals, trees, flowers, or grass, not even a single dried shrub. All plant life went dormant during the six years of winter. Besides marine life, there were no native animals.

All that snow and ice reminded me of northern Minnesota. At least Oconto had deciduous and evergreen trees, and winters that only lasted five months, not six years.

I was twelve when Dad and I first arrived in Oconto Village. The snow was halfway up to the second floor windows. Someone had dug a tunnel through the snow to our front door from the road. I was positive the huge amounts of snow would never completely melt. I sank deeper into depression at the thought of never seeing another flower bloom again.

As Dad unloaded the car, I stood in the house. Even with the lights on, it was dark and dismal.

Looking at Akiane's barren ice world, those same feelings of hopelessness rose up in me. I feared I'd fail to accomplish my mission and I'd be stuck here for the rest of my life trying to work things out. I'd never set foot on Earth again.

The only sign of life on this frozen world came from volcanoes that quietly breathed gases into the atmosphere while others spewed molten lava, creating islands that would one day become large masses of land. Steam rose as the red-orange lava liquefied ice and surged into exposed water. In some cases, the resulting steam spread like dense fog. A few volcanoes looked dormant, but for the most part, this was a new world still forming and constantly changing. I knew from the files I'd read that just under her surface, Akiane was still very much alive.

The pilot banked.

I slipped. Jorg's shoulder caught me.

His body heat caressed my shoulder, and ran down my arm, making my fingers itch to hold his hand.

He'd pushed his parka sleeves up to his elbows. My eyes traced his forearm, his hand.

Don't. I sidestepped away.

I dropped my head and closed my eyes, took a deep breath and slowly let it out.

In the beginning of our relationship, I thought Jorg was interested in me, by the way he looked at me, the way he paid attention to everything I said, and the way he smiled when he saw me. But he treated everyone the same. I was no one special.

We were just friends.

I'm not sure what I would have done if he was interested. The idea scared me. I wanted love, but I knew it wasn't real, not for me. If I let anyone in, dropped my guard, let them get too close, let them know the real me, they'd abandon me.

It was best to be just friends. There'd been too many betrayals, too many broken hearts — all of them mine.

If he knew me, knew who I really was, he'd ... I couldn't stand it. Not again. Not him.

The warmth of his body faded.

I raised my head, opened my eyes, and looked out the window.

We were flying over a disordered ice ridge the size of a mountain range that seemed to stretch from east to west horizons. The ice ridge was slammed up against an unblemished sheet of ice. Akiane didn't warm up enough to melt its poles. This undamaged ice covered Akiane's North Pole.

The thick ridge of ice looked as if someone had tried to shuffle gigantic ice blocks like a deck of cards, but gave up and dropped them in a jumbled mess. Some chunks were crushed into pieces only a few meters in size, but others were huge, kilometers long.

Every once in a while, a piece of ice, angled just right, reflected a flash of star beam like a beacon signaling, "Welcome," or "Stay away." I wasn't sure which.

"That must have been some storm," Jorg said.

I shook my head in wonder. "Do you really think a storm did that?"

"What else?" he said. "Look at it, they're piled one on top of the other. They're smashed into each other and frozen in place."

A shiver of fear swept over me. "If a storm can toss an ocean of ice like that, I don't want to be around when it hits again."

Jorg chuckled. "Spoken like a true adventurer."

The pilot swooped past the ridge, banked south and flew over the frozen ocean. Most of the ice lay smooth as though the waters had been tranquil when the big freeze hit.

"I wonder what that is," Rona said. Like every other scientist, she wanted to know what everything was, whether it was related to her field of study or not.

"What?" Jorg asked.

"That." She pointed down to a red line, several kilometers long. It meandered through the ice like a river.

"What do you think it is?" I asked.

"I have no idea," Rona said. "But wouldn't it be fun to find out?"

No, I thought, *it would not!*

"Some kind of plant life. Algae, maybe," Jorg said, hopefully. What a find for him if there was a river of algae.

39

He laughed. His laugh always lifted my spirits and made me want to join in.

"Olivia, have you ever seen anything like that back on Earth?" Jorg asked.

He was one of the few who would attempt to engage Olivia Zeller in conversation when it wasn't absolutely necessary. Olivia's know-it-all arrogance was off-putting to almost everyone else.

"What is it?" Jorg asked.

"Don't know." Olivia shook her thick copper curls. The head oceanographer admitting to not knowing something? Highly unusual.

"The people who live here must know," I suggested.

"Of course they know. How could they not? It is their planet after all." She shrugged, dismissing me. "I think it's a river of fish caught in the ice and frozen.

"On Earth fish migrate looking for plankton to eat. Many different kinds of species will gather in the millions. It's a most impressive sight." Once Olivia started talking, she could go on for quite some time. "In the Northwest Passage, there are so many fish, polar bears and seals can swim together and eat, without fear of attack."

"There she goes again," Rona whispered genially.

It didn't bother her when someone like Olivia rattled on endlessly. In her mind, there might be something to be learned.

"Plankton can double in size in one day. In just a few days they can become as large as eight tons covering a thousand kilometers then die out in 72 hours."

I tuned Olivia out.

For Jorg's ears only, I said, "Once inside the habitat, I'm not leaving."

"For two years?" he asked. This was difficult for him to understand since his plans were to spend as much time outside doing as much research as possible. His field of study was snow, snow ecology, and algae.

I, on the other hand, didn't need to be outside for any reason. "If I get stuck here, yes. I'm staying inside until the next transport comes."

"You'll get cabin fever."

"The habitat was built so that 5,000 people could comfortably live in it. According to one of the messages I received from the colony, it sounded as if there were a lot less than that living in it. WSC sent 100 scientists, two cooks, and me. There'll be plenty of room for me to roam about. I'll be fine," I said, with definite assurance.

He looked at me with confused disbelief. "But, why?"

"I have a major aversion to the cold," I said.

"You're from northern Minnesota. You should be used to the cold."

"When Mom left, Dad moved us to Oconto Village. It's only a few hours farther north than our home in St. Paul, but those latitudes had a major affect on temperature. It was colder, the blizzards lasted longer, and the snow piled higher. One year, the snow was so bad I had to crawl in and out of the house by an attic window. I didn't just hate it. I loathed it. And there was nothing I could do about it."

"Why Oconto?" Jorg asked.

"Dad said he wanted a quiet place to write."

And there it was, that look of recognition. It had finally dawned on him who I was.

"You're Loy Hewett's daughter," he said with full admiration.

"Yes." I turned away, steeling myself against the emotion.

"All this time. Why didn't you tell me?"

I shrugged.

"Jessie, I read all his books. It's because of him I study the ecology of snow."

"Good for you. Personally, I never read any of them."

"Why not?"

"I hated the cold. I hated Dad for dragging me to the end of nowhere. I hated Mom for leaving. I hated me."

"You, Jessie? Why did you hate yourself?"

I didn't answer. How could I tell him what an awful child I'd been?

He didn't press, instead he said, "May I ask why she left?"

"Mom preferred a career as an art director to being a wife and mother," I said. "She wanted to inspire conceptual ideas that worked in different media formats."

"And did she succeed?"

"Dad and I were too far off the beaten path to know. We lived in communication isolation." It was funny now, but back then I was angry about it. "Believe it or not, there are still places where one can live unplugged from the electronic age."

He gave me a half smile, one of those charming smiles that melted my insides. Once again, I had to remind myself that we were just friends.

"No, I didn't know there were places like that left in the 25th century. My father would have loved it. He always made me leave my virtual games behind when we went on vacation. Drove me crazy," Jorg said.

"I had serious withdrawal that lasted for weeks," I said. "Although, I have to say, moving us there was a bit of an oxymoron."

"Why?"

"He typed all his manuscripts digitally and communicated with his publisher electronically."

Jorg raised a questioning eyebrow. "I read his books digitally and they made me dream of coming to a place like this. I'm surprised he was so anti-innovation."

"Yes, well, he knew he couldn't stop the future. Dad said computers had their place, but they shouldn't rule one's life.

"I didn't have a choice; I read everything the traditional way. A book with pages I could hold in my hands. Books are still printed, for those who want them." I'd never admit it out loud, but I still preferred traditional books. But with limited space on a ship, I had to leave all of them behind so all my books were now digital.

In my mind's eye, I saw my books neatly sitting on their shelves, and I jumped back to my bedroom in St. Paul. We lived just off the southern end of Cleveland Avenue, a few blocks from the Mississippi River.

A memory of Dad laughing and chasing me around in our backyard flashed before me. We never played like that in Oconto. There were a lot of things we never did after we Mom left.

"I think he really moved to the edge of nowhere hoping to forget Mom. The divorce was a lot harder on him than he admitted, but I knew."

"Children are more aware than their parents think," he said.

It had been over ten years, and still I wasn't ready to talk about Dad, or admit to my part in his death.

"I remember when he died," Jorg said. "It was a terrible accident. I'm sorry you had to go through that."

Whenever I thought of that day, I could smell the salty sea; I remember screaming and my stomach spiraling. I never cried; the tears wouldn't come.

43

Jorg didn't know the whole truth. No one did, but only because the media didn't know. Otherwise, they would have spread my shame across the world. I'd never told anyone what really happened or the real reason why my fiancé left.

I couldn't stomach looking at him. Not after that day.

All those old feeling were coming back. I needed a diversion before I dissolved into haunting memories.

"Olivia, will you include the mysterious red line in your studies?" I interrupted her in the middle of whatever she was prattling about.

She glared at me before she answered. "I wanted to, but was told not this trip. The colony isn't anywhere near it. And if you were a researcher," she just had to add, "you'd know there's too much to learn near shore to risk venturing this far out."

"So only the water near the colony is worth studying" I asked, purposely needling her.

"No," she retorted. "There are underwater volcanoes, which melt rock and release mineral to feed local marine life.

"The brine produced in the Antarctic affects ocean currents on Earth. Our ocean currents regulate Earth's temperatures." She paused to take a breath. "The amount of brine produced here when the ocean freezes must be unimaginable.

"How does it affect the Akiane's ocean currents? In what directions do the currents flow? How do they ..."

"All right already." I didn't need a list of everything she planned to study.

"In other words, there is plenty to study, but we have to start somewhere and, in this case, that somewhere is going to be at the colony," she tartly finished.

"Besides," Jorg chimed in, before I had time for a rebuttal, "spring is coming and in a few months all this will be water. Wouldn't want to get stuck out there when that happens."

I knew he was trying to prevent a verbal clash, but I couldn't stop myself. "Even though I might not be a researcher, Olivia, I'm smart enough take a shuttle out there just to see what that red line is before everything ice melts and it disappears. I might even take samples to study."

She glowered. Few people got along with her. I wasn't one of them.

"If the ship was staying, you could," the pilot interrupted.

"Right, I almost forgot. You're not staying," Jorg said with a sigh.

Everyone on the shuttle abruptly quieted at Jorg's words. We knew the ship was leaving, but somehow it hadn't become real until that moment.

Another cold shudder passed through me, as I thought of the crew forsaken some 318 years earlier. To know that for the rest of your life, you would never feel the warmth of sun or family again. What loneliness!

The thought of being left on Akiane, light-years from Earth for two years, rekindled the resentment over my orders. Why me? I didn't understand.

"No, the ship's not staying," the pilot said, over her shoulder. "We'll be here for a week to make sure you're settled, then we head back. As you know, there's a ship right behind us, arriving in a little over two Earth-Standard years. It will take anyone ready to return to Earth." She twisted her chair around so she could face her passengers. "Make the most of your time here. If your work is not finished and you miss the next transport, there won't be another ship for nine years."

"Two years isn't nearly enough time to study this planet," someone complained. Every scientist mumbled his or her agreement.

"Your choice," the pilot said, returning to the panel of computer monitors and control buttons.

The crowd shared a disgruntled moan. It would take a lifetime to fully explore Akiane's unique, alien composition and conduct the fascinating research these scientists wanted to do. They'd have to spend their lives on this planet to accomplish everything.

Akiane was a serious commitment. If someone decided to go home for a visit, it was another six-year, five-month trip back to Earth and six-year, five-month return trip to Akiane. During that time, someone else would work on their project, making discoveries they'd miss out on.

It could be a tough decision: stay on Akiane for the rest of your life with the possibility of never seeing Earth again, or go home and potentially miss out on the greatest discoveries of the century.

I was glad I didn't have to make that decision. When my job was completed, I was going home. Nothing, not even a command from Captain Norris, would change that. If I had to, I'd resign.

Jorg pulled me from my thoughts. "So, Lieutenant Jessie, two years. Think we scientists can get anything done in that amount of time?"

"I have no doubt that you will."

The shuttle rose up as it banked, circled, pointed downward, then leveled.

Another, "Look at that," resounded, followed by several, "Wows."

At the equator, morning light shimmered on a path of 30 kilometers of open ocean. I had no doubt that the open water circled all along the equator.

The ragged ice edge jutted in and out like a puzzle missing pieces. Broken and chipped ice floats varied from the size of a mansion to the size of small countries. Rivers of water ran across the top of the ice, waterfalls flowed over ice cliffs into ice lakes or into open ocean water.

The warmth of Kahair was melting Akiane. Spring has sprung, I thought with little enthusiasm.

"This section of ice was its own environment," Jorg said with admiration. "I'd love to study it before it all melts."

CAPTAIN'S LOG

WSC HAWK
Captain Matvey Petrov
Landing site on Akiane
Earth year 2144, November 1

WSC HAWK *was the first to arrive on Akiane. We landed on a section of land near the equator where there was open water. Except for 30 kilometers around the equator, all surface waters of the oceans are frozen.*

Hawk *carried the power source for the new colony. We unloaded it with the intention of having it set up before* Eagle and Falcon *landed. We'd already begun assembling it.*

But we made a calculation error and settled too close to the ocean. We only thought of being near open water and fishing. The land was good for farming once the ground thawed.

We saw Eagle *explode. It was like a bright flash in the morning sky. We didn't know what it was until* Falcon *radioed us.*

Later that same day, we suffered horrid earthquakes. At first the quakes were gentle and only lasted for seconds. As they increased in intensity, it was thought people would be safer outside in the open where nothing could fall on them.

But then the ocean ice shattered. Almost immediately, monstrous waves with the speed of shuttles rose up and flew toward shore. They battered the ship and land.

The quakes continued to become more forceful. The ground shook with such intensity it rippled as if it was water. I thought the planet would come apart.

By the time it was all over, everything that had been unloaded was lost, including the power source. Everyone who was outside ... lost.

Hawk's *engine was damaged. She will never fly again. The main ship may be able to move to a new location, but nothing more. Life support is minimal.*

Captain Matvey Petrov's Private Quarters
"Sir."
Captain Matvey stopped recording. "Anything?"
"The beach was swept clean, Sir."
"Thank you. You may go."
The lieutenant turned to leave.
Matvey stood and walked to the door.

He hated this planet. He'd not set foot on it, and it had already stolen all he loved and his reason to live.

Their first child had been born on the ship. Amanda was 23 months and 14 days old. She and her mother, like so many others, were on the beach enjoying the fresh air when it started.

Eight hundred sixty-eight people, mostly colonists, had been outside when the world shattered. They should have immediately run back to the ship. Some might have made it. Instead they froze as the ground shook and they dumbly stared at the ocean when the ice shattered. By the time the first wave rose up, it was too late.

The waves took everything and everyone out to sea.

Only the thirty-two crewmembers who were still on duty in the ship survived.

The colonists had come with the hope of new beginnings, but had slammed head-on into death. What more tragedy did this place hold?

Matvey would never know. He picked up the last holophoto of his family.

He was still holding it when he locked the door. There was no reason to ever set foot on Akiane. He would join his family instead.

Chapter 5

Jessica Hewitt

Life in Minnesota

I MUST explain why I so adamantly *hate* cold weather.

It brought back too many painful memories and deep emotions. Every snowflake reminded me of what a horrid child I was.

In the year 2432, I was twelve years old.

Minnesota was a nice place to live. It was mostly warm year-round. In the summer, I ran barefoot through thick grass sprinkled with clover, climbed trees, rode bikes, and played softball in 95 degrees Fahrenheit. The air was soupy with humidity.

The heat and humidity didn't stop us, we were children, and children are oblivious to weather.

The year before, my cousins and I discovered an interconnected virtual role-playing game (IVR Games) called *Master Runners*. From then on, my cousins and I spent most of our time playing indoors.

In the game, I was a girl with dragon blood. In the heat of a battle, I could change my appearance to green scales and grow a tail. I brandished a sword and breathed fire. I was a mighty warrior.

The virtual game was such that I could feel it when I got hit or when my sword sliced into a fantasy creature. The real person felt a twinge, but not the actual cut. I could also smell a monster's odor or when a character in the game farted. Blaaa.

There were rougher IVR Games where someone could get seriously hurt. We weren't allowed to play them.

But we did play *Master Runners* every day, *every single day* right after school, before dinner. We had already conquered the first seven levels and had almost finished the eighth when Mom left and Dad decided to move out of St. Paul.

When one was not there to play the game, the game continued with whomever was playing, but the absent player's avatar stood still until its owner returned. Last I saw my dragon girl, she was standing in the middle of a battle.

I remember those days with sadness, mostly because I can't go back. And mostly because I learned at an early age that the unexpected dominates life.

My childhood was better than any scripted program or novel. Mom, Dad, and I were together. We were an average, normal, happy family.

At least for me, that's how I remember it. I was completely oblivious to the impending doom.

Logically, I know it wasn't the volcanoes' fault, but they were the climax of the worst year of my twelve-year-old life. I had no idea that my adult life would be so much worse.

Most of the eleven volcanoes on Iceland have unpronounceable names, and are not capable of disrupting the rest of the world when they erupt. But some have caused the worst flooding Earth has ever seen. Europe was shut down more than once, because volcanic ash clogged all machinery, airplanes, jet crafts, farm equipment, hovercrafts, and lungs, if inhaled.

I was 12 when three such volcanoes erupted, each several times, within a year of each other, affecting the entire northern hemisphere. It was a worldwide economical disaster. The Northern Hemisphere shut down.

The Arctic Ocean froze all the way to the state of Oregon on America's the West coast and New Brunswick, Canada on the East Coast. There was ice and snow across America all the way down the Mississippi River to its southern end into New Orleans.

The pleasant Minnesota weather came to an abrupt end. The volcanoes changed everything. Ash blocked the sun, which lowered the temperature. For the next ten years the weather in Minnesota was miserable.

That first winter, several blizzards hit St. Paul; each dumped over 90 inches of snow. Snowplows were not able to keep up. They were barely able to keep emergency roads clear. Some neighborhoods were lost under the snow. By the time the plows did reach them, there was too much snow to get in and clear it. Neighborhoods had to dig themselves out. Roofs of houses and businesses caved under the weight.

In the spring, when the snow melted, creeks and rivers flooded small towns, major cities, and farmland. Tributaries of all the major rivers contributed to flooding the Mississippi River, which flooded the surrounding the Midwest.

But that wasn't the most miserable part of the year.

Just before my thirteenth birthday, on April 12, Mom left.

She wanted to be a multimedia artist. She used digitally enhanced photos and combined them with her paintings. One day she got an award at a community art festival. The online news reporter

Communiqué did a feature story. A St. Paul gallery wanted to sell her work. Soon she was having her own one-woman shows.

Dad and I were proud of her and supported her efforts.

At least that's how I remember it.

But Mom decided she'd rather be a full-time artist rather than a wife or mother. One day she said she'd had enough of us and left. As an adult, I now know there must have been more to it than that, but Dad never talked about it. So I don't know what really happened and now I never will.

At first, Dad and I were in denial and believed she'd come back. She didn't.

Dad accepted reality first. That was when he decided to get away from the memories—a restaurant, a frequented street, their bedroom (after she left, he slept on the couch), the kitchen, and pictures on the wall, many of which disappear. I never saw them again.

He quit his high school teaching and counseling job and moved us to Oconto Village in the Boundary Waters. A place in the far northern Minnesota woods near Superior National Park and the Canadian border, where people lived "unplugged." They wanted a simple life without interconnections. Of any kind! They wanted to return to nature. To me, they lived a primitive life in the woods.

Don't get me wrong, the village was modernized… somewhat. Houses had electricity and running water. But no one had a smart house. They had to turn lights on and off manually.

Those people were mostly disconnected from the virtual world. There was a connection through the schools and the library. They didn't want their children to be completely ignorant about the world's technological advancements.

Children were taught to use their minds to be creative in areas from art to engineering. They read traditional paper books and played outside, but did not spend hours playing virtual games. I hated it.

The far North Woods was one of the last nationally protected wildernesses of forests and lakes. No paved roads or electricity existed within the park, the area was filled with lakes and rivers with rocky shorelines, dense forest, and sharp bluffs.

In the summer, one could ride horses, hike trails, or canoe. In winter, one could dogsled or jet craft through the woods. There was fishing year round.

Every year, urban adventurers came from some big city to Oconto Village to pit their skills against the elements. Most people were prepared, but there was always someone who truly did not understand the dangers. They'd read the books and would ignore the advice to take a guide. Every year, there was at least one whose "adventure of a lifetime" was their last.

I was forced to leave my family and friends behind. On my dad's side of the family, I had thirty-five first cousins. They were all my best friends, every one of them. Most of them lived close enough for me to see weekly.

Auntie Lucy, Dad's sister, lived a few blocks away. She made me homemade fudge and stovetop popcorn, both long-lost arts. When I was little, she held me on her lap and read interactive mysteries solved by fictional third graders. I would change obstacles and tactics, which would create different outcomes for the end of the story.

My avatar stood motionless in *Master Runners* as a memorial to me. My friends said they'd kept her for the day when I'd rejoin them. I never did. For all I know, my dragon-girl is still there.

How was I to leave all that behind?

I had been living in a wonderland, unaware of what the real world was like. Then someone shattered the glass, all the glitter floated away, and I learned the truth about life.

No amount of crying, pleading, or begging changed Dad's mind. We moved to the end of the world, completely cut off from everyone. I became the new kid at school with no friends.

I cried for days, then weeks.

One night Dad came into my room and sat on my bed. I lay with my back to him. Tears wet my pillow.

He was quiet for a long time. Finally, he said, "Tears will not bring her back. At some point you have to move on. Your mother has left us." He sighed. "We both have to move on."

He placed a hand on my shoulder. He might have hugged me, but I swished my shoulder. His hand moved away.

After a few more minutes of silence, he left and softly closed my bedroom door behind him.

I kept hoping Mom would contact me, or come and find me. She didn't.

I wrote her a letter asking her what I had done to make her leave. I poured my heart out to her. I told her how much I loved her and missed her. I asked her to forgive me. I promised to be good. But I didn't know how or where to send it. I hid it under my pillow. Dad found it when he changed my bedding.

I came home to find him sitting on my unmade bed crying. We hugged and cried together. It was then I realized how much he was hurting too.

That was the day I resolved never to cry again. I decided to move on and not hurt Dad with my tears.

I became torn between fearing that Dad would one day walk out on me and being angry with him for dragging me to Oconto. I was torn between being a pleasant, compliant child or screaming at him for the most insignificant reason and not being able to stop myself.

My teen years were miserable for both of us.

I was nineteen when I finished college, and decided to take a little time off. I went to Baja, California, to get away from the cold. I fell in love and decided to stay for the summer.

Before summer was over I was a permanent resident.

I became a guide for urban warriors. I took them camping in the Baja Desert, surfing and scuba diving in the Pacific Ocean. There were more than a few macho men who had trouble keeping up with a slip of a girl, 5 foot 8 inches tall and 128 pounds.

It was the best time of my life, except when I think back on it. Then the guilt and shame over Dad's death comes rolling in.

Chapter 6

Lieutenant Jessica Hewitt
First Morning on Akiane

WITH JORG and Rona at my side and the other scientists standing around, I didn't feel a particular degree of loneliness. Still, the dread remained, one of being abandoned in the middle of an alien world with no hope of escape.

I turned my attention to the scene before me.

The colonists had built their habitat in some sort of crater. We stood on a makeshift landing area overlooking the building complex and an uninteresting landscape, white snow, dark colored rocks, and cloudless blue sky. To our west was a small mountain range.

From the ship we'd seen two moons orbiting Akiane. They seemed relatively close together, but standing on land, we could see only one moon in the western sky, which was about to slip behind a small mountain range. It looked much like Earth's moon at the first quarter.

"Where's the other moon?" I asked.

Jorg looked up. "What other moon?"

"From the ship, we saw Akiane traveling with two moons. Where's the other one?"

"It's out there, Jessie." He glanced up. "It's just not where we can see it." His attention returned to the scene before us. I followed his gaze.

Dad used to take me on dogsled rides in the hopes I'd see how wondrous the land was. The whole time we were out, all I could think was how cold it was. It didn't matter how warm he dressed me. I was cold. After being lost in a blizzard and almost dying of hyperthermia, I feared frigid temperatures.

"Beautiful, isn't it, Jessie?" Jorg asked.

"Beautiful, Jorg?" I asked. "You've got to be kidding."

He looked at me as if I was the one who didn't get it.

"Look at it, Jessie," he said, waving his hand over the landscape.

"It's white," I said.

"It's not just white. The snow reflects the colors around it. The sky is a deep morning violet; the mountain range folds in and out of shadows; the snow's highlights are pristine with jet-black rocks peeking through. Look how the snow subtly changes from white to blue to lavender to gray as it dips and rises. And over there," he pointed north of the habitat, "see the algae?"

"What?" I asked.

"The blotchy colored snow is algae."

I expected to see small barely distinguishable patches of color. To my surprise, there were fields with shades of reds and yellows, and where the two colors mixed, oranges. It wasn't one continuous color, but faded in and out of the snow like waves or ripples of color.

"Jorg, how much algae is there?" I asked.

59

"Looks like there are acres of it. I've never seen so much of it in one place before. They must be cultivating it," Jorg said. "It is a great source of vitamin C."

"Is it frozen?" I asked.

"No, Jessie."

"That doesn't seem logical," I said. "Shouldn't it be frozen?"

"It's cold tolerant," he said.

"It looks like there's plenty of it for you to study."

"Yawper," he agreed. "Back on Earth, algae is just about everywhere from the Arctic to the Antarctic and now we've found it here on another planet."

"Resilient little buggers," I said.

"Yes, Jessie, they are," he said, with pride.

It's amazing how one's interest causes people to see different things. Jorg, who loved the snow and cold as much as my father, saw more than white. He saw color, beauty, texture, and multi-colored algae.

I saw Akiane as an inhospitable alien landscape of death.

"I don't understand why they came here in the first place," I said.

"You mean why not a warmer planet?" Jorg asked.

"Yes."

"At twenty-seven light-years, this was the closest to home," he said. "And we're still in our galaxy, the Milky Way."

"Closest to home," I said. "Jorg, you mean with all the planets out there, this is the only one they could find?"

"For every star, there is at least one planet orbiting it, usually there are more. In fact there are more planets than there are stars. Those same stars are probability able to support some sort of alien life. But this is one of the few planets that can sustain life as we know it."

"Human life?"

He chuckled. "Yes, Jessie, human life."

"But they had folded space. Why not go somewhere more hospitable with a warmer climate?" I asked.

"Scientists are willing to work on a project that they might not finish in their lifetime. They know the next generation will build on what they started. But a politician is thinking of his career. Money-backers are thinking of their investment," he said.

"They want results they can see," I concluded.

"Right," Jorg said. "And since projects like this need politicians' approval and are funded by their nation's money, scientists often have to produce results in a reasonably quick timeline."

"So Akiane was picked because of its availability."

"Yes," he said. "If it had succeeded, then folded space would have been further developed and we'd have reached more planets. This one is in a collection of stars known on Earth as the Pegasus Constellation. If we had developed folded space travel, we'd be in the Pegasus Galaxy by now, which is 300,000 light-years away. But since the colony appeared to have failed, politicians were hesitant and money dried up."

"This is all Asa's fault." I signed unhappily.

"Who?" he asked.

"The astronomer who discovered this planet," I said.

"I'm not sure I know the story."

"Well, let me tell you," I said as if I were the authority. "While looking for giant planets, she noticed the one in this star system dragged."

"Dragged?"

"For a 40 hour period, it slowed down for a few seconds."

"Seconds?"

"That's all it took," I said. "She watched it for 48 years. The planet slowed down every 11 years. She guessed there was a smaller planet involved. There's more to the story, but she got permission to send a probe and discovered there was indeed planet and it was habitable."

Jorg laughed out loud. "Seconds. It doesn't take much to get a scientist excited. And here we are." He spoke with pride.

I wasn't as amused. I wanted out of the cold. My real interest lay in the stone habitat that rose out of the mounds of snow. It would be warm in there and it would protect me from blizzards and subzero temperatures.

"The habitat is huge," I said.

And it was. The habitat looked almost two-thirds of a kilometer in diameter. It looked like a monstrous ball that had been buried in the ground and only the very top was visible.

"I mean, I knew, but until you see it…" I trailed off in awe. I guess I never thought about how large it was.

"You don't really get a feel for the place," Jorg finished my thoughts, "until you see it in person."

Two main ships were enclosed in an area surrounded by a stone wall with a glass ceiling.

"See those two round protrusions rising out of the dome? They look like the top of space ships," I said.

"Could be. The main section ships, of their time, were the average size of 48 meters in height and 322 meters in length," Jorg said. "It looks like they built a wall that circled the main ships and enclosed the entire area."

I did the conversion in my head. Each main ship was 157 feet in height, 1,056 feet in length, and with a 35-foot wall surrounding them.

After a pause, he continued, "I can see them using the ship's engines as a power source while they built the habitat. An ingenious move. But why keep the ships? Why not build homes and a city within the dome?"

The top of the stone wall curved in toward the center of the dome, which was made of gray-smoked glass. They finished the habitat with six seven-meter long tunnels leading in and out of the habitat.

It didn't look like much. There weren't any windows or doors in the walls. All of their natural lighting came through the glass ceiling.

I imagined what it looked like inside: all steel and stone. It would be sterile, with even less personality than the planet. Jorg was right. I was about to develop a severe case of cabin fever.

"It looks like they closed-in one area between two of the tunnels to make one large room," Jorg said.

"Why only one?" I wondered. "Why not enclose all the areas between all the tunnels?"

He shrugged. "Maybe they haven't gotten around to building the others just yet."

I turned to see what else people were focused on.

Dad always said a person's interest caused them to see different things even though they were all looking at the same scene.

Volcanist Spago Jorgson stood, his attention fixated on a distant mountain range.

He was one of the many who thought himself superior to the others. After all, most of the rest of the geniuses had received their first PhDs in their late teens. He received his first PhD at fifteen. At twenty-two, he was the youngest team leader.

"What do you see, Spago?" I asked.

"The colonists built their habitat in a caldera," he said.

"What's a caldera?" I asked. "I thought we were in some sort of a crater."

"A caldera is what's left after a massive super volcano eruption," he said.

"A *what*?" Several people asked.

He continued as though he'd not heard their concern. "The caldera appears to be 18 kilometers wide. Those mountains," he said, pointing to a small mountain range to the west of us, "were once active. It's that volcanic activity that built the mountains. But they look dormant now."

"How can you tell from here?" I asked.

He considered me as if I'd asked the most stupid question in the world. "For one, we just flew over them and there was no sign that they were active, and second, I doubt these people were foolish enough to build in an active caldera."

He turned back to the mountains. "But I won't know for sure until I examine them."

"Well, as long as they're safe," Jorg said.

To Jorg, I asked, "Think there's algae in the mountains?"

He called to the volcanist. "Spago, think I could go with you to the mountains and check for algae?"

Irritated that we were disturbing his train of thought, Spago turned his thin frame back to us. "Once I checked it out. Those mountains look exceptionally rugged. Wouldn't want you wandering around and have you slip and break a leg."

"No, of course not," Jorg agreed, not at all put off by the younger man's arrogant tone. He continued, "Anytime you want a tour of snow, I'll be happy to oblige."

Spago thick eyebrows almost met as they frowned. "I have no need for snow."

"A hot-blooded Italian like you? No, of course not," Jorg said, smiling broadly.

Spago turned away, but not before we saw his cheeks blush under his olive skin.

"How does the algae color the snow like that?" I asked.

"Fine little hairs. That's what I've come to study: snow, fine little hairs, and worms."

"Worms?" This surprised me. "Worms live in snow?"

"Yawper. Worms, spiders, and fleas. Snow has an ecology all its own, you know."

His whole face beamed. I wasn't sure if he was teasing or not.

"Yes, siree," he said. "I've come light-years to study snow, hairs, and worms. Heck, if I find a new species of worm, I could have it named after me."

"Interesting. A whole ecology. That's a lot of work to do in two years, my friend," I said.

He placed his hand over his heart, and with a look of martyrdom, he said, "To have my own worm, I'll make the sacrifice." He wiped a fake tear from his eye.

I liked Jorg's unfailing humor. He rarely took anything too seriously, yet he was dedicated to his field. I had no doubt he'd find his worms.

"So, why worms?" I asked.

"Why?" Jorg's eyes lit up. "They're fun."

"Worms are fun?"

"Scientifically, yes. They're good for more than just fishing, you know. What we've learned from them has helped advanced the study of the human race."

Was he serious? "I don't believe it," I said.

"The worm was the first DNA to be mapped. From what we learned from that, we were able to map the human genome. By studying the worm immune system and how it contributes to immunosenescence—"

"Immuno what?" I asked.

He grinned like one would when explaining things to a layperson, like me.

Another reason why we shouldn't be together, I thought. *I don't understand half of what he's talking about.*

"We learned how to extend human life with the help of worms," Jorg said.

"Really?" I asked. "So what do you expect to learn from Akiane's worms?"

"That's the fun part. I don't know." He shrugged and his smile broadened.

"But you're going to find out," I said.

"They're amazing little creatures." He brought his thumb and first finger near each other and said, "They can make themselves short and fat or ...," moving his fingers apart, "... long and thin."

I gave him a "Who cares!" look.

He chuckled. "Okay, did you know a worm is either a hermaphrodite or a male?"

"I thought all worms were hermaphrodites."

"No, one-fourth are born males."

"Any born females?"

"They are either males or hermaphrodite," he repeated, "which means they propagate by themselves. Males cannot reproduce unless they mate."

"If they propagate by themselves, why have males?"

Jorg winked and gave me a wicked smile. "Jessie, a partner is always more pleasurable."

I shook my head in mock disgust.

With a gentle touch, he pushed a strand of hair off my forehead. Our eyes locked. I quickly looked away, afraid my feelings might betray me.

Jorg shifted his weight, then called, "See anything, Olivia?"

Olivia Zeller stood at the edge of the landing area and stared out over the land. The breeze ruffled her short golden-copper curls. It didn't matter that it was above freezing, just watching her bare head made me feel colder. I pulled my hood tighter and tied it in place.

Rona stood with Olivia, also seemingly oblivious to the cold.

I had no idea what they were looking at. They couldn't see the ocean; we were too far away and we were at the bottom of a crater, caldera. Olivia would have to walk several kilometers to get to it, carrying her equipment with her, not something she would be looking forward to. She preferred swimming to walking.

I guess that was why she got an amphibious hover vehicle that traveled over land, and under water.

Olivia walked over to us and stood on the other side of Jorg. "I don't know why they didn't just build near the ocean instead of here."

"I'm sure they had their reasons," Rona said, standing next to me.

"Maybe they liked the mountains," I said.

"Or the algae," Jorg said.

Ignoring my comment, Olivia asked, "Why build near algae?"

"Food. Salads. Lots of vitamin C. Keeps scurvy away," he said. "But I think they planted the algae near the habitat, not the other way around."

"There's plenty of food in the ocean," Olivia said, "and seaweed can keep scurvy at bay." She spoke in that irritating know-it-all tone of hers.

"Not if you can't get to it," Jorg said.

And they were off on one of their long, drawn-out scientific conversations on probabilities. Over the last year-and-a-half, I'd learned that scientists like to show off their knowledge and compare ideas. They enjoy a good debate. It didn't matter who won, they just liked hearing themselves talk.

Many of them were so obsessed with their studies, their eyes glassed over if I tried to turn the conversation to something else. There were only a few, like Jorg and Rona, who could talk about something other than their field of study or science in general.

"Olivia says there are two kinds of ice," Rona said, "land ice and sea ice."

"There's going to be a lot of discussion about snow and ice, isn't there?" I asked.

"Not to worry, Jess. As soon as I give the colonists physical examinations, there will be plenty of discussion on human physiology too," Rona said.

"Oh joy."

She grinned at my lack of enthusiasm. "You really are going to be bored, aren't you?"

"I fear you may be right."

"We'll have to find something for you to do."

"Oh, Rona, I hope to be finished so I can return to Earth with *Britannia* or this is going to be a very long two years for me," I sighed. "I don't even know how to negotiate. Now if WSC was looking for someone to fail, that would be me."

"Jess, you're not going to fail," Rona said.

After almost one-and-a-half years as roommates, she still didn't know me.

"These colonists just need to meet us, see that we don't bite, and they'll change their minds," she continued. "Think what your father would have done."

In a moment of weakness, I had told her how my father had a gift of helping people with their personal relationships. He was the town mediator, marriage counselor, and domestic referee. People came to him because they trusted his judgment. He'd listen to both sides and give a fair assessment of the situation. *He* would have made a perfect negotiator.

"I didn't sit in on his sessions," I said.

"But he must have imparted some wisdom to you, Jess."

"If he did, Rona, I wasn't paying attention."

CAPTAIN'S LOG

WSC FALCON
Captain Faris Assetti
Landing on Akiane
Year 2144
Day one on planet

WE HAVE taken on the 31 remaining crewmembers from the Hawk. *Of the 2,038 who started this journey, only 852 survived. All other crewmembers and colonists have been lost.*

I am the only captain left alive.

I have a negative feeling about this place. The colonists have lost everything. Their building supplies, DNA for future livestock, and seeds for farming: all were on Eagle. *All the colonists have left is the* Hawk; *even their power source was lost.*

The ship has been severely damaged and battered. She will never fly again. Fortunately it does have the ability to move to a new location. Life support is barely able to keep the surviving crew from freezing.

My preference is to take everyone back, but the colonists on Falcon *came to start a new colony. They wish to stay and fulfill their mission.*

I think they are foolhardy.

Colonists have chosen a new place to build. After several scans to make sure it was safe, they decided to settle in a caldera created by a super volcano explosion. Probes estimate another explosion, at that magnitude, is not due for more than 100,000 years. Colonists plan to move before then.

The colony is now 5 kilometers from the ocean, close enough for a hovercraft to transport fish, but a safe distance from monster waves the next time they return.

Falcon *was only a transport ship and was not scheduled to be part of the colony. After the colonists were settled, we were to return to Earth.*

The crew and I have discussed it. We cannot in good conscience leave the colonists like this. We will stay and use Falcon's *engines for a power source until they are able to connect with geothermic energy the hot springs will provide.*

My crew and I will return on the ship coming in two years, 2146. I have sent a message advising WSC of the situation.

We moved Hawk's main ship to the caldera and have landed Falcon's main ship next to her. Falcon's engines now power both of them. Each ship has its own hydroponics, both of which have been expanded. Produce will not be a problem. We have fresh fish from the ocean. Everyone is helping with the fishing, cleaning of fish, gardening, and cooking and clean up.

There are plans to build a habitat to enclose the area around the ships, which will be built to protect the colonists from the six-year winter and to withstand the type of gravitational storm we encountered when we first landed. The ships will sit on the northernmost wall so there will be room to build their future city inside the habitat, then the ships will be dismantled and removed.

But we are first reorganizing living areas. We have divided into two groups, one group in each ship. We will expand rooms so everyone has plenty of space and no one has to live with another unless they want to.

Personal log

This is not what I expected. A twenty-four year round trip was plenty long enough. Upon my return to WSC, my entire military career as captain would have been on one ship.

Now it seems I will not even accomplish that. I was a captain until we landed. Now I'm helping a colony to establish itself. On my return trip I will be a passenger on another's ship.

By the time I return to Earth, what will I have accomplished? Very little.

My dog Harrie seems to enjoy the freedom of the outdoors to being cooped up in my cabin. My father gave her to me to keep me company on the long journey. He made sure she was genetically enhanced so she would live for the duration of the roundtrip.

Her name is really Henrietta the Spitz, but by his strange sense of humor, my father called her Harrie. I decided to keep the name. Every time I think about it, I remember him.

In some ways Harrie makes me home sick for my family, especially my father. In other ways, she eases the homesickness.

I am thankful for her friendship and salaam, peace.

Chapter 7

Lieutenant Jessica Hewitt
Habitat

SPAGO PASSED his hand admiringly over the tunnel's wall. The tunnel was made of black lava in meter-wide, hexagon blocks. "Each of these stones has been cut, or made, to fit perfectly together." One might have thought it was a technical marvel by the way he spoke. "I would guess there are several layers. Each layer overlaps the others. It makes for a very strong wall."

Jorg and I stopped to look. Indeed, the hexagon did appear to all be exactly the same size and were fitted together seamlessly, as smooth as glass. The wall looked 42 centimeters thick, presumably filled with the layers Spago suggested.

There was a well-trod snow path to a set of steps leading into the tunnel.

Before he took the steps, Spago dug in the snow with his hands on the outside of the entrance. The rest of us stood and watched in wonder.

"See, there is a base that comes up to the middle of the wall and extends downward at a 45-degree angle. They did the same on the inside of the tunnel, but there wasn't enough room to make a full triangle base so they filled in the floor of the tunnel and built steps to get into it," he said, approvingly. "I'll venture to say the entire wall of this habitat is fortified in the same manner. This kind of construction is not only strong, but durable. An earthquake couldn't bring this place down."

"Earthquake, on Akiane?" Olivia asked, nervously.

Spago smiled. "Okay, Akianequake."

"I'm not concerned about technical terms," Olivia said. "Will there be another earthquake?"

"This habitat is built in a caldera. A caldera is a crater created by a super volcanic explosion, and with volcano explosions comes earthquakes, or in this case Akianequakes," Spago painstakingly explained. "And if they built their habitat to withstand Akianequakes then I'd say, yes, there is a very good chance that there will be more quakes at some point during our stay here."

Olivia paled. "Super volcano."

"Not to worry. I would venture to guess that another explosion like that will not happen for hundreds, or even thousands, of years, but there must be smaller explosions," Spago said. "These people are used to quakes. I'm sure they've built the habitat to withstand the roughest of quakes."

"But you said the mountains were inactive," I reminded him. I didn't like the possibility of being caught in an earthquake any more than Olivia.

"I also said I have to take a closer look to be certain. There could be cycles of activity," Spago said, "which could be years or hundreds of years apart."

He jumped up the stairs and started down the tunnel. The rest of us stood in stunned silence.

I'm sure all of us were wondering just how often Akianequakes occurred.

One by one, we slowly followed.

"Wow." Spago stood staring at the inside of the tunnel wall. "These people combined medieval, 20th, and 21st century technology."

"Explain," Jorg said.

"They constructed the triangle base from medieval times, and hexagon blocks from 20th century. Together they create an extremely strong building," Spago said.

"This we already know," Olivia said. "What else?"

Spago took out a small hammer from his pocket and tapped the wall with it. Then he hit it as hard as he could.

Everyone gasped.

The hammer created a small indentation that almost immediately disappeared.

"The building material isn't just lava, as I first thought. This is smart building material. It was first invented for military use in one of the Middle East Wars, I forget which, but at that time it was called battlejacket technology," Spago said. He was genuinely impressed. "The technology advanced from there. The colony's engineers infused nanotechnology into the lava to make it smart building material." He pulled his attention from the tunnel's interior wall to look at us. "This habitat repairs itself."

"What?" several of us chimed at the same time.

"If there is a crack because of a quake, the wall will immediately repair itself as if the crack was never there. You know what that means don't you?" he asked as if he were the proud engineer.

76

"No," Olivia said. "What does that mean?"

"This building will survive anything for no less than a thousand years," Spago said. "In the beginning of this colony, they had one smart engineer."

As we walked through the tunnel, the temperature warmed by several degrees. I pulled my hood back and unzipped my jacket.

The first sign of plant life was long, spindly reddish vines running along the tunnel walls. I guessed they were red from lack of sunlight. Farther in, the vines sparingly produced tiny reddish leaves with green tips. As we drew closer to the inside of the habitat, the vines thickened. The thumbnail leaves became finger length. They were fat at their base and thinned into a point. As the leaves thickened and grew larger, they also became greener. The red receded to the base while the green spread from the point inward.

Soon I smelled the sweet scent of flowers.

Everyone who stepped into the habitat's entrance abruptly stopped. Jorg, Rona, and I, with Olivia following close behind, pushed our way through to see why.

If the outside was a frozen hell, the inside of the habitat was heavenly.

Before us was a small pond about a city block long and half as wide. Beyond it was a hill covered with well-manicured lime green, gold and rust colored bushes. It looked like fall on America's Eastern seaboard.

To the left were two copper-leafed trees that towered over the bushes and one emerald green tree just to the right of center. The branches from those trees gracefully stretched out and up. The way they grew was too perfect, too artistic for nature. They looked purposely shaped for their esthetic beauty like gigantic bonsai trees.

There were many flowering bushes, some with white flowers with large lacy petals and pink centers; others were clusters of scarlet, tiny flowers; and others were jewel-like indigo flowers.

Rock steps descended from the trees to a path along the water's edge.

On the hill's left side, water fell like a ribbon onto flat rocks that were tilted at different angles to direct the water to the next rock before it swept over a group of pebbles, like a brook spilling into the pond.

Smaller plants on this side of the pond's edge enhanced the scene's beauty, but didn't obscure the view. A huge rock slab wrapped around the pond's left side.

We stood on a walkway made of black crushed lava rocks mixed with bits of pink granite stones that made the path glisten. The path ambled through the grass and around the pond to a bridge that crossed over a creek, which slipped into the habitat.

"These people have been busy," Jorg said.

"Well, they've had more than 300 years," I reminded him.

"They certainly have not been sitting around doing nothing," Rona agreed.

I never imagined anything so exquisite. It was a place of peace and tranquility, where one could sit and quietly contemplate life. But instead of sky there was a glass ceiling and a wall to keep the outside, outside.

No birds flitted about or twittered in the trees. No squirrels chased each other or jumped from one tree branch to another. No fish swam in the water. Not a ripple marred the perfect glass-like effect, not even a reflection of sky or clouds. There were no butterflies, nor bees. No annoying flies. No breeze rustling the leaves.

The trees, flowers, and pond were beautiful, but lifeless.

"Most impressive," Spago said, but he wasn't looking at the trees and flowers.

I followed his gaze to the ceiling. The hexagon-stone wall curved up and over us. Where it stopped, a hexagon metal brace held up the glass ceiling. When the star Kahair was high in the sky, its light would nourish the garden with photosynthesis.

Interesting, but it was those who were already here that caught my attention.

Scattered around this side of the pond, sitting in the grass or on rocks, were the forty scientists who had come in the two shuttles before us. Among them were six white dogs with reddish tufts; one had larger spots across his sides and face, each weigh about forty-five kilos. Two dogs had all white puppies crowding around their feet. All of the dogs received some sort of affection from the lounging scientists, such as tummy rubs, or ear scratches.

Great. Dogs. Dogs were my least favorite animal. They are too dependent on their owners. I much preferred independent cats.

"What are you still doing here?" I asked. "Shouldn't you be in your new quarters unpacking by now?"

"We're waiting for the 'spirit' to move someone to escort us in," Mathieu Rutger, one of two medical doctors, said. He was soft spoken, easy-going, and overweight. To look at him, one would have thought that he was an average Joe, but once you got to know him, you realized he was usually the smartest and most logical person in the room.

At least that was what it was like for him as a child back on Earth, but on the ship, he was finally equal among his pears.

"What are you talking about?" I asked. "What's preventing you from going in?"

"The dogs," Lu said. "They won't let us pass."

Dogs were nothing more than bullies. I hadn't met one yet that wouldn't back down when I stood up to it.

Dad always said, "Let them know who's top dog, and they'll respect you." He loved his dogs and they loved him, but they knew he was master.

"Didn't the pilot tell you? We're to wait here until someone comes to escort us in," Mathieu said.

"How long have you been waiting?" Olivia asked.

"Since we arrived," he said. "Almost an hour ago now."

"That's ridiculous," I said. "Just go in." And I proceeded to show them how. I had a mission to accomplish. Time was marching. I had to convince these people they were WSC colonists so I could go home.

Jorg's face flashed into my mind. I'd return to Earth without him. He was staying here. I shook my head. It was for the best. He'd forget all about me before I left Kahair's system. Would I forget him? It would be a long trip home without him.

Three of the dogs immediately left those doting over them and surrounded me. A set of puppies tumbled over themselves as they hurried after their mother. I tried to step around. They growled. Their menacing jaws were even with my thigh.

"That's why," Mathieu said, motioning at the animals.

"They bite," Lu warned. This surprised me because I knew Lu was a full-blown tomboy. When she was younger, her mom was afraid of her dirty clothes. Once, a garter snake slithered out of a pants pocket. From then on, her mom ordered Lu to empty her pockets every night when she undressed for bed.

"Don't be such a fraidy-cat, Lu. They're just dogs." I again tried to move past them. But while I was looking at Lu, four more appeared, seemingly from out of nowhere. Their growls grew more intense. They bared their sharp teeth. I stopped.

80

"Better stay here," Mathieu warned. "I've already had to treat one bite." He held up his hand. "Good thing I'm a doctor and had my bag with me." He patted the brown leather shoulder bag at his side.

He must have used a self-healing nano-kit because I didn't see the bite or a spray on bandage.

"They're friendly if we just sit here," Lu said.

I didn't want to sit with a dog lounging across my lap. I wanted to find Akiane's leaders and settle the negotiations so I could go home.

The dogs reminded me of my father's sled huskies and their incessant barking, if you'd call the noise they made barking. They whined and howled as if trying to speak. They whined every time I exited or entered my house and yard. They howled at anyone who came within meters of our yard, and that included almost everyone in Oconto. They howled when other dogs howled. There was always at least one dog making some kind of noise, somewhere in town.

Many nights, I went to sleep with a dog barking, somewhere in the village, only to wake up in the next morning with him still at it.

Now ten growling dogs surrounded me. I could stand up to one dog, but not a pack of them. And more came down the path toward us. *How many dogs did these people have?*

It was a little embarrassing to have to back down after I'd made a show of being tough. But it would have been a whole lot worse if they'd attacked me.

One dog, all white, except for a red ear, slightly smaller than the others, showed his affection by rubbing against my leg much the way a cat does.

"Leave me alone," I said to the mutt, and used my leg to push him away.

He cocked his head and turned as he looked at me. His one red ear pointed straight up.

"Hey, dog," Jorg called to him. "Come here." It trotted over to him. Olivia joined Jorg. Together they ruffled the mutt's fur.

I considered trying to find the alpha dog. Dad had showed me how to grab a dog by the scruff of his neck and flip him on his back. Once he submitted, the others would follow his lead. I smiled picturing the scene of me fighting a mutt for hierarchy.

I decided it might be best to wait for our escort.

Since Mathieu had already been bitten and didn't appear to be interested in dogs, or they in him, I joined to him.

"Where do the mutts come from, anyway?" I asked.

"Native?" Mathieu suggested.

"There aren't supposed to be native mammals on Akiane. Only marine life," Lu said. "I checked. But they might be offspring from the first dog Captain Assetti brought with her."

"Dog?" I asked. "As in one?"

"I don't know. The logs said the captain only brought one with her," Lu said. "Another wasn't mentioned."

"What did you read?" I asked. "It couldn't be the captains' logs. There aren't any. I checked."

"No, I read the WSC logs from that time period," Lu said.

"I'm positive those same WSC logs must have mention that there was more than just one dog," Olivia's tone indicated Lu was stupid. "After all, someone must have brought another on board to keep the captain's bitch company."

Lu ducked her head. "I-I d-d-don't think so." Olivia was making Lu feel insecure. "The c-c-captain's Sp-pitz was named H-H-Harrie, with an "ie" as in, she was female."

"I thought the dog's name was Henrietta," Rona said.

"Then the captain should have called her Hennie, Henry, or Etta," Olivia said.

"Spitz?" I asked ignoring her. "A Spitz is a small furry lap dog." I looked around. "Some of these dogs are size of a bear cub."

"Didn't I read somewhere that the captain had a genetically enhanced dog so she would live for the duration of the trip?" Jorg asked.

"Yes," Lu said. "I read the same thing."

"I guess if we humans can live longer, there's no reason our pets shouldn't too," he said.

"That still doesn't explain where all these dogs come from," Olivia protested.

"The logs also said the first ships brought DNA livestock," Jorg said. "Cattle, pigs, chickens, sheep, and the like. Maybe there were pets like dogs in with the livestock. And if they brought different breeds that would also explain the size difference."

"I wonder where the other animals are," I said.

"Penned up somewhere. You don't think they'd let cattle roam in a place like this, do you?" Olivia asked.

"No, Olivia, I didn't," I said. "This habitat is too small to graze cattle, pigs, goats, and chickens anyway. I'd think the colonists would have built a separate habitat for livestock. So where is it?"

"Well, maybe they have all become vegetarians," she said.

Thankfully, Larry Gino ended that fruitless exchange by diverting our attention to his conversation.

Chapter 8

Larry Gino
Project Leader

"DON'T LET me do all the work," Larry Gino bellowed. He was always bellowing about something. He was bent over, back straight, with one bare hand reaching for the lava path. He wasn't limber enough to touch it. "The ground is too far away. I can't reach it."

Larry Gino was a grumpy old man with a loud voice and a wicked little laugh that matched his wicked sense of humor. He had a sly mischievous grin and a twinkle in his eye. At 82, he was still a kid at heart. He was of average height with a little pouch of a belly. He had bright gray eyes and a hint of rosy cheeks.

Gino (as most people called him) was a man out for adventure. Usually the young were willing to trek across the stars, even with the possibility of never returning to Earth. The more mature were, well, more mature and more cautious. They had families and were at the age to settle down.

Not Larry Gino.

The Akiane scientific team was young, late teens to mid-twenties and early thirties. They were just starting out in their careers, and none had started their own families as of yet.

World Space Coalition decided that Akiane was a young person's adventure. Research would be new so they decided that those studying the alien planet should also be new and young. It was hoped the young would stay on the planet and have many years of research ahead of them.

In the first proposal, only thirteen year olds who had already earned their master's degrees would be selected. On the six-year journey, they could work on as many PhDs as they wanted while they grew up. They'd be nineteen when they arrived and ready to begin their studies.

Gino laughed in their collective faces while showing them the error of their thinking. The children might have been geniuses, but they were babes with little life experience.

"Someone should have at least some seasoning under their belt," Gino had told them with little grace.

WSC's Akiane Project Committee changed their policy and also decided that Dr. Larry Gino, geologist should be the project leader.

He had the most experience. He'd worked on the Moon and Mars colonies, and had helped establish the Europa colony.

He agreed, thinking he would not have much to do until he reached Akiane.

Instead, he became "father" when young scientists became homesick, counselor of romantically broken hearts, disciplinarian over disagreements, and teacher to those with PhD studies.

"I'm not being paid enough," he'd grumbled more than once.

Gino said he was going to spend the next phase of his life on an alien planet leisurely studying Akiane's geological structures.

His wife of fifty-nine years had passed away. He'd left three sons, two daughters-in-law, and seven grandchildren behind.

The granddaughter with the most spunk, who Gino called Sunshine, and her two younger brothers, Gunner and Sweet Baby Ray, loved dirt and rocks. They loved his cross-space holo-communications. They begged to hear about his interplanetary space adventures.

Sunshine had loudly declared that as soon as she was old enough, she was going to Mars University for her masters in geology, and her brothers declared they were going with her. Lastly, she informed Grampy in no uncertain terms that he was to meet them on Mars.

When the call came, he'd answer it, move to Mars, and raise the next generation of Gino geologists. He figured he had a good fifteen years before that call came. Sunshine was only 5 years old when he'd left Earth. Fifteen years was a long time and who knows how many times the mind of a five-year-old would change.

"How could you leave them?" he'd been asked more than once. "You'll miss the little ones growing up."

"They can send photos," he curtly said. In truth, if he thought of it too long, he became teary-eyed at all he'd miss. But when he thought of all he'd miss by staying home, he was grateful for the chance to be in the thick of things.

Since the average age for humans was now 150 years, he'd make it back to Earth, and his family, long before he passed away.

Volcanist Spago knelt down where geologist Gino pointed.

"Get those gloves off," Gino yelled as he straightened. *The boy was brilliant, but didn't have lick of sense*, he thought. Out loud, he said, "You can't tell anything with those on."

Spago was usually a bit stand-offish, but not with Larry Gino.

Obediently, Spago whipped his gloves off and placed both hands on the ground. Then with his rear up and his nose to the ground, he took a big sniff.

He couldn't keep a straight face, Gino laughed heartily.

The younger man tilted his head to look up at Gino and chuckled. The older man flashed that kid-like grin. Those two were always playing games.

That was the real reason why Gino had come. His own boys lacked any scientific interest. Gino loved his biological sons, but these scrappy brainiac scientists were his real children.

"What do you think?" Gino asked. He felt like a schoolboy who'd found a mud hole and wanted to show it to his best playground buddy. The idea was a little old fashioned, but that's how he felt, like a kid. Playing in the dirt as a child is what had originally spiked his interest in rocks.

"I think you're right," Spago said, just as eagerly. He sat back on his heels.

"Right about what?" Mathieu half-whined that he'd been left out of playtime.

"I wanted Spago to feel the path to see if it's warm. We think the colonists pipe hot water throughout the garden to heat it." Gino did his happy jig. Feet firmly planted, hips swaying with his arms moving back and forth. "This place is going to be fun to figure out," he said with enthusiasm.

Spago spoke with the same passion. "We think their heating system is not man-made."

"What is it?" Jessica asked.

"Geothermal heat!" Spago and Gino said in unison as if they were two boys who had just found a large bullfrog in their mud hole.

The volcanist and geologist stared at each other for a second then burst out laughing. One might have thought they were father and son, though they looked nothing alike.

Both were of average height, but Gino was fleshy with age, while Spago had a young man's thin frame. Gino had light brown, graying hair. Spago's hair was dark brown. Gino's face was wide. Spago's face was narrow.

"There is a massive lake that resides underground," Gino said, "which is heated from magma."

"How do you know there's a lake?" Jessica asked.

"Hot springs," Spago said. "Has to be a lake to feed them."

"I'll bet this pond and the hot springs outside are a part of the chain fed by the same underwater lake," Gino said.

"What hot springs?" Jessica asked.

"Didn't you see them, Jessica? The hot springs outside the habitat?" Gino asked. He couldn't believe that she'd missed them. The springs were situated between the mountains and the habitat.

Jessica stared at him with a puzzled look, trying to remember.

Gino shook his head. That was the trouble with the young; they miss so much of the world around them. They were too self-absorbed.

"Jessica, how could you miss them?" Gino asked.

She shrugged. "I was checking out the algae."

"What algae?" Olivia asked.

The young, even the brilliant, pay attention only to what interests them to the exclusion of everything else around them. Gino sighed in disappointment.

Jorg said to Olivia, "I'll take you out later and show you the algae patch."

She nodded her approval.

"And I'll take you outside, Jessica, and show you the hot springs," Gino promised.

She frowned.

Disappointed, Gino remembered Jessica was military, not a scientist. Exploring something scientifically worthy might not interest her.

"Jessie's not going outside," Jorg said.

All eyes turned toward Jessica.

"Not going outside? For how long?" Gino said.

"Until she goes home," Jorg said.

"Why?" Olivia asked. She was sitting on the ground with a dog lying across her lap.

"You came to study Akiane. I didn't," Jessica said. "I'm here on orders. I don't have to go outside. And since I don't like the cold, I'm not going outside until it's time for me to go home."

"Bit touchy, aren't we?" Olivia said.

"Now, now," Gino interrupted before the two got into it again. "Jessica has a right to her opinions."

And that seemed to be Gino's real job, babysitting adults.

❧ ❧

Two-and-a-half hours later, after all 103 of them were assembled at the entrance, and everyone was good and bored, three men appeared.

Gino, who never lacked for words, was speechless.

The *Britannia* crew, who had brought their personal gear and equipment to Akiane, told Gino and the others that the colonists looked a bit strange, but they were humans from Earth. It had only been 318 years. How much could they have changed?

Two of the men were a full head and shoulder taller that Jorg, who was an even 2 meters. The third man was older and slightly shorter.

All three were big men with big hands.

They wore shiny bright green, pajama-like clothes. Their sleeves were long, their shirttails hung out, held secure by a wide leather belt, their pant legs were wide and flowed as they walked. They each wore identical thin green gloves.

The middle-aged men looked like he'd just swallowed acid. His mouth puckered, his nose wrinkled, and his eyes narrowed in displeasure.

The youngest looking man smiled politely and looked pleased to see them. Worry lines etched his pleasant face.

The third man's skin was blotchy and his hair was graying. He looked weathered with age, but his smile said the hardships of life had not soured him.

The men stood without speaking and stared at them as though the scientists were the aliens.

"Lu," Gino softly asked. "What happened to their skin?"

"I don't know," she said.

"Think it's something they eat?" he asked.

"I don't know."

"If we eat it, will our skin change like that?"

"Larry, I don't know, but if it is something they eat, and we eat it, and if our skin does change, it will change back as soon as we stop eating it."

"But, Lu, they're maroon."

"I know, Larry."

Chapter 9

Adumie
Invaders

INTRUDERS SAT on the rocks staring wide-eyed, mouths agape, not moving, as if Adumie and his companions were the ones who were strange.

They sat on rocks that had been purposely chosen, shaped, and lovingly placed for their beauty. Those of Earth walked and sat on grass, giving no concern about the permanent damage. They had come to conquer and they had started with the gardens.

Adumie fumed.

Off-worlders were an alien-looking group, all different sizes and shapes, tall, short, thin, heavy. Adumie reasoned they must have a very complicated hierarchy.

On Akiane, things were simple. Adults were a uniform shape and height and a head shorter than the priests, except for those who were too ill and had lost their ability to maintain their size. The children were different sizes because they were still growing and had not yet learned to control their shape.

Their skin coloring was also different. It ranged from as black as lava to brown as soil, and from pale granite-pink to chalk white. Not one of them was maroon. Even their hair was different shades of black, brown, red-orange, and yellow. Some wore their hair long, but some wore it ridiculously short. Not one wore the distinguished priestly braids.

Everyone on Akiane was born with black hair and black eyes and their skin colorings were shades of maroon. The priests wore their hair in many thin braids. Everyone else's hair was straight to their shoulders. No one was humiliated by variance. Except Nu Venia, there was uniformity.

Only the color of her skin said Nu Venia was one of them, but her yellow eyes and white hair said she was different.

One child stood among the Intruders. That one had straight black hair and black, oddly shaped eyes, not round like the others. Why would they bring only one child? It did not make sense.

Not one of the Intruders wore gloves. Adumie did not want to think of the trouble that caused.

"Welcome," Cameron said, with a respectful bow. "I am Cameron, this is Jecidia." He waved a hand toward Jecidia. "And this is Adumie."

Adumie asked, "Who speaks?" He wished to quickly be done with this. Identify the priest. Let that one make World Space Coalition demands. Deny the demands. Then all will know their place.

"Well?" Adumie demanded.

One of the tallest, with hair color of Kahair's morning light, stood. Presumably, this one was in authority.

"Do you speak?" Adumie asked.

"I'm sorry, who do you want?" that one asked.

"Who are you?" Adumie asked.

"I'm Jorg Krause."

"Do you speak?"

Jorg Krause looked confused. "I don't understand."

"I believe you are asking for me. I'm Larry Gino." That one stood and walked with determination toward them, but he was only shoulder high to the Jorg Krause.

Adumie held up his hand. Larry Gino stopped. Somewhere in his heart, Adumie knew this one was not the one.

"Are you from World Space Coalition?" he asked.

"Well, we all are," Larry Gino said.

"I think he means you, Jessica," a rounded, curly copper-haired one said.

"Me, Olivia? Why?" That one's voice had the sound of irritation.

"I think he's asking for the person they specifically requested," the copper-haired one said. "That would be you,.."

"Olivia is right, Jessica," Larry Gino said. "You do speak for WSC."

The tall one reached a hand out to the one called Jessica. Jessica took Jorg Krause's hand for all to see — without shame!

Adumie diverted his eyes. He would not look upon such blasphemy.

The Jessica took a few steps forward. "I am Lieutenant Jessica Hewitt."

Lieutenant? What sort of name was that? The name rolled off the tongue refusing to end. What was the significance in using Lieutenant when the others used Jessica? A name revealed a person's nature. What did Lieutenant reveal?

At one time Adumie spoke his name as A'Dumie, which meant vitality or fullness. When he was young, A'Dumie was alive with hope and possibilities. That was another person. Another life.

Adumie meant void, empty, just how he felt now.

The name Lieutenant sounded harsh. Lieutenant looked harsh, furrowed forehead, eyes narrowed, mouth set in hard edges. This one was a little taller than Larry Gino, but shorter than Jorg Krause. World Space Coalition had sent a person of no importance.

"You speak for God?" Adumie demanded.

"What? Speak for God? No." Flustered, Lieutenant's face turned red. That one's eyes darted about, looking from Adumie to Cameron then turned to those behind.

Jecidia and Cameron exchanged glances. Jecidia had requested a priest. Why send a priest who does not speak for God?

"I am Lieutenant Jessica Hewitt," that one repeated.

So many names for such a small person, of no significance, a priest who does not speak for God. This one was a subordinate, a *xia ji*.

"I am here to negotiate," the *xia ji* said.

Adumie did not like the sound of "negotiate."

"What is negotiate?" Jecidia asked.

"I came to speak for World Space Coalition and decide on the terms of your colony," Lieutenant *xia ji* said.

"Terms? Negotiate? You mean demands," Adumie declared.

"Demands? No. I'm here to …"

Adumie did not let Lieutenant speak. "I know why you are here and why you have been sent. I will not be so insulted by a *xia ji*." He abruptly turned and left.

Chapter 10

Lieutenant Jessica Hewitt
Cultural Differences

SECONDS, THAT'S all it took, I'd failed in mere seconds.

Adumie had looked at me the way my mother used to. Her eyes would narrow then harden and seemed to say, "You're not worth loving."

One afternoon, I'd stood before her, on my best behavior, after having done all my chores. I'd made her a card expressing my love. She handed it back, saying, "What am I supposed to do with this after you used my paints? Without my permission. Clean up your mess. And make sure you put things back where you found them." She turned and walked away.

I was broken hearted.

Adumie walked away in the same manner of rejection.

His eyes had said, "You're not worth speaking to." And my insides shriveled. I'd tried to look at him while I spoke, but I couldn't stand his disapproving glare.

I never knew what I'd done to make Mom dislike me. Now, this alien man, who had never met me before, felt the same way. What was wrong with me?

"When Adumie calms down," Cameron began, but Jecidia cut him off.

"We will show you to your living area now," he said.

Cameron didn't respond. He didn't so much as give Jecidia a reproachful look for interrupting him. Instead he stood stone faced as if nothing had happened. Clearly, Cameron was not the one in charge or the one I needed to smooth things over with.

"What was that all about?" Olivia asked. One might have thought she was the one who had just been rejected. She spoke loud enough for our guides to hear. Perhaps she thought to insult them further, but neither responded.

"What did he call me?" I asked, more to myself than anyone else.

"*Xia ji*, that's Chinese for subordinate," Lu said.

"Why am I subordinate?" I asked.

"I don't know," Lu said.

"You're only a lieutenant," Olivia said, still not lowering her voice. "Maybe he expected an admiral."

"No, I think it has something to do with cultural differences," Lu also spoke in hushed tones.

"Who cares?" I voiced my irritation.

"You do," Lu said. "For some reason he thinks you're a subordinate and I don't think he means military."

"Technically, she is," Olivia retorted. "A lieutenant isn't that important."

"Olivia. Sending a lieutenant to speak for the admiral is the same as actually sending an admiral," Jorg said.

"Maybe to us, but clearly not to Adumie," Olivia said.

"I think it's more than your rank, Jessica. I think there's something else bothering him," Lu said.

My thoughts exactly. He seemed to hate me, even before I opened my mouth. I cringed. If he did hate me, how was I supposed to sit down and negotiate with him?

"Bothering him?" Jorg asked. "Such as?"

"I don't know," Lu said.

Our guides escorted us through the habitat to the far side of the habitat from where we'd entered. We walked at Jecidia's pace, and stopped several times so he could catch his breath. What should have been a thirty-minute walk took us almost fifty minutes. Amazingly, no one complained. The slow pace gave us a chance to examine the habitat.

We stayed on a lava path that meandered though the gardens. The inside of the dome was one large garden, with trees, bushes, flowers, and rocks of all kinds and of various sizes.

The path kept us away from the only buildings in the dome, which seemed to be the two outdated space ships. The shape of the ships was different from modern sleek ships. They were almost round. The hull was no longer shiny. The paint was a faded deep gray, instead of the now classic blue gray.

I could only assume the colonists had turned their ships into their cities, and everything outside were native gardens.

We passed a mound of rocks taller than our hosts. Water spouted from the top of the pile and flowed into a large bathtub like container. As it filled, the water descended into another pool and then another until the water filled the last pool at ground level, which was the size of a professional swimming pool. The water was clear and inviting. If I had to guess, it was a pool to swim or bathe in.

Spago and Gino softly discussed the rocks and water.

"Think the water comes from the underground pool?" Spago asked.

"Yes, in which case that water is scolding hot," Gino said.

"Agreed. And the pools are to cool the water to a usable temperature," Spago said.

Olivia's voice shattered the quiet of the moment. "Notice the columns? Why use columns? Why not ..."

Someone overrode her with one word and sent a shiver up my spine. "Earthquakes."

The colonists must have had the technology to balance a building this size without the use of columns, even if there were quakes. But if the quakes on Akiane were frequent and intense, they might need reinforcements to keep the building standing. I didn't want to think about it. Though the next time we passed one I did take a closer look.

The center of the column was hollow and wide enough for a small person, like Lu, to comfortably stand in. Three thick metal rods the size of my wrist curled up in an S pattern toward the glass ceiling. Another set of rods circled up in the opposite direction. The columns looked like colossal springs that help hold the dome up.

The farther we got from our original entrance, the less the gardens were manicured. By the time we'd reached our living area, it looked as though no one had tended these gardens for a long time. The tops of trees had been chopped off so they didn't grow into the glass ceiling. The sides along the path had been similarly chopped off so one could easily walk the path. But that seemed to be all the care they'd managed to do. Here the gardens looked like a wild forest.

Lower to the ground, vines were trying to creep over the path. Saplings were pushing up through the rock path.

Something was wrong. I couldn't imagine that these people hated us so much they would neglect their precious gardens. No, there was another reason why this area had been neglected.

When Jorg and I were on the landing field getting our first look at the habitat, we'd seen six tunnels leading into the habitat. For some reason the colonists had only enclosed the area between two of those tunnels. By my navigational skills, I guessed we were heading for that room. It looked like we'd been banished to the far edges of their complex so we wouldn't be underfoot.

The entrance to the room was the width of three normal doors. Just above the opening, someone had just freshly painted over something. The paint was black like the dome wall, but the shine was clearly noticeable. I'd bet this room had a name that had been erased because of our occupation of it.

"This is for you," Cameron said referring to the room.

It wasn't much to look at.

The floor was a dingy faded blue, worn with age. It was one large room the same length as the tunnels, but only half as wide. There was a wall down the length on the left side of the room, with two doors on either end. Our living quarters couldn't be on the other side of that wall; there wasn't enough space for all the rooms we'd need.

There were no windows, offices, or cubicles. The only light came from a glow radiating from the ceiling. The room was empty except for the piles of luggage and crates of equipment the *Britannia* crew had delivered for us.

There were another two doors in the right wall near this end of the room. I had no idea what they were for.

"I thought our things were supposed to be in our offices and labs," someone said.

"I think this is our offices and labs," another said.

"Better not be," Rona said, angrily. "I can't work in here like this. I need dust-free workspace."

"So do I."

"Me too."

"Well, I'd better get one."

One person speaking their opinion wasn't enough. Every single one of them had to voice their opinion, even though it was the exact same thought as everyone else.

"Enough!" Gino bellowed before they had all spoken.

To my surprise, they abruptly quieted.

Lu, Rona, and a few others walked over to the crates and began to inspect the pile.

"I think we should deal with this first," Zhoa said.

"What?" I turned to see what he was referring to.

Behind us, just to the right of the entrance were several large hooks. Hanging from one of those hooks was a piece of meat the size of a polar bear.

It had been skinned, beheaded, and gutted. Its four legs hung lose. At one time it must have been a magnificent animal.

"What is this?" Zhoa asked our guides.

Jecidia turned to face him. "Who are you?"

"I'm Zhoa. My brother, Vong, and I are cooks."

Jecidia nodded. "Will you not be eating meat?"

Zhoa blinked; the question stumped him. "Yes, we eat meat. But why is it hanging on the wall?"

"As a courtesy," Cameron said.

"I don't understand," Zhoa said.

Cameron said, "We are unaware if you have the skill to hunt."

Vong chuckled. "These people are brilliant, but I don't think they're very good hunters."

Our guides didn't acknowledge his humor. "This meat is tupilak," Cameron said.

"Tupilak?" I said.

He nodded.

"Where I come from, tupilak is an Inuit mythical creature that lives under the ice. It grabs little children, pulls them under, and drowns them," I said.

"Here tupilak live in the ocean under the ice. We hunt it. Eat it. Blubber is used for heating and lighting when one camps outside. Its fur is used for warm clothing," Cameron said.

"Will you always deliver the tupilak like this?" Zhoa asked.

Cameron said, "We will provide you with meat, yes."

"What about fruit and vegetables?" Zhoa asked.

"Your *ashag* is there," Jecidia pointed to one of the doors to the right of us. "The room here, you will prepare your meals." He indicated the other door.

"Excuse me," Vong said, "but what is *ashag*?"

"It is the fields where food is grown," Jecidia said.

"I'm thinking hydroponics," Zhoa said.

"Are the bees in there, too?" Vong asked. "Will we have honey hives?" His face brightened at the thought.

"Bees?" Cameron asked.

"Yellow and black insects that fly around with tiny wings. Bees to pollinate the flowers, vegetables, and fruit," Vong explained.

"Ah," said Cameron, with a nod of understanding.

"Yes, there are brushes," Jecidia said.

"Brushes?" Vong croaked.

"Brushes," Cameron agreed with a slight nod of his head.

At Vong's look of dismay, Cameron asked, "Is something not to your liking?"

"You don't have bees?" Though Vong spoke politely, his voice sounded a bit strained.

I didn't understand why the lack of bees would stress him.

Zhoa caught his brother's arm before he could say more. "Brushes are fine," he said.

"But ..." Vong started to object. Zhoa shook his head.

Softly, Vong continued to express his feelings, "If there are no bees, someone will have to pollinate each individual flower." Clearly he was not looking forward to the tedious task.

"We will make do," Zhoa just as quietly said.

"I think everyone should help," I said.

All heads turned towards me and groaned.

"We don't have time to pollinate flowers," Olivia said irritably. "We have projects."

Several people took a step away from her, not because they disagreed with her, but because she was so loud. Her voice seemed to bounce off the walls.

"You do if you want to eat," Gino said. "We will all help Vong brush flowers."

Olivia glared. "I didn't come all this way to brush flowers. It's not my fault they won't share their bees with us."

"It's not that they won't share," Zhoa told her. "I don't believe they have bees."

"That's still not my fault. I have a job to do. I'm not going to squander my time futzing with flowers."

"How about if we discuss this later, after our hosts have gone." I didn't want our hosts to know that Olivia had come to study marine life. If they objected, Olivia would be the one to start the first intergalactic war, not me.

She rounded on me. "Don't cut me off like that. I will not be quiet just because you tell me to. Who do you think you are to

102

order me around like that? I have an opinion and I have a right to express it. You don't have any authority over me. I'll …"

I stepped up to Olivia, got in her face and said, with full authority, "Enough!"

She stiffened, shrunk back, and blinked several times. She couldn't believe I'd just yelled at her, but she kept her mouth shut.

"Please continue," I said, politely to our hosts.

After a light nod, Jecidia said, "This area is yours. The rest of Endurance is ours."

"Endurance?" I asked.

"The name for the place in which we live," Cameron explained.

"The entire habitat? This building and the gardens?" I asked to be sure I understood him correctly.

"We live inside Endurance, yes," Cameron confirmed. "We named it Endurance for we have endured much."

The name of the habitat was not in the files I'd read, but I could understand why they named it Endurance. After these people were stranded here, light-years from Earth, they needed a place to survive and thrive. So they built this habitat. This habitat helped them endure the harshness of the outside weather.

The name reminded me of Sir Ernest Shackleton, captain of the ship *Endurance* in 1912. He and his crew sailed for the Antarctic, but never made it. Winter came early that year and trapped the ship in the ice surrounding the Antarctic. The ship and her crew became famous for the incredible journey they endured and the fact that they all survived. Just like these people.

It was beginning to look like the colonists had brought much of Earth's different cultures with them and incorporated them into their lives here: such as the Inuit tupilak and now Shockleton's Endurance.

My father would have loved it here. He'd have fun untangling their cultures and lifestyles. It was the kind of thing he liked to do and was always talking about. I wished I could trade places with him. But I realized if he were still alive, there would be no need to trade places. I wouldn't be here. I'd still be on Earth with him.

Cameron stared at me as if he might be reading my mind. It made me nervous.

Zhoa asked him, "Will you also provide fish?"

Our guides stepped back in horror. "We ... You ..." Jecidia stammered.

I was surprised their composure and confidence could be so easily shaken.

"We did not anticipate your asking for fish," Cameron said.

Zhoa was now equally taken aback. "I didn't mean to offend. Do you not eat fish?"

"Fish are for chovis," Jecidia said.

Chovis? That was a word I had not heard before. I was about to ask what or who a chovis was when Cameron confirmed, "No, we do not eat fish."

"Then neither will we," Gino said, quickly stepping into the conversation.

A few voices from the scientific fish-eating crowd objected.

"We will not offend our hosts by eating fish," he said loudly.

Reluctantly, the crowd subsided.

Cameron nodded.

Now Jecidia studied me, also trying to understand something about me. I didn't like the way those men scrutinized me. It made me feel small and insignificant. I ducked my head.

Lu ran to Gino's side, out of breath. "La-ary, t-t-the toilets a-a-are dr-rainages. S-s-stalls don't have d-doors or cur-r-tains." She sounded on the verge of hysteria.

"Get a grip, Lu," he said.

Rona ran up and grabbed his arm. She practically yanked him off his feet as she pulled at him.

"Come," she said. "You have to see this. You all do." She proceeded to drag him through the room, around the pile of crates and into one of the doors to the left of the room.

We all followed.

As soon as Gino saw why Rona and Lu were so distraught, he pulled his arm out of Rona's grip and grunted, "This is not going to work."

Chapter 11

Larry Gino
Accommodations

BEHIND THE door was another room the exact size as the first room. In it were five rows of perfectly aligned bunk beds. Gino didn't need to count. He knew. There were 103 beds, one for each scientist, the two cooks, and Jessica. These colonists expected them to live, bathe, dress, and sleep, men and women, all in one room.

This was why the luggage was in one large pile. The military movers thought each person would choose the bed they wanted and place their things next to it. They should have said something. Maybe they thought this was funny.

"Well, this will be interesting living arrangements," Gino said, with a slightly uneasy laugh.

"No," Lu scolded him. "This is no time to be joking."

"Lu, don't be so dramatic," Rona said, "Gino doesn't like it any more than we do."

No, he wasn't joking; he was nervous. People didn't do well with everyone in one room. No one would want this. It didn't matter if it was the year 2450.

"Where are the bathrooms?" Olivia demanded.

"Against the wall." Lu groaned.

Faucets for washing hands and showerheads stuck out all along the far wall. Underneath each was a drain. There were no dividers or curtains.

"Don't these people know what year this is?" Olivia asked. "We have modern conveniences. We even have new technology."

"Yeah, but they weren't on Earth for all of it," Mathieu said.

"We're supposed to shower in the open for all to see." Olivia wrapped her arms around her plump body. "No," she said weakly.

"And we are to pee and crap for all to view," Gino said. "Personally, I have no desire for anyone to watch me, man or woman."

"I agree with Gino."

"I don't relish the thought."

"Well, I'm not going to."

"I don't care how progressive we've become, I'm not sharing a room with sixty-eight men," Olivia said. "Larry, what are you going to do about this?" Olivia is one of the few people who call Larry Gino by his first name.

Gino braced himself for a fight. He feared Jessica would tell Olivia and everyone else that this was a military operation. Sometimes, you have to put up with crap while under orders. Instead, she crunched up her face in disgust. She didn't like it any more than the rest of them. He let out a soft sigh.

Evidently, feelings were mutual. A couple of the younger people thought it was funny, but they were quickly shut down.

Sharing a room with several men would be bad enough, but 103 women and men would not do at all. The thought of bathing or dressing in front of so many people was creepy.

"Jessica!" Olivia rounded on her as if this was all her fault. "What are you going to do about this?"

"Me? Why me?" Jessica jumped with surprise.

"You're in charge, aren't you?" Olivia said. "You're the lieutenant from WSC. You're the negotiator."

"Enough," Gino said softly, "I am team leader. I'll talk to them."

"Well, you had better," Olivia demanded.

Before he spoke to their hosts, Gino thought it best to first deal with Olivia. He took her by the arm and gently pulled her to one side.

Speaking under his breath, he asked, "Olivia, what's the real problem?"

She leaned in so close, her curls brushed his face, and quietly whispered, "I can't dress in front of men. I can barely do it in front of women." Anything else she might have wanted to say seemed caught in her throat.

She wrapped her arms around her chubby body as if he might see her naked.

He wouldn't have thought Olivia had a vulnerable bone in her body. Still, he couldn't blame her. He didn't relish the thought of all those women watching him tramp around in his under draws.

"I will deal with this, but you have to keep your mouth closed," he said. Olivia had a problem with expressing herself appropriately, often insulting those around her. He was afraid of what their hosts might do if she insulted them. "You'll make things worse for our living situation."

She nodded. "You take care of it and I'll stay out of it." He hoped she'd keep her promise.

Gino hurried back through the crowd to find their guides, but they were gone. As he ran into the garden, faster than even he thought possible, Gino realized he was panicking.

"Wait!" he called to the men just as they were about to disappear around a corner of bushes.

They stopped. Cameron took a few steps toward him.

Gino almost insulted them himself by bellowing in his usual manner, *What do you think you're doing? Just how far does your dislike for us go? Just ... Just ...* He realized he sounded like Olivia. This would not do. Before he created an interplanetary rift, he took a deep breath to calm his nerves.

His wife's face loomed in his mind's eye. She would have objected to his sour attitude. She always did. But it was in him to yell and be gruff. He was rarely angry, truly angry; he just wanted to make people laugh and not take life so serious.

Gino knew these men would not understand his brand of humor. He needed to speak calmly. He took another deep breath.

"Is there a problem?" Cameron politely asked.

"Ah, yes," Gino said. "We can't all live in one room."

Everyone had followed Gino and now stood in a semicircle behind him, waiting for the outcome.

"Explain." This was good, Cameron seemed genuinely concerned for their needs.

Pointing in the direction of their living area, Gino said again, "We can't all live in the same room."

"Why not?" Jecidia asked.

"Because it is unacceptable for us to do so," Gino said.

Jecidia looked mystified. They both did.

109

Gino's stomach did a flip-flop. *Please, help me make them understand,* he silently prayed.

"What is the problem?" Cameron asked. Did he really not know?

Gino's mind raced. He was good at bellowing, but that wouldn't work here. He needed to convince them without offending them.

"In the same way you do not eat fish," he said, "it is not socially acceptable for us to live together in one room."

"We live in one room." It appeared that Jecidia's mind would not be easily changed.

"All of you?" Gino asked.

"All of us," he confirmed.

Pausing to considerer his next words, Gino said, "It's socially improper for us to do so."

Jecidia had just said it was socially improper for them to eat fish; they should understand the predicament.

The crowd around them murmured and scuffled about nervously.

"You require how many rooms?" Cameron asked.

Good. He understands, Gino thought.

Lu pulled at Gino's sleeve. He tried to ignore her. She continued to pull.

He had told Olivia to remain quiet. He now realized that he should have told all of them to stay out of this conversation.

"We only need ...," he began.

"Many," Lu blurted out.

"Many?" Jecidia asked, surprised and alarmed.

Gino inwardly moaned. Lu would make things worse if she didn't keep quiet. They'd be stuck with that one large dormitory. He glanced at Olivia. He would be the one blamed, not Lu.

There'll be no controlling Olivia now, he feared.

Lu whispered. "Each married couple needs their own room."

At launch, there had been only two married couples, but thanks to Cupid's arrows of amore, and the captain's authority to perform marriage ceremonies, there were now nine, not to mention those who were in relationships, though not married, each desiring their own private space.

Gino had been young once. He knew couples had a knack when it came to finding privacy.

Maybe he could get three rooms, one for women, one for men, and one for the married couples to share as they pleased.

Rona whispered in his other ear, "We need dust-free work areas."

He didn't look at her. The workroom was large enough for all of them to set up individual workspaces. These young ones demanded too much. They were going to get kicked out of Endurance and sent home in defeat before they even started their research projects. Gino hadn't come all this way just to be escorted back to the transport ship empty-handed.

With a pleading gesture, he said, "We require three rooms for our living arrangements, and please, our work area requires special consideration." He quickly gave Rona and Lu a look of warning that said no more comments.

Jecidia gasped. Cameron's shoulders slumped slightly. He bowed his head in disappointment.

"We hunt for you. You expect us to pollinate your plants. Now we are to rebuild your living area?" Jecidia sighed unhappily. "Perhaps Adumie is right. You think us servants."

"No! That is not our intention." Gino was both surprised and appalled that they would think such a thing. "We need your help to meet some of our needs. That is all." He motioned toward the scientists around him. "We are willing to compromise." They groaned in concern for what he was about to suggest.

He turned back to their guides. "For right now, we will settle for one more sleeping room other than the one you have given us."

He raised his hand before anyone could object. To Gino's surprise, they quieted.

"As we get to know each other better, and with your help, we would very much like to discuss different accommodations for our needs," Gino said.

"We have survived for 318 years without your interference. Now you come expecting us to obey your every command?" Jecidia said.

"No!" Gino exclaimed. "That is not at all what we want."

"No?" Jecidia echoed.

Cameron pulled Jecidia into a huddle.

It was a tense moment as everyone watched the two confer. But by their animated gestures, it seemed to be more of an argument. Once finished, Jecidia stiffly shuffled off. He had trouble walking.

Cameron returned to Gino.

"In time we may discuss different accommodations," he said. "But, for now ..." he waved toward the their rooms, and bowed his head apologetically, "... you must overcome your differences." He turned and left.

As soon as the two men disappeared from sight behind some bushes, questions erupted.

"How can they say *no*?"

"Don't they understand?"

"How can they all live together?"

"How can we all live in one room?"

Someone asked, "Why do they think we want them to be our slaves?"

"I have no idea," Gino answered.

"They are a bit testy, don't you think?" Olivia asked.

"What are we going to do?" Rona asked.

"Jessica, do something. You're WSC," Olivia demanded. She frequently demanded her requests.

"You work for World Space Coalition just like I do," Jessica said. "*You* talk to them."

"You were ordered here as liaison," she said. She kept talking, pressing her point. Jessica turned her back and walked away.

And yet Olivia kept talking. Only now she'd turned on Gino. "Are you even listening to me? What are you going to do about this?"

"Olivia, it won't do any good," Jorg said. "They don't want to help us. Gino did the best he could."

"He didn't try hard enough," Olivia said. "Maybe Jessica should have yelled at them instead of me. Maybe then Gino would have gotten something done. He's so fond of yelling, maybe he should have yelled at them." She jabbed a finger out the bay door. "I'm not living like that."

"It's no one's fault, Olivia," Rona said. Hopefully, she could shut Olivia up before someone slugged her.

But Olivia was not the type to just let go.

"Someone should have demanded action," she insisted in her gravelly, grating voice. "Someone should make them understand. I can't live in conditions like this."

"Enough already." By the roughness of his voice, Gino was tired of Olivia's complaining. "Their minds were made up before we got here. Nothing Jessica nor I could have said would have made a difference."

Olivia asked, "What are we going to do?"

"Make the best of a bad situation," Jessica said.

Olivia's eyes were wide with disbelief. Her mouth opened and closed. For the first time ever, nothing came out. She looked like one of her fish.

"You people are supposed to be problem solvers. Are you telling me you can only solve scientific problems? What about solving life's problems?" Gino asked.

"Fine. You want a solution? Have *Britannia* make us walls," Olivia loudly declared.

"That's brilliant," Gino said.

She smirked.

"Lu, are there drains and showers along the entire length of the far wall of the dormitory room?" Gino asked.

"Yes," she said.

"There are thirty-five women. We'll move thirty-five beds to one side of the room, then move the rest of the beds to the other side," Jessica said.

"But we'll still all be in one room," Olivia whined.

"Yes, but we'll call *Britannia* and ask them to make dividing walls before they leave," Jessica said.

"Why not just give us an Object Builder?" Rona asked. "Then we can make work areas, too."

"Because the machine is built into the ship and *Britannia* has more need for it than we do," she said.

"We'll ask them to build two walls across the dorm room so there are three rooms. Then divide the third room into three rooms for couples," Gino said.

"Only three rooms?" someone asked.

"Sorry, it's going to have to do. *Britannia* doesn't have the time to make a lot of separate rooms," Jessica said.

"But only three? Who gets them?" Sean, a newly married engineer, asked.

"You'll have to make up a schedule," Gino said.

The couples looked dissatisfied, but one of the women said, "It's better than not ever being alone." Slowly, reluctantly, the others agreed.

Good. At least one thing was settled; only a thousand more to go, Gino thought.

"We should stack the crates and boxes against the wall and make cabinets out of them. We know what's in them and who needs to get at what. We'll organize them accordingly," Spago said.

Universally, some moaned their objections. "Why bother?"

"To get them out of the way so we can move around," Jessica said.

"We need clean rooms," voices objected. "Our work will be contaminated."

Jessica ran her fingers through her hair. She was becoming stressed over these unexpected circumstances. *But she is handling it well*, Gino thought.

"Here's how I see it. You can quit now, return to *Britannia*, and go home. You all know that's my first choice," Jessica said. "Or you can learn how to work in primitive conditions."

As if they didn't understand her words, no one spoke.

Gino didn't know what to do. He couldn't imagine any of them going home defeated, or sitting for two years doing nothing just because they didn't have dust-free areas.

Then he had a thought, and said, "For crime's sakes. Some of the best scientists worked in far worse conditions: Darwin out on a ship, the *Beagle*, in the middle of the ocean; Leonardo de Vinci worked in a hot, un-air-conditioned, candle-lit, poorly-built wooden room; Einstein worked in his head. Now there was a disorderly mess." He chuckled.

A few smiled.

"Don't forget Stanzas on Mars." Gino looked around the room to make sure all were paying attention. "He certainly didn't have a dust-free workspace and look what he accomplished. There are now colonies on the Moon, Mars, Europa, and here, on Akiane, all because of him."

Gino bellowed in his best old-man voice. "Are you young people going to tell me you're not as good or as dedicated? You're on an unexplored planet about to make discoveries that will affect scientific history, and you're crying about dust?"

Sheepishly, they diverted their eyes. Their brain-gears started whirring as they considered his words. They glanced around to see what the others thought.

"What do you say?" Gino's voice easily spun around the room.

"I guess," one timid voice said.

"It's better than doing nothing," another said, more confidently.

"I'm not going home empty-handed."

"Sure, why not?"

Each person spoke with increasing confidence.

Gino winked at Jessica. Together, they had diverted their second catastrophe. Then he turned to the cooks, brothers Zhoa and Vong, "Where's the kitchen?"

They pointed to a door to the right of the hanging meat. "In there, I think," Zhoa said. "We haven't checked it out yet."

"Deal with the meat before it goes bad," Gino said.

"Dinner will be ready before you've sorted the crates," Zhoa promised.

"Good," Jessica said. "Zhoa and Vong will need help finding their kitchen equipment in that pile of crates." She pointed to the hundreds of crates of all sizes piled in the middle of the room. "Would someone please help them move everything in their kitchen."

"Let's go," a few voices chimed.

"Do we have hinges or door handles?" Mathieu asked.

"Probably not," Jessica said. "Why?"

"We could make doors for the crates if we had some," he said.

"*Britannia* might have them," Lu suggested, "or they could make some."

"Lu, contact *Britannia* and ask them if they have anything we could use for hinges and handles, and don't forget to ask them for our walls. See if they can also make tables and chairs, and cubicle walls," Gino added.

"It will be my pleasure." Lu turned to do as he'd requested.

"Oh, hang on." Jessica had a thought.

Lu stopped in mid-step and turned around.

"Ask them to contact Earth to let them know you'll need supplies to build clean rooms," Jessica said. "See if the next ship coming to Akiane can accommodate you."

"Will do." Her hand came up for a quick salute. Her heels clicked.

The rest of the scientists began unpacking and constructing the wall of cabinets.

Rona stepped in front of Gino.

"I have a question," she said.

Several people glanced in their direction.

"What?" He tried side-stepping her, but she refused to let him pass.

"How do we clean our bedding and clothes?" Rona asked. "If these people used third-world bathroom services, how advanced could their laundry cleaning be? What are we going to do?"

Everyone stopped to look at him for the answer.

Gino cringed. *These children are going to be the death of me yet.*

Chapter 12

Adumie
Insulted

ADUMIE ENJOYED the quiet after the caretakers finished tending the *ashag* and picking produce for the day's needs. He liked the smell of lemons, the taste of tiny tomatoes, and the feel of the freshness of the hydroponics. He needed this time to undo the after affects of meeting Invaders from Earth.

After the habitat was completed, it was decided that the grounds would be used only for pleasure and to allow native plants to grow. The hydroponics became the *ashag*, the fields of produce.

Eagle carried seeds for every kind of fruit and vegetable that grew on Earth. When it exploded, all of it was lost. Everything they had to eat came from the fields that were on *Falcon* and *Hawk*. They only had the basics, but it had been enough. The ancestors went through great pains to keep the same integrity of fruit and vegetables as that of Earth.

Adumie chose a peach and bit into it. Did it taste the same as on Earth? Delicious. What did he care if the fruit tasted the same or not: it was now fruit of Akiane.

The gardeners carefully nurtured each plant. This tree was close to ten years old. The tree was one and a half meters tall with roots the size of his fingers. Its trunk was thick, snarled and folded over itself, and twice the size of his forearm. Its branches were weighted down with bright crimson peaches.

Along the same table were other trees just as old and older. Saplings grew on a nearby table.

He lightly touched the leaves of a tomato plant. Its stalk was also thick and gnarled. Vines were allowed to grow until they stopped producing, then they were pruned back in preparation for new growth.

New growth was the promise of future.

"There is disappointment that one such as you wished not speak to the priest from Earth," Jecidia's voice crushed the peace of the moment. Why would the old one not leave him alone?

"I will not be so insulted." Adumie seethed not just at the thought of the Earth priest, but also of being disrupted during his short time of serenity.

"Perhaps their ways are different and they are unaware of our ways. That one could be smaller to show respect," Jecidia suggested.

Jecidia was always seeking the best. He forgives too easily and does not clearly see reality, Adumie thought. *I am not so deceived.*

Adumie continued his walk in the hopes of leaving Jecidia behind. Jecidia tried to keep up.

"That one ..." Adumie would not speak the name Lieutenant, a name with no meaning. "A priest was requested. A priest was granted who does not speak with God's authority. Nor does that one stand as a priest should. Why send such a one?"

"Perhaps they do not value height as we do." Jecidia gasped for breath. One of his legs seemed to be giving him more trouble than usual. He began to limp. "Did you not observe their many sizes? They might not be like us."

Adumie snorted. "As Cameron has said, 'They are not so different from us.'" Yet if they were different, it was an excellent reason to convince the community not to associate with them.

Besides, once the Invaders learn the truth, that they were no longer fully human, those of Earth will be appalled. Adumie imagined the looks of disgust on their faces. His people had done what was needed. Earth did not have understanding of their struggles to survive.

Adumie had come to the *ashag* to be alone, not to think about Invaders, but this one chose to be intrusive. Adumie hastened his pace.

As Jecidia fell behind, he spoke louder. "Did you not notice how all of them are shorter than our priests? Is that not a sign of respect?" Again he spoke of harmony.

"They came to dominate, not show respect." Adumie would not be calmed. Suddenly stopping, he whirled around. "World Space Coalition proves their disrespect by sending *xia ji*."

Jecidia halted, gasping for breath.

"Did you see how they held hands without shame?" Adumie demanded as he stomped back toward Jecidia.

Dropping his head as if in shame, Jecidia said, "There are no explanations for such an act. They may be more different than we ever expected. Sadly they might not hold purity in the same regard as we do."

"We are a holy people. We are not to associate with blasphemers," Adumie said, standing before him. "Does it not say, *'Do not be unevenly yoked with unbelievers'?*"

Jecidia raised his head and looked Adumie in the eye. "Is it their touching of hands or their size or that they are from Earth that most offends you?"

Adumie walked past Jecidia. If he would not leave Adumie alone, Adumie would find another place to walk. Perhaps outside. Jecidia could no longer tolerate the cold as he once did.

But as Adumie was escaping, he found Qorow Low, Halmahera, and seven other life-givers standing before him.

Qorow Low smiled tentatively. Adumie chose not to respond. Disappointed, her smile faded.

The pain of disappointment was all too familiar to Adumie. It was better this way. Qorow Low's emotions would wane from lack of encouragement. Such affections brought only problems. Wishing things could be different proved nothing.

"Speak," Adumie said more roughly than he'd intended.

Qorow Low flinched.

He closed his eyes. One more regret. He truly liked her, but she wanted more than a priest's friendship, something he could not give for fear of consequences.

Halmahera spoke. "Minds are wondering if those of World Space Coalition have knowledge of how to save our children from the slow dying illness."

Division among the community, Adumie thought. *This is Cameron's fault.*

"Intruders are not here to help, but to rule over us," he said. "They claim all that we have built as theirs."

"They may have new methods of healing," Qorow Low said. "How many more children must die?" She often spoke her mind without thought. It was that which frustrated Adumie most about her. If only she would listen to him and not be misguided by Cameron's false hopes.

When a life-giver became ill, she could no longer birth a child. It was happening to too many life-givers. Many were dying young—too young or they died while giving birth. Their numbers were dwindling. Soon there would be no more life-givers. Without children, the community would cease to exist.

Soon everyone would be dead.

"I want to have many children and I want all of them to live," Qorow Low said, with a little cry of fear in her voice.

"My first child has died," Susa said, as she pushed through the crowd of life-givers.

"As have mine."

"And mine."

"My second child has died. I'm fearing to have another," Susa continued.

"What are you doing to save our children?" Halmahera asked.

What could Adumie say? *I have prayed, but God's answer is death.* He could not speak such truths out loud.

"Those of Earth only bring discord," he said. "They have no care if we live or die. They only want what we have built and all we have created."

"How can you be saying that?" Qorow Low asked.

"We sent a message asking for their help. I sent the message myself. It took twelve of their years for them to decide to answer," Adumie said. "By that time, so many had already died." Like the one closest to his heart: Petra.

"They are here now," Qorow Low said. "Ask them."

"Yes, one should be speaking to them," Susa pleaded.

Their faces were filled with anxiety and grief. It tore at Adumie's heart, making him hate those of Earth all the more. Intruders brought the hope of help, knowing full well they would not do so. Those of Earth were the same people who had sent them here 318 years ago and then abandoned them.

The ancestors sent many messages and patiently waited for reinforcements. None came. Earth sent one robotic ship 26 years later. By then it was too late. The change was beginning. They feared their children would not be welcomed; they could survive on Earth; not once they had become children of Akiane.

World Space Coalition sent no more ships, sent no messages. Earth became silent, not interested if any survived or died. Earth was pitiless.

"I don't want any more of my children to be dying," Halmahera said. Her child was about to come-forth. She had already lost four. How many broken hearts could one endure in a lifetime? Adumie didn't understand why she continued to try.

If only her child would be born healthy, Adumie silently prayed. Unfortunately, no one was listening.

"I honestly do not believe Intruders care about our children," Adumie spoke gently. His words were difficult to say yet they needed to be spoken, heard and followed. "Not one of those of Earth tries to make amends for abandoning us so many years ago. World Space Coalition lied to the first of us. Promises were made to send ships and more people. And any who wished to return to Earth could. Those promises were never kept."

"Still, we should be speaking to them," Qorow Low insisted. "Perhaps they are not understanding because no one gives understanding." The gentleness of Qorow Low, which Adumie admired most, would be her undoing.

"They blaspheme." The words came from Adumie's mouth before he had time to stop them.

"Explain," Qorow Low said. Her eyes were fill with suspicion. Did she think he lied? Or was it that she did not believe his words? Her lack of trust stabbed at him.

"They touch," Adumie said. "In public for all to see."

The life-givers gasped in horror.

Qorow Low's eyes narrowed in continued disbelief.

"How can they be doing such a thing?" Halmahera angrily spoke.

"They have no shame for such blatant displays of touching. Gloves do not cover their hands." Adumie looked directly at Qorow Low. "Do you think God would be pleased if we ask help from such people?"

Qorow Low pulled her gloves tighter and would not look directly at Adumie, but softly quoted, "*Our bodies are a living sacrifice unto God. We should be holy and pleasing unto God.*"

"Do not waste your time trying to win over those who will not be won over," Adumie said.

"Adumie is speaking truth. Those of Earth do not care. Intruders must be made to leave," Mercener said.

"If only there was knowledge of how to make them leave," Adumie said. "Do not go near them. They bring harm." Adumie gently directed the life-givers back toward the Blood Vines. "Return to your children; speak of life to them. Ignore Intruders." He wanted to say with full faith, *Leave them to God.*

If only God cared enough to deal with them, Adumie thought. For he feared God would do nothing.

Halmahera immediately did as Adumie said and quickly turned, no doubt to check on her child. Others followed, some with less enthusiasm. Mercener almost ran out of the *ashag*. She was on a mission.

Qorow Low was the last to leave. Without raising her eyes from the floor, she spoke quietly. "I hope you speak the truth of God's words and do not speak from bitterness of heart."

He did not answer her. How could she know of his wounded heart? He'd told no one.

"There are decisions that must be made by the whole community," she said.

He wanted to say no. But the word caught in his throat and would not come out.

He saw her pain. He could not scold her, nor could he deny her. Perhaps she was right. A meeting should clear thought and bring unity, but they'd already had several meetings and still nothing had been decided.

As high priest, the final decision should have been Adumie's, but every time Cameron overrode him.

So once again, another gathering. "We will meet in the morning after first meal. Tell the others," Adumie said.

She bowed respectfully and turned to go.

Suddenly, Jecidia stood at Adumie's side. "That one cares deeply for you, and plainly sees the truth of your heart." He sounded proud of Qorow Low.

"That one's feelings are inappropriate," Adumie snapped.

Jecidia said, "I do not presume to judge."

"No, Jecidia? Clearly you do judge me. Otherwise, you would not be continually doubting my abilities. You are no longer leader. I am. I will do what I think is best." Adumie spoke directly into Jecidia's face as if such closeness would finally make him understand. "Intruders do not come to bring health. They come to dominate and insult."

Swiftly, angrily, Adumie left Jecidia standing alone.

"How would you feel if they stood taller than you?" Jecidia's voice trailed behind.

Such a comment could not go unchallenged. "How would they appreciate it if I sent Nu Venia to welcome them?" Adumie demanded.

"I think Cameron would be pleased. I do not believe Nu Venia would be so willing." Was that humor in Jecidia's voice?

"Cameron," Adumie snorted. "That one has no reasoning."

"That one believes God will rescue us," Jecidia said.

Adumie did not answer, but stopped, too angry to continue.

Slowly, Jecidia caught up to him.

"I'm remembering a time when you once believed, Adumie."

He turned away. "You may remember, but you have no understanding." Adumie walked off, determined not to answer any more of Jecidia's words and not to stop until he was clear of the old one.

Jecidia did not follow, but he did continue to speak, "Tell me, Adumie. I will listen."

This was something Jecidia could not fix with simple ideology.

"Speaking troubles of the heart cleanses the soul," Jecidia called after him, "and brings forgiveness."

If only Adumie's sins could be so easily forgiven.

CAPTAIN'S LOG

Akiane Colony
Captain Faris Assetti
Year 2144
Day six on planet
Beginning construction

It has been decided. Plans have been drawn. Akiane will provide a good source of building supplies. There is plenty of lava and we have the technical ability to reshape it to our needs. The enclosure will be 2.21 kilometers in diameter. The main ships will sit on the northernmost wall so there is room to build a future city inside.

Construction details will be found in the engineers' logs.

Since we have only the three doctors from Falcon, Beasley *will train a new medical team. He is using the computer medical data as his curriculum. There is more in his medical logs.*

Chapter 13

Adumie's Lament
Morning after Intruders' Arrival

DEATH SHOULD be bittersweet. Bitter because it hurts to lose the one loved; sweet because it should be a time to celebrate a life well lived. And so it was when there was an occasional death, but when death comes every few hours, there is only grieving and fear.

People feared to sleep. They were afraid of who might not wake up. They feared *they* might not wake up. Death was no longer a promise into God's presence. It not only took loved ones. It took joy and hope. It took and took and took, until Death was no longer welcomed.

Cameron said the deaths were the product of a mysterious disease. He believed God had brought the Intruders to find a cure.

More than once Adumie had cried out to God, "See, Lord, how distressed I am! The torment within disturbs my heart. Do not punish your people for my sins. Punish me only."

But *God does not answer the prayers of the wicked.* And Adumie was wicked. These deaths were his fault.

The Word also said: *The visions of the false priests are worthless. Their oracles are deceptive.* Cameron's sin was to be misled by false hopes. Instead of trusting God, he wanted to trust strangers who had once abandoned them.

Adumie's footsteps echoed quietly as he walked. Endurance's hallways were once filled with life, joy, and laughter, but no longer. Now they were desolate.

There was to be a community meeting this morning, but death continued to rule. The meeting would have to wait.

He stopped to look into a sleeping area. One hundred fifty beds set in neat rows. Pillows waiting for someone to rest their head upon lay neglected for lack of use. At one time, every bed had been occupied. Now this and too many other rooms were vacant. All that was left were the memories painted on family walls.

He could not bring himself to look upon those drawings.

Those who still lived chose to live all together in one room. They tore down a wall between two rooms to make one room.

Adumie entered that room. Everyone stood in somber silence waiting for him. Bereavement filled their faces. Their hearts were deprived of joy. Illness and perpetual grief dimmed their eyes. There had been too much death. More had died during the night.

I weep. Tears overflow my eyes. There is no comfort. No restoration of soul. The Holy words echoed in his being.

Tears welled in Adumie's eyes. Crying was not for high priests. There had already been too many tears. A few more meant nothing.

"We are ready," Jecidia informed Adumie.

This morning five adults and three children, all taken before their lives were fully lived, would be laid to rest.

The bodies lay on their mats on the floor. Each was wrapped in a dull yellow funeral cloth ready for their final journey.

Leven, Adumie's sibling, was the last to be prepared. Most of her hair had fallen out and her skin had turned ash gray. She had withered to skin and bones.

The first three of Leven's children lived. The next two had already died. The last child had been stillborn. It was unclear if Leven died of the slow death or of a broken heart.

It was for the high priest to say final words. What was there to say? That this was God's will? That God called them to Himself because of love?

No. There was nothing to say.

Too many had died. Endurance had lost its luster and was falling into dust for lack of caretakers. There were few gardeners, hunters, fishers, or butchers. Few left to tend the Blood Vines. Fewer chrysalises survived the vines. Soon there would be none left.

Out of respect for his station, everyone reverently waited for Adumie to speak.

The torment pounded at his heart. Words failed. He shook his head. "I cannot," he whispered.

No one pressed for last words. They understood all too well. Emotions and words were all consumed by grief.

A lone, plaintive flute began to play. Its tune drifted through the room and around the people, but no one sang along. Another flute joined in, then a third. As if by the combined efforts of the flutes, one voice was inspired to sing:

When Kahair rises, we will praise our God.
When Kahair sets, we will praise the Giver of Life.

With an upbeat tempo, an instrument made of strings of tupilak gut and a set of bones would join in. This was a song of praise, but today, it was a song of lament. More voices solemnly joined in.

We return the cherished
to the One who has given them to us.
Be not sad.
Look to the day when we are reunited
in God's love and glory.

Adumie did not sing. The lyrics stabbed. If God loved, why do nothing while people, so many people, died? Did God not see anguish? Did He not care? How many would die before this trial ended?

All energy had drained from him. He wanted to lie down and sleep and not wake until death had completed its work and taken him.

Six people for each adult, four for each child, lifted the moss bedding and stood in a line. Soon there would not be enough people left to carry the dead out. What then? Lock them in an empty room to rot?

When they were many, only family and friends walked alongside the dead, but now that they were few, everyone who could came. No one wanted to be alone or be left behind. Even the sick came, which meant the procession moved slowly and stopped often for them to rest. It would take three times the normal time to get there. So they took sleds. It was quicker and it would be easier on the sick.

Only the sickest, who could no longer stand, and three caretakers stayed behind.

Adumie led the way from the family room to the outside exit.

A new day was wakening. The pale blue sky gave way to lavender, pushing back the dark of night. It would be a few hours before Kahair appeared over the rim of the caldera, but his presence was easily seen.

The funeral procession walked one slow step at a time, out the exit farthest from the unwanted guests. This time had been picked so Intruders from Earth would not see. They slept while the dead were laid to rest.

The procession traveled across snow-covered land and over land-locked ice to open water. Temperatures were warming. Ice was thinning and receding. The journey was getting shorter.

Open water put moisture in the air. Moisture brought snowstorms and blizzards, but this day was calm.

It should have been a sign of encouragement, as if God were welcoming the dead. In reality, God had deserted them. Prayers for mercy and healing were not heard. People continued to die.

Adumie no longer believed or prayed. What was a high priest without faith in God?

In the past, when one died, there was a celebration. That one would never be cold again and would never know the terror of The Storm. They now resided in the City of Heaven. They walked among angels and family on streets of gold.

Yes, they were missed, but the joy of knowing where they had gone, eased the pain of loss.

Death no longer brought that hope or peace.

They rode in silence, but as they unloaded the mats, they began to sing again. The procession moved to the rhythm of their lament:

> *If I rise on the wings of dawn,*
> *if I settle on the far side of the horizon;*
> *Your hand guides, Your right hand directs my course.*

Chovis also walked quietly.

They did not playfully wrestle or chase each other. They understood the solemnest of the moment. Those who had formed a bond with the one who was now dead, walked under the body.

As the procession reached water, people spread out. Everyone viewed the ocean as they sang one last verse:

> *I remember well my affliction and my wondering;*
> *yet, I call to mind,*
> *by the Lord's great love,*
> *my soul is not disappointed.*
> *Each new morning brings God's mercy;*
> *great is God's imminence.*

Unhurried, bodies and bedding were placed in the ocean and pushed out to sea. Gradually, the bodies drifted away.

The living mournfully watched.

Nine chovis jumped in and swam around the bodies. The mats slowly sank as they took on water. Two chovis whined and yelped in concern. Chovis loyalty did not stop because of death. Leven's chovis dived in after her.

Adumie knew the chovis would follow Leven too deeply and drown, or a tupilak would attack and eat the chovis, which seemed odd since chovis did not eat tupilak.

Two more chovis dove in to follow the one they had walked with.

The last body sank.

Six chovis swam farther out. Chovis often jumped into the water, swam too far, and were unable to return. No amount of calling could convince them to come back. No one bothered to call to them now.

Eighteen chovis sat staring at the water. Several looked as if they might jump in, but for some reason did not. Those with pups would not. They would return to Endurance.

Every one of these, Adumie thought, as he looked over the community, *every one of them will die before their time. And there is nothing I can do to stop it. Then it will be my turn. I will be the last to die and there will be no one to cover my face.*

Chapter 14

Adumie
Fishing

"NOW WE fish," a fisher said, as if life continued without Leven and the others.

Adumie would have preferred to stand and stare for a while longer at the blue green water and its slowly melting ice casing. The water had quieted as if they had not laid loved ones to rest and chovis had not been lost.

Life dragged Adumie along, no matter who or how many died.

Chovis ate fish, not tupilak. Since few chovis survived swimming in ocean waters, fishers caught fish for chovis.

Fishers slung their nets over their shoulders and walked along the edge of the ice. They would not fish near the dead. They were looking for another open water spot filled with shoals of fish. Priests followed. All but one sled returned to Endurance with the others. The last would carry fish to be dried and stored for when the fish disappeared for the summer. Most chovis stayed with the fishers. They knew what was coming and were eager for their first meal of the day.

To Adumie's amazement, Jecidia came along. No one would have blamed him if he had returned with the others. Jecidia was too weak to help in case of an attack. Yet he did not use his weakness as an excuse to shirk duties. That was why Jecidia had been such a great leader and was so well loved. It was difficult living up to such standards.

Jecidia was good hearted and giving. Adumie was heavy hearted from long held secrets.

Adumie slowly followed and watched as sixty fishers spread out along the edge of the ice and cast their nests. Twenty-three priests casually talked and stood as they watched over fishers.

One of the priests dropped a bundle of spears on the ice.

Hopefully, they will not be needed, Adumie thought. He was too tired to even think of an attack.

Tupilak made fishing dangerous. The sea creatures looked a lot like chovis, only they were red and were much larger. Chovis were affectionate, protective, and loyal. Tupilak were aggressive killers. They attacked and ate not only fish and chovis, but fishers as well. Priests protected the fishers from tupilak. Then hunted them. People ate tupilak, not fish. But Adumie doubted there would be any hunting today.

Akiane was warming; ice was melting. During winter, tupilak lived on land near the open equator waters. Once the ice melted, tupilak left the area and would not return until Akiane refroze. They were already seeing less tupilak these days.

They had already gathered and stored enough meat to last them for the warm years. It was hoped the off-worlders also had enough meat to satisfy them.

It was good that hunting season was nearing an end. Adumie was tired of death and killing. He walked alone along the edge of the ice looking out over the open water.

A chovis nudged Adumie's hand. He knelt to scratch behind the chovis' ears and down her white — apricot tufted neck.

The chovis' tail happily wagged. A velvet tongue licked at Adumie's hand and face. As much as he enjoyed chovis, none had ever attached herself to him. Even though Adumie knew not everyone had a chovis follow them, he couldn't help wondering if it was another sign of how inadequate he truly was that none followed him.

The tongue abruptly disappeared. Her tail froze. Her head dropped. Her ears pointed up. A low growl came from deep within the chovis' throat.

Adumie stood.

Something was wrong.

Chovis had been eagerly anticipating their next meal, and had been under fishers' feet, playfully wrestling each other for the best place to watch for nets laden with fish. Now they were pacing the water's edge, growling. Chovis life-givers moved their pups to safety, and hurriedly herded them toward Endurance.

Fishers nervously watched the chovis and the water. They pulled their nets in and moved inland.

Priests pulled their fur jackets, gloves and green shirts off and dropped them on the ice. Bare-chested, they stood like finely chiseled red-garnet soldiers, ready to respond to the threat. They even took their green gloves off so their hands could grip their spears without slipping. Their arms were free to accurately throw the spears.

Disappointed, Adumie also pulled his jacket, shirt, and both gloves off, in anticipation of an attack, and dropped them on the ice. He had hoped for a quiet day. It seemed no such day was forth coming.

He quietly wondered, *Would things ever returned to normal?* Then he wondered why he would think such a thing, when he knew no such day would ever exist again.

Jecidia moved to the spears, untied and arranged them so they stood with the shape ends pointed up. He gave each priest a spear as they ran past him. He was useful after all.

Fishers dragged their nets in. If the nets were full, they secured the fish as quickly as they could and ran. Any other time, a net would not be left unprotected. Chovis would rip it to shreds to get at the fish. But at this moment, chovis were preoccupied with the threat in the water. Tupilak were near.

Some fishers released their haul and ran, pulling their empty nets behind them.

Chovis continued growling and pacing the water, looking for the threat.

Timus and Telto, two from the same life-giver, were having trouble hauling their net in. It seemed to be stuck on something. They pulled. Timus moved to the right side and knelt on the ice to get a better look. Foolishly, she leaned over to pull at the netting.

"Timus, don't!" Adumie yelled.

A tupilak could easily leap up, snag her with its teeth, and pull her into the water.

But she couldn't hear over the chovis growling. Timus pulled a knife out and leaned farther over in an effort to cut the net free. Adumie let out a sigh of relief when she stood and shook her head. The net was still snagged. Perhaps now those two would move from the water's edge.

Adumie thought to go to them, but decided to stay where he was. The tupilak could come up anywhere. He stood in a good place to run in either direction. If he went to Timus and Telto and the sea monster came up from the other direction, Adumie would be at a disadvantage to help.

Suddenly a deep red tupilak leaped out of the water as easily as a child would jump onto a large rock. It stood on all four paws, not bothering to shake water droplets off its fur. With raised head, its jaws opened wide to showed large pointy teeth capable of shredding a person as easily as it could shred ice with its claws.

The creature stood between Adumie, and Timus and Telto. He should have gone to them. He regretted not having a spear. He was too close to the water and too far from Jecidia.

The tupilak sniffed the air and saw those running. The animal looked around as if assessing the situation and appeared to be considering chasing after a group of fishers. It took two, three steps toward them.

A person being chased was supposed to run toward the protection of the priests, hoping that the sea monster would follow them, and the priests would kill it.

"Good," Adumie spoke softly. "Follow the fishers and we will kill you."

Chovis ran toward the monster, yelping and growing. Next to the huge tupilak, a forty-five kilo chovis looked like a pup. It seemed not to mind them. It was contemplating what it wanted to do or whom to chase.

The monster stood as its head swiveled to the right and saw Timus and Telto still by the water's edge. Its body followed its head slow and easy.

Timus and Telto saw the sea monster eye them. They dropped their net. It quickly slipped into the water — lost. It would take days to make another.

With a show of its large teeth, dripping with saliva, the tupilak growled hungrily.

Telto bolted toward the priests. Timus stood frozen. The creature started for her. She panicked, turned, and ran along the ice shelf away from the sea monster, and from the priests.

Adumie moaned in disappointment.

The tupilak stopped. The creature watched the priests running toward it, but all were too far away. Tupilak had been known to run from priests and retreat back into the water. This one did not.

It gracefully pushed through the chovis surrounding it, and with a trouble-free gate, pursued Timus as if it had plenty of time to reach its victim. If it did reach Timus first, all it had to do was grab her and leap back into the water where she could not be rescued.

"No!" Adumie yelled and ran. He was the closest. He forced his size to grow until his pants and boots were too tight to allow him to grow any larger. His longer legs took longer strides, the extra power moved him faster, but it felt as if he was running in place. Timus seemed no closer.

If only she would grow in size. She could easily out run the tupilak. But she was too afraid to think of it.

Priests had been spread out and had not been on alert. They had been lax in thinking they were fishing in a new place where there were no tupilak. Adumie should have known and been prepared. Tupilak were everywhere. Instead of mourning the past, he should have been prepared for the possibility of future disasters.

Chovis tried to distract and slow the monster down, but it tore through them like a large, red boulder rumbling across ice. It sent two chovis skidding. One managed to stop in time, but the other

141

slipped off the ice into the water. It came leaping out of the water just as easily as the tupilak.

Telto looked over her shoulder to see Timus running in the wrong direction. She yelled at Timus to turn, but she did not hear or look back to see Telto frantically waving her toward the priests.

If only Timus had not panicked and run the wrong way.

Adumie was strong and healthy, a good runner. Even if he didn't have a spear, he hoped he would make it in time. He thought to distract the monster until the others arrived.

The tupilak quickened its steps. Its four paws moved in rhythm with each other.

Two chovis, Poulas and Addle, ran with Timus. They yelped, encouraging her to run faster. They even tried to redirect her steps toward the priests. Timus stumbled over them, almost lost her footing, but kept going. Fur boots were made to keep one's feet warm, not to run in. Timus' arms pumped her forward, but the heavy boots slowed her.

The monster was gaining. All it had to do was lunge and the two would plunge into the water. Timus would be lost.

Furious chovis seemed small and ineffective beside the tupilak. They nipped at paws almost the size of their heads. It ignored them and kept going.

Poulas jumped on the tupilak and tried to dig her teeth into the thick muscle at the top of the tupilak's back. With one shake of its massive body, Poulas slid off.

Priests also wore fur boots, which also slowed their running.

Adumie feared they would not be in time. "Please, God," he prayed, "not Timus." His heart could not stand another death. Not this day. Not ever again.

The tupilak's right paw swiped at its victim's legs, but missed.

Timus leaped and yelped in fear.

Poulas and Addle ran in between the tupilak and Timus. The monster snapped at Addle. The chovis bounded out of the way and landed on Poulas. They tumbled to the side. Immediately, Poulas was up, running and snapping.

Addle shook her head as if trying to clear her thoughts. Instead of joining in the chase, she sat with her tongue hanging out and watched.

Timus was running out of energy. Her next step crumbled. She fell forward. Arms flayed as she tried to keep her balance. She landed hard on her stomach. For a moment, Timus looked as if she had been knocked out, but then she scrambled to get up.

A large paw slapped at Timus, knocking her feet up in the air. Her forehead bounced off the ice. The sea creature used both of its front paws to swipe at Timus, playing with her. It spun her around and rolled her over.

Terror distorted Timus' face. Her eyes bulged as if they might pop out. Timus raised her hands in an effort to ward the creature away.

Adumie's heart pounded. "Please, God, NO." He ran harder.

A priest's aim with a spear was true and could bring the creature down. Even though the tupilak was on all fours, one should have had a clear shot, but chovis leapt around and onto the tupilak. They were in the way. One could not get a clear shot. The tupilak easily whacked at the chovis, sending one spinning out of the away. Immediately, they came back to defend Timus. Poulas again leapt onto the side of the monster. She clawed her way up its back. The tupilak rose up and easily shook Poulas off.

Poulas couldn't hold on. She unceremoniously dropped off. She twisted around just in time to land on all fours and strike again.

Adumie saw a spear fly at the tupilak. The spear should have caught the creature in its right side, penetrating its lung. But at that same moment, the tupilak lunged forward, with jaws wide opened, and sank its teeth into Timus' stomach.

The spear swished into the animal's back shoulder.

Timus screeched in terror and pain, then abruptly quieted. She lay in shambles on the ice. Was she already dead? Were they too late?

Four more spears flew at the creature, but missed. One spear caught a chovis in the hind leg. It cried in pain. Chovis scattered out of the way.

Two more spears sliced into the tupilak's side. It roared in aggravation as it turned from its meal. With one paw, it reached around its side and snapped the two spears free, but it couldn't reach the one in its shoulder. It swayed with the creature's movements.

Chovis again crowded around, leaping up at the tupilak, making it difficult for one to throw any more spears.

Standing on its hind legs, the tupilak tried to reach the spear in its back, but couldn't. Now priests had a clear target. Three spears found their mark, one in the tupilak's right chest and two in the stomach. The monster lifted its giant head, and roared as if the sound of its fury would ward off those attacking. The creature was a fearsome sight.

The tupilak clawed at the spears in its stomach. They too snapped off. The sea creature slapped a paw down, crushing the back of a chovis. It yelped once in pain and died. The monster rose to its full height and gave a mighty howl. But it seemed less fearsome. The spears had wounded it.

Finally, Adumie reached the creature and threw himself at it. He grew in height. The seams of his pants were stretched to their limit. It was a disgrace to force one's pants to rip open, but Adumie didn't care and he doubted if anyone else would. Timus' life was at stake.

Jaws snapped at Adumie. Somehow he managed to stay out of its reach. He smelled sweet copper, Timus' blood. He saw fresh pink meat between its teeth, Timus' flesh.

All his frustration, all his sorrow, all his hate took over. Adumie had the strength of the tupilak.

The claws of its left paw raked across his back, but he didn't feel the pain. The monster pushed Adumie away and turned again to Timus.

Adumie jumped on the animal's back. He grabbed the spear in its shoulder with both hands and twisted. Its left front leg went limp and it fell, slamming its left shoulder into the ice.

As he rolled free, Adumie held onto the spear. It threatened to wrench from his hands. He tightened his grip. The spear left the beast's shoulder with a sickening sucking sound.

The animal rose to its feet with a furious roar of pain and anger.

Adumie also rose to his feet. The creature was too close to use the spear. He dropped it and raised his hands in time to catch the creature's one good paw as it swung toward his face. He twisted the arm between them as a shield to keep those jaws from ripping into him.

Then a thought came and everything slowed down giving him time to think.

All Adumie had to do was loosen his grip, just a little. The tupilak's arm would be free giving the jaws room to strike. Its claws would rip his chest and stomach. The creature might drag him into the water. But Timus would be saved.

145

No one would know that he had given up. They would not believe he would do such a thing, but they would believe that he would do everything he could to save Timus.

He could loosen his grip, just a little. It would all be over within seconds. Everything would be someone else's problem. He could, but his hands would not.

He could not force them to open. They would not obey.

Then Cameron flew under his arm, moving at full force, smashing into the tupilak.

The creature fell on its back.

As Adumie stumbled, he bent to pick up the spear, stood and readied to strike.

Sensing the kill, chovis yelped louder. They bit at and pulled out chunks of fur and skin, and spit them on the ice.

Back claws racked at Cameron. Only his fur pants protected his legs.

Holding the spear in both hands, Adumie quickly moved around the monster and slammed the spear into its heart. The tupilak went limp.

Cameron stood.

Chovis leaped on and off the creature as if they had brought it down.

Several priests arrived at the same time. The tupilak's paws lay lifelessly at its side. Its breath was shallow and raspy. Blood darkened its red coat and surrounding ice. It looked up at those standing over it. With one final act of defiance, it weakly growled.

The last priest to arrive thrust his spear in the animal's heart next to Adumie's spear.

The creature ceased to live.

Addle leaped onto the tupilak's stomach and stood with her head held high as though she alone had brought it down.

Adumie turned to see Telto knelling over her sister, holding her hand.

Barely breathing, Timus' eyes no longer focused.

Chovis circled Telto and Timus until they found a good place to lie down and silently watched the two. Poulas, the chovis who walked at Timus' side, lay next to her and rested her head on Timus' leg.

Adumie knelt to check the wound. It was deep. Part of the stomach muscles were missing or lay in shredded bits on and around Timus. Her bowels were badly ripped and hung outside her body. Vital fluids seeped into her exposed wound and onto the ice to mingle with her blood.

Once again, God had not answered his prayer. Adumie slumped to the ice. He looked into Telto's worried face, and shook his head.

Telto knew and drew a weary sigh. She did not cry. Not now while Timus needed her to be strong, but later when the truth of the event and the realization that this was the last of her immediate family fully sunk in, Telto's emotions would come.

All the priests and fishers gathered around the two and waited in silence with Telto for Timus' last breath.

They did not bring the body back to Endurance. Telto lifted Timus and carried her to the water's edge. Telto knelt and gently dropped Timus into the water. Timus' chovis, Poulas, jumped in, following her into the water.

As Timus' body sank and faded from sight in the clear water, Adumie noted there were no yellow funeral cloth, no moss mat, no flutes, no singing, and no words spoken.

CAPTAIN'S LOG

Akiane Colony
Captain Faris Assetti
Year 2144
Day 156 - 5 months on planet

The ground is thawing; nights are warming. This land is harsh and desolate. There are no trees, not even a blade of a weed sticking out of the snow. Except for my dog Harrie, there is no wildlife. No sounds other than the ones we make. The quiet is unsettling.

The only good is the star with plenty of light and the hope it will one day bring life in the form of native plants. I have named it Kahair, Arabic for good.

The main ships are no longer two separate ships, but one colony. We have built several passageways at different levels to make moving from one to the other easier.

We are learning to work together for the good of everyone. People are dividing up according to their skills and likes such as: gardening produce; fishing; cleaning and gutting of fish; preparing and cooking meals; cleaning up afterward.

We are learning who of us are better cooks, better farmers, and who are better fishermen.

Today we completed the base of the wall that will enclose the habitat. It should withstand the next gravitational storm. If it does not ...

One must not dwell.

There is plenty of lava rock. We pulverize it into a fine dust and make lava concrete. We have formed meter-long hexagons, which fit perfectly together.

Fear creeps in, fear that we will not succeed, or that the next gravitational storm will destroy all we have built. Seventeen people decided this new life was too overwhelming. They took the easy way out, the coward's way, and committed suicide.

I have declared that it is not good to dwell on what could happen, but dwell on the possibilities of a successful future.

Sometimes it seems that all we do is work. The habitat must be finished before winter returns in five years. If I do not push, I fear it will not be finished in time.

Father Striken says we need some relief. It's not as if we can go on vacation. He says I should declare a holiday, a reason for celebrating, but there is so much to do. We need to begin building scaffolding from the left over parts of Hawk's *main engine casing so we can start on the wall.*

Faris' Speech

Faris climbed up onto the base and walked along its length for several meters. She stopped and turned to face the crowd of people gathered below her.

"This is a moment of pride," she said.

The crowd gladly agreed.

She was proud of them, those who had chosen to fight for what they wanted and refused to fail. "We should be overjoyed of what we have accomplished so far. We have endured much." Faris projected her voice for all to hear. "But we are prevailing. We have finished the base of the dome."

Cheers.

A sleeping baby, startled by the sudden exultation, cried out in objection.

"Yes," Faris said, with a wide smile, "let's not forget all of our greatest accomplishments. In the five months we have been here, 23 children have been born. Evidently, the colony was truly started aboard ship."

Laughter.

"We must now work on the wall so it will be finished before winter returns."

The crowd became sober.

"But we will start tomorrow." Faris raised her voice and loudly declared, "Today we eat, drink, and be merry, for tomorrow we work."

The crowd erupted into cheers, cries of startled babies, laughter, and music. Soon there was dancing.

Personal Log

I cannot help but be proud of all we have accomplished. WSC should be similarly pleased.

I am torn between wanting to stay and see this colony succeed and returning to Earth.

I have left so much behind. Things I do not have here like friends, a trusted companion I can truly confined in.

If I return, I will leave much behind here. The beginnings of a new world, starting from scratch, literally from the ground up. Back on Earth, I could only read reports. It would be nothing like actually being a part of the colony's history.

Insha'Allah I must trust God and place my life in His hands to help me make such a monumental life decision.

Chapter 15

Olivia's Problems
Day Two

OLIVIA AND her crew of five had brought six large aquaria in six oversized wooden boxes almost three meters long and two meters high, including the stand, and a little less than half a meter wide. The aquaria were to hold seawater and marine life for her research.

"Why six?" I'd asked. "And why so large?"

"Not all marine life is compatible, Jessica," she said testily. "They tend to eat one other. I have to keep them separate. The aquaria are large so the fish have room to swim."

It made sense, but it seemed like a lot of work to bring all that water and fish from the ocean to here. I was glad it was her project and not mine.

"Those crates won't fit neatly into the cabinet wall," someone said.

"We could leave them out," one of Olivia's teammates, Kai, volunteered.

"We have little room as it is. It would be better if we could incorporate them in with the rest of the crates," Jorg said.

"What if we use them for the base?" Kai suggested.

And so it was agreed. The aquaria were unpacked. The crates were placed on the floor, lengthwise, against the wall on the work area side of the room.

That first night had been rough. Most people slept in their clothes. I laughed to myself at all the whining. If they had been military, they might have been expected to live all together for their entire stay. But the captain was gracious. Before lights out, he'd sent a team to install rods and curtains so each stall had its own privacy.

I would never have admitted it to the civilians, but I was glad for their whining and the change in our living arrangements.

By mid-morning of the second day, *Britannia* sent fabricated walls for the dorm area, but not a construction crew. It was up to us to make all improvements.

We divided the dorm room into three parts: one each for men and women, and one for couples. The couples' section was then divided into three smaller rooms.

But as the dorm walls were being installed, Olivia quietly disappeared with her team. They took the opportunity to assemble her aquaria in the middle of the work area. She wasn't considerate enough to place them against the wall. She placed them in the middle of the workspace, right where other people planned to set up their research workstations.

The aquaria were made of metal frames, thick clear acrylic walls and a metal stand. Two already stood facing each other with enough space to comfortably walk between them. Olivia was just starting on the third when someone noticed what she was doing and loudly complained. Her aquaria would take up most of the work area unless someone stopped her.

"I have to observe from all four sides," she exclaimed.

"But did you have to take up all the work area?" I yelled.

Everyone was standing around us. No one was happy.

"Move them," I ordered.

"I can't. They're too heavy," she yelled back.

"Then take them apart and rebuild them," I said.

"I can't. We glued them together."

"And why did you do that?" I asked. I knew. She didn't want us to force her to move them. She wanted them to stay right where they were.

"It makes them stronger," she said. "They'll be holding large volumes of water."

"Well, you're not building any more. Two are plenty," I said.

"You're not the boss. I can do as I please." Olivia held her head high in defiance. She was a full 5 centimeters shorter than me. It wasn't much of a height difference, but she was so full of herself, I guess she thought she was more intimating if she stretched to her full height. She wasn't.

She took a step closer and looked up at me. "I'm assembling them and there is nothing you can do about it."

I took a step closer. "I'll find a hammer and smash them," I promised.

"You wouldn't!" Her eyes narrowed, threatening.

"To whom would you complain?" I asked.

"I have plenty of picks and hammers among my equipment," Gino volunteered with a little chuckle. "You may have your choice, Jessica, my dear."

Olivia gave him one of her all too familiar glares, then she turned to look at the others. The atmosphere was one of anger. No one would defend her. Even her teammates had deserted her. They'd stepped away from her and the aquaria. They knew she was wrong. I imagined they'd tried to explain it to her, but she wouldn't be deterred. If she built all six, there'd be little room left for anyone else.

She was one person I would not miss when I left this place. Olivia only thought about herself. As long as she was happy, no one else mattered.

"I've already started this one. I have to build at least one more aquarium," she complained.

"Then build it against the far wall," Gino said.

"What do I do with the rest of the equipment?" Olivia asked.

"Pack them back in their crates," he said.

"We can't fit everything into its crate once we've taken everything out," she said.

I wanted to slap her smug face. If I'd had less self-control I would have.

"Maybe not everything into one crate," Mathieu said. "But you could use two crates per aquarium."

God bless him.

"And we'll help," Jorg said, flashing that smile of his.

God bless the both of them.

Olivia growled. It was against her nature to be outnumbered and outmaneuvered. Begrudgingly, she relented.

Once her last aquarium was completed and the others were repacked way, the next project was placing all those crates against the wall in the form of cabinets.

They chose the long wall next to the dorms.

But a cabinet made of different sized boxes was a major ordeal. They started the cabinet, took it apart, and rebuilt it three times before they decided it was acceptable.

155

It was like a jigsaw puzzle trying to get odd sized boxes to fit in an orderly fashion. But worse, these people were scientists. They had to have everything just so. Large crates had to be on the bottom. Certain crates couldn't be too high or someone short like Lu couldn't reach it. Some smaller crates were pushed farther back. Some larger crates were pulled out so those could be used as tables while getting into a different crate.

I would not have been so precise, but I'm not a scientist.

Sometimes, they made my head spin.

"No don't put it there!"

"Why not?"

"Because ..."

"What if ..."

"It should be this way."

"No, this would be better if ..."

"If you do that, then we should ..."

Everyone had an opinion. And when they couldn't agree, they looked to Gino to make the final decision. To my surprise, they listened to him.

Nothing was exactly where everyone wanted it, no one complained, except for Olivia. She demanded the wall be rebuilt to suit her needs.

By the end of the next day, no one was willing to go through that a fourth time.

Olivia had not yet been forgiven for her aquaria. Each scientific group arranged their work area right up to the aquaria. If she had built them along the wall, she could have had all six and she could have easily walked around them. Now she could only walk between the two of them. The third one was erected *against* the far back wall. She couldn't even walk around that one.

Olivia complained late into the night that her aquaria were not where she wanted them. I guess she thought if she was persistent, someone would hear, or maybe she thought to wear the others down. Her whining was ignored.

CAPTAIN'S LOG

Akiane Colony
Captain Faris Assetti
Year 2144
Eight months

Our Oceanographer Adryel says the cold ocean waters will delay the warming of the planet a few years. He has also warmed that with the open waters, and with temperatures above freezing, comes snow.

A simple snowstorm is nothing. We continue to work on the habitat.

We are confined inside when a blizzard comes. One can last for days with winds that make it impossible to stand up straight.

Nerves get on edge. Fights break out, which leads to more deaths.

There have been two murders so far. One murderer killed himself. The other is in the brig. We are unsure as to what to do with her. Seven have died of despair. They went to sleep and didn't wake up. Four more committed suicide.

Akiane is killing us. 31 have died from a strange disease. 92 others are sick. Beasley says it's a virus that is rewriting our DNA, but it has no new DNA information. It's the lack of information that is killing us.

He's having trouble pinpointing where the virus has originated. More details in medical logs.

I do not like this place. I want to go home. I think all of us are tired of working on the dome. But we have no choice. For the moment, we are stuck here and have no way to leave.

Chapter 16

Larry Gino
Morning of Day Four

A COUPLE of centuries ago, people would have retired long before reaching their eighties. But not now, modern technology and medicine had extended human life to at least 150 years.

Gino was a little stiff at times but at eighty-two he felt as spry as a fifty-year-old and as mentally as sharp as a twenty-year-old.

He chuckled to himself. *Hopefully with a little more maturity.*

Gino was standing outside the same habitat entrance he and the others had entered when they'd arrived three days ago. He looked over the hot springs and snow-covered mountains to the west. They'd finally settled in their new living quarters. Now they could begin their research.

Jorg stood at his side. "Just imagine," he said, "we're standing on an alien planet."

It didn't look alien. It looked like the rugged, snow-covered Canadian Rockies.

Even though this was not his first alien planet—he'd been on Earth's moon, Mars, and Europa—Gino was as excited as if it was his first time. "Virgin territory," he said. "We will do the research the colony didn't have the time to do when they first arrived. These are exciting times, my boy."

"Indeed they are, old one."

Gino laughed.

Jorg patted him on the shoulder. "I'm headed out to the vast algae patch to see how similar it is and how it differs from Earth's algae, and see what kind of ecology it has."

"Spiders and worms?" Gino asked.

"Spiders and worms," Jorg confirmed. With his work pack slung over his shoulder, he headed out.

Gino turned to see Olivia and her team rolling toward the edge of the caldera in their small aquatic hovercraft. She was ready to fill her three aquaria with seawater. Eventually, she and her crew would take the aquatic-craft underwater to investigate the bottom of the alien ocean.

She'd release robotic cameras to film marine life, which would produce sharp realism digital images. At some point she'd go scuba diving, collect alien coral life, and try to recreate it in her aquaria so she could more closely study them. She was also working toward the possibility of bringing an aquarium of marine life back to WSC as a museum piece for the galactic zoo they hoped to start.

The astrophysicists and astronomers had already set up their ground telescopes. They'd begun mapping the night sky from Pegasus' point of view. They were also building a Very Large Telescope (VLT) or an astronomical interferometer. They had plans for the next ship to set the VLT in orbit around Akiane. The telescope will have extra resolution capable of picking up very small objects and will continue to look for extrasolar planets, or exoplanet planets, outside Kahair's star system.

All information from every project on Akiane would be sent back to WSC. Hopes were high that they would make significant scientific discoveries. And Gino was in the thick of it.

"What are you doing standing here?" Spago came trudging out of the habitat. "We have a mountain to study. Get a move on!"

"I'd already be there, with a week's worth of work done, if I didn't have to wait on punk kids like you," Gino bellowed.

"Excuses, excuses." As Spago hurried past Gino, he glanced over his shoulder and said, "You coming or are you planning on standing there all day?" He continued on as if to leave Gino behind.

It would be a few more decades before Gino was too old to keep up.

∽∾

Geologist Larry Gino stood on the side of Akiane's mountain surrounded by a chaos of rocks. He turned a garnet rock over and over in his hands. It looked beaten and battered. Pieces had broken off.

"Whatever happened to you, my diminutive fellow, must have been traumatic," he said to the rock.

So far, his findings made little sense. The base of the mountain looked like a construction pile of rubble. Geological formations eluded him. Every kind of rock classification seemed not to relate to the rocks surrounding them. Gino and his team marked the areas they planned to excavate.

Gino had never seen anything like this on Earth, the moon, Mars, or Europa. Nothing made sense.

Rocks congregated according to their geological timetable. There might be a slight mixing because of erosion, earthquakes, or human intervention, but there was still a clear line as to which time period one was studying. But here, everything was all mixed up.

Good, Gino thought, *wouldn't want an easy project. Need something that's difficult and mysterious. It will produce better results and make for more interesting research.*

The team took digital images of the marked areas. They had labeled the most interesting rocks and marked their positions, and were in the process of analyzing what they'd found.

Realism imaging was remarkable, almost as good as the real thing.

Up until the middle of the twenty-second century, the only way to study rocks was to carry them back to a lab and carefully saw them open. Then cut wafer thin cross-sections, which was then cut into smaller pieces. Those pieces were examined for mineral content and carbon dating.

But with realism imaging, Gino took holographic pictures that could recreate the rock in an exact 3D image. Deeper 4D imaging allowed him to feel the roughness of the rock, taste, and even smell it. Digitals in 5D showed him the interior of the rock and its mineral content all the way down to its molecular structure.

Spago's seismic readings would do the same on the interior of the mountain.

Volcanoes are notoriously noisy, which increased as it prepared to erupt. A volcano would have repeating mini-earthquakes that could not be felt or heard above ground, but underground, there would be as many as one every second to every half second. As the threat of eruption neared, the quakes happened so fast it sounded like one long scream. Newly developed 6D realism imaging recorded those quakes so they could be seen and heard.

Geologists used to dig core samples out of the ground, which could be hundreds of feet long. They would be cut and saved in manageable lengths, packed in crates, and carefully shipped to a storage facility where someone could check it out and study the interior rock formation.

It would take hundreds of core samples to fully understand one area of land. Each core was individually examined to obtain the needed information to assimilate a hand drawn contour map. As technology advanced, the images were computer drawn with more exact specifications.

Hundreds of thousands of samples had been drilled over the centuries, and no matter how carefully the cores were stored, they degraded over time.

Spago was setting up his seismic equipment now, placing the instruments along the base of the mountain 15 meters apart. The seismometer would bounce sound waves off underground rock, which then created an interior rock image.

He could project the image and see Akiane's rock structure with 3D, 4D, 5D and 6D quality. He could project the image to actual size or shrink a part of it down to page size. One could walk though a life size image and extract information at any precise point then print images of the most interesting sites at any scale desired.

Data of Akiane would be sent back to Earth. Researchers would take a virtual walk through the images and make valid discoveries without ever setting foot on Akiane.

Gino picked up another rock. He turned it over in his hand, ran his thumb over it, then the tips of his fingers. The surface was rough. He picked at it with a fingernail. Little slivers fell away. He smelled it, and tasted it with the tip of his tongue, salty.

Realism imaging might be amazing, but it was nothing like smelling the air, feeling of a breeze on his face, or feeling the warmth of an alien star on his back, or the beating of his heart as he actually walked an alien planet in real time.

"Looks like junkyard geology," Spago said as he joined Gino.

"Just what I was thinking. It looks like a giant has been piling rocks with no particular order to them." Gino stood and stretched his back.

"It seems to be the same everywhere," Spago said. "Of course we are in a caldera. A massive volcano explosion could easily do this."

"If that's true, when do you guess it happened last?" Gino stood.

Spago shrugged. "At this point, without more information, everything is just a guess. A thousand years? A hundred years?"

"Yeah, my best guess too. An explosion like that could have caused a junkyard effect, but I get the feeling there's something more," Gino said. "It's too early to settle on a conclusion."

"Well, we should have some good readings by the time we get back," Spago said. "But I can tell you this mountain is not completely dormant. There are a lot of rumblings down there."

Gino lifted one questioning eyebrow.

"Nothing dangerous."

"Just enough to make things interesting," Gino said.

"Exactly."

"There's a puzzle here, Spago."

"Looks like a messy puzzle, Gino."

"The greater the mess ..." Gino smiled.

"... the greater the excitement untangling it," Spago said.

165

Chapter 17

Adumie
Guardian Angel

ONE COULD not see Kahair's actual rising from the bottom of a caldera. Adumie came to the top of Endurance to watch the morning's effects. The darkness faded into pinks and oranges then to light blue.

It was times like this when Adumie could forget death and Invaders. Instead he rejoiced at the beauty of the land and the vastness of God's glory. It was a time to reflect on God himself.

Adumie turned to the west to the ever-changing mountain range. At the moment, it was bathed in Kahair's morning light, a mixture of soft reds, yellows, and blues that blended into unnamed hues only God could imagine. The mountains were peaceful. Soon The Storm would return and the volcano within would awaken to fume poisonous gases and bleed lava.

But this morning, all was quiet except for the angry eruption in Adumie's heart.

Intruders were gathering outside. Why did they not stay in their own living quarters?

They were like fungus exiting from Endurance, spores drifting on the wind spreading over Akiane, laying hands on all that was valuable, infecting everything they touched.

The tall one with yellow hair walked to the algae fields, infiltrating and contaminating them. No one would pick algae from those fields ever again. New fields will have to be secretly planted where the tall one will not find them.

The short red-haired one, and several others, took the path to the coast. They traveled in an enclosed vehicle that moved without the help of the wind or chovis.

Intruders in their strange orange suits rode in an opened cart to the mountains where they crawled over the mountains like flying insects oblivious to the mountain's grandeur and might.

Biblical words seemed to foretell of Intruders' coming: *They will take what we leave behind. All that we have will be handed over to those we cannot tolerate.*

One day, Intruders would be the masters over everything Akianes had built and had once loved.

Adumie was helpless to stop them. Helpless. His prayers went unanswered. His voice unheard among the community. He could not protect his people from invasion or heal them from this illness.

With all his heart, Adumie wished he was a guardian angel. In the name of God, he would cut down the unholy Intruders and cut out this slow killing disease, thereby saving his people.

This was all his fault. If he'd been a better person, a better leader, he might have known how to stop those of Earth from coming. If he had been a better priest, sinless, if he was more of what God wanted then God might have answered his prayers and there would be no deaths.

CAPTAIN'S LOG

Akiane Colony
Captain Faris Assetti
Second year, Day 2

We have ended the year in tragedy and seem to have begun the New Year no better. Forty-eight more people have die of the virus. All told, 172 have died since we have landed. They have not all died from the virus, but also from despair, murder and suicide.

Now at the start of our second year, the fish have vanished. They were becoming sparse for the past several months, but now they are all gone. If we had arrived at this time, we would have thought there was no marine life on this planet. But we know there is.

We think they left because the ocean waters have opened up.

We are mounting an expedition to learn where the fish have gone and why they left. We leave in the morning.

Fish is one of our sources of protein, besides beans, soy, and nuts. We plan to find a school of fish, net as many as

168

we can and bring them back to the colony where we will gut, clean, and preserve them for future meals. When we run out, we'll execute more fishing expedition as needed.

We are twelve and will take a shuttle for a quick trip. We should be gone for no more than a few days.

Father Striken

There was a gentle knock on Faris' office door. "Yes?"

The priest entered.

Faris stood. "Father Striken, may I help you?"

"Please, call me Joseph, or Joe."

"Father Joseph then," Faris said.

"You offer me far too much respect. I am a member of this community like any other," Father Joseph said.

"Sorry, but my grandfather taught me to respect the priests of all religions," Faris said.

"Not all religions have priests," he said.

Faris nodded. "You know what I mean. May I help you with something?"

"You look tired," Father Joseph said.

"I am fine." Faris felt not just tired, but also old, but she was unwilling to admit it to any one, especially this priest. She didn't need his counsel; she was leader and must stand strong. "You came here for a reason, Father."

He understanding that he was not to peruse that line of questioning. "I wish to go on your fishing expedition," he said.

"I had not expected this from ..." she stopped in mid-sentence. It was not good to insult, but he didn't seem the sort who worked hard. Fishing was hard work.

"A priest?" he finished. "Do you think I only pray and read all day?"

That was exactly what she thought. "We will only be gone for a few days, Father. There is no need for a spiritual adviser."

He tapped his heart. "I feel in here that I should go with you." He paused. "I feel that it is important."

"I already have eleven people to help with the nets when we find the fish," Faris said. She really didn't want him along. For some reason, she didn't feel comfortable around him. It probably had to do with their different views on religion and Allah. She knew it didn't make sense, but there it was.

He smiled mysteriously. "Counting you, there will be twelve people. I will bring good luck by being your thirteenth member."

She knew he was trying to lighten the moment. Neither of them were superstitious.

His strength of faith shamed the weakening of her faith. It wasn't that she had stopped believing, she just didn't understand why so many bad things had happened. It almost seemed as if Allah had forgotten them.

Yet the priest firmly believed that Allah would turn things around and they would prevail.

It annoyed her that her faith was not as strong as his.

That was the real reason she didn't want to bring him along, but there was even less reason to deny him.

"Fine," she relented, "you will be our lucky charm. We leave at first light."

Chapter 18

Adumie
Coming Forth

ALL IN the community had gathered with life-giver Halmahera. Her chrysalis was hardening.

If the child was too weak to break through, the chrysalis would be ceremoniously wrapped in a yellow funeral cloth and reverently placed in Akiane's waters.

Adumie's emotions seemed to have dried. He felt nothing, neither hope nor sorrow, but stood and watched as the porous membrane sealed itself closed into a hardened shell.

Worried faces intently watched. Mouths were turned down instead of up in joyful smiles. People stood in mournful silence instead of excited chatter. Some were filled with the regret of a child they'd recently lost. Though they crowded in together so all could see, no one touched another.

Two small hands gripped the edge of the nest soon two inquisitive eyes peered into over the edge. Tremont was trying to get a better look, but her life-giver, Japiehern, pulled the child back.

"You will get your gloves sticky," she said.

The vines of the nest perpetually leaked a milky substance that fed the child in the nest.

"But I cannot see," Tremont complained.

Japiehern lifted her child. Tremont wrapped her arms around her life-giver's neck. Small, gloved-hands laced fingers together.

As Adumie's eyes scanned the community, they rested on Nu Venia. When she noticed he was watching her, she slipped behind Cameron and peered around him.

Even the sight of that one had no affect on him this day.

"The chrysalis has finished," someone said.

Emotionless, Adumie turned his attention to the fully hardened chrysalis.

They could hear as the child inside lightly pushed outward, but the chrysalis did not give as it usually did. The child gave a muffled whine as she tried to stretch, the brittle membrane cracked slightly, but held the child firmly inside.

Little feet kicked in frustration. Cracks increased. The chrysalis was now completely opaque. It was no longer possible to see the child's shadow as it moved. But all could hear irritated grunts. A foot kicked harder. More thin cracks.

The child became silent. Either it was thinking what to do or … it was too weak.

Life-giver Halmahera squeaked in fear, but she made no attempt to free her child. To do so would kill. The child must free herself to live.

Simultaneously, Adumie and Qorow Low moved to stand on either side of Halmahera.

"Do not fear just yet," Qorow Low said.

"But my child does not move." Tears choked Halmahera's voice.

"Give the child a bit more time. I am sure it is exhausting work to break through a chrysalis." Qorow Low encouraged.

It is good advice, Adumie thought. He could not have spoken better, though he couldn't help wondering if this was all the child had to give.

Too many other children had not been able to free themselves. In desperation, a life-giver had torn the chrysalis open only to find her child dead or too near death to be revived. That was why they no longer opened the chrysalis, but released it into the ocean.

Seconds seemed like minutes. Still they waited. No one spoke. No one wanted to suggest the inevitable.

Adumie realized he was not breathing. He almost feared to breathe as if the release of one's breath might curse the child.

Suddenly, both legs kicked outward. One end of the membrane shattered as several pieces fell away. Chubby legs wiggled about with their newfound freedom. The skin coloring was bright, deep pink, like the sky at Kahair's early rising.

Adumie leaned in to check for signs of illness.

There were no gray blotches on the child's legs. This child was healthy and strong. He nodded his approval.

Faces eased into expressions of relief. The crowd gave the child an encouraging cheer. Even Adumie couldn't help but smile.

The little legs stretched, relaxed, and lay still.

A fist came bursting out of the side of the membrane followed by the other on the far side.

This time, Halmahera squealed in delight as more of the casing crumbled. She leaned in to help remove her child from the casings leftovers.

Qorow Low was right. She has more faith than a high priest. Adumie cringed at the thought.

Halmahera picked pieces of the chrysalis off and finished freeing her child, but she had no new clothes to dress her child in.

No one made clothes for their children until after the child came-forth and were living in the family quarters. Before the fear of death, there would be many little shirts and pants, even fur suits made in preparation for the little one coming-forth. But now, to make clothes beforehand was to curse the child. The joy of making the clothes was lost. There was much disappointment when unused clothing were given away or stored for lack of a child to wear them.

But this time Halmahera would have great joy in making clothes for her.

A charming smile spread across the child's face. She knew nothing of the troubles of this world, but only saw her life-giver. Adoringly, the child's black eyes focused on Halmahera. She extended her arms upward.

"Kagan." Halmahera could not contain her giggled excitement as she bent to pick up her child. They hugged for the first time. Such touching was only permitted between life-giver and child, not between adults.

A healthy child almost eased the pain of life's troubles. Adumie felt a wave of relief.

Halmahera knelt and stood Kagan on the floor. With Qorow Low's help, Halmahera tied a small green wrap around the little one. Avoiding palm-to-palm contact, Halmahera held Kagan's wrists and helped her to stand.

The child's legs wobbled. Kagan swayed, sat with a thump and began to cry. The expression of surprise was so cute it was impossible not to laugh.

It was the first time Adumie had laughed in a long time. It almost felt as if it was the first time he had laughed in his entire life. It was pure joy.

Tearful Kagan looked around at faces filled with joy and laughed too.

With a little coaxing from Halmahera, Kagan tried to stand again. It didn't take long for Kagan to walk, but it would be several more hours before she would walk without Halmahera's help.

A child had been born healthy, the first in so many births. Adumie could have cried with relief. Perhaps the illness had passed and the next generation would live.

Encouraged, Adumie walked through the Blood Vines to see life-givers hovering near their nests, hoping that their children would also come-forth healthy.

Adumie pushed back leaves to check several chrysalises. None were dried or discolored, another encouraging sign. He watched children's shadows as they moved within their protective casings.

Then the inevitable happened, a mournful cry pierced Adumie heart. Could trouble come so soon? He followed the sound of the grieving back to Halmahera.

Sobbing, she held a crying Kagan at arm's length so Adumie could see the child's back. Kagan's hands opened and closed in an effort to draw her life-giver closer.

On the child's strong muscular back, along the spine, tiny, barely noticeable gray blotches were forming. This child would die before she was fully grown.

Chapter 19

Rona Montgomery
Afternoon, Day Four

IT HAD been eight years since Rona and Lu first learned they'd been chosen for the Akiane Project. They'd trained together for the mission. They'd studied and worked together on their PhDs in microbiology while in route to Akiane. They'd planned their research strategy.

Now like new buds coming forth with the freshness of spring, they burst forth ready to get started and give their first physical examinations. They especially wanted to collect DNA samples from every colonist and follow their genetics back to their respective ancestors. They planned to show colonists holophotos of their ancestors.

They wanted to see what, if any, effect the planet's environment had on the colonists' physical structure, that and the colonists' DNA a limited gene pool, had an affected the genetics of a population. The goal was to see how the colonists' DNA had changed during their 318 years of isolation.

Every twenty-five generations, the father's DNA line would produce small mutations in the family DNA, nothing major, just small, insignificant mutations. It wasn't a sexual issue. It was the way of genetics. The mother's mitochondria had its own properties. It was by mitochondria that researchers were able to extend human life to 150 years.

A generation was defined as the time from when a girl was born to when she gave birth to her first child. That time changed according to culture. It's considerably shortened when women had children by age fifteen. The time was lengthened if it was normal within a culture for women not to give birth until their thirties or forties. The unknown length of a generation for colonists was often a discussion topic between Rona and Lu.

Lu had already outlined five papers they'd write and publish back on Earth. She bought a frame for the Nobel Prize diploma they'd share. Rona had smiled at the gesture. Then to Lu's delight, she created a mock Nobel Prize diploma to put in the frame wrapped it and gave it to her. It was better than Christmas.

Now finally, four days after they'd landed here, they were ready for first contact. Their computers were synchronized with files to take notes, store data, and hold digital images. Lu carried the non-intrusive Handheld Medical Scanner, HMS, to take body and blood readings.

Blood samples were best. They gave more accurate readings. The HMS could tell blood type, map DNA, and identify a disease. It might take much longer to gain these people's trust before they would be willing to give blood samples.

All they needed now was to befriend colonists, learn about their living habits, and gain their trust.

They left their area to explore.

When they saw three women walking in the gardens, Rona thought they'd encountered triplets. The women were so similar in size and dress.

The boots were leather and looked as if they had been turned inside out so the fur was on the inside. The top of the boot was turned down to make a fur cuff. The gloves were also turned inside out with a cuff. The fur on the coat and pants were turned outward with a fur cuff on the bottom coat hem and on their hoods.

All three women had black hair exactly the same shoulder length and were exactly the same height, a little taller than Jorg. They had stout bodies, although Rona thought it might be their fur jacket that made them seem so round.

Their dogs were mostly white with apricot tufts, while the women's clothing was mostly red with a few white tufts.

As she and Lu drew closer, the women turned to look in their direction. Their faces were wide with high cheekbones, flat noses, and maroon skin. Though they had similar facial features, they were not triplets. Rona wasn't even sure if they were sisters.

Their hoods rested on their shoulders, their jackets were opened. They'd just come from outside. Underneath their jackets they wore shiny, sateen-like, green shirts. While they each wore thin green gloves, they also carried a set of fur gloves.

As soon as the women saw Rona and Lu they promptly trotted away like deer spooked by hikers, their dogs followed close behind. In turn, each woman glanced over her shoulder to see if they were being followed.

"Hi there." Lu waved at them. "Wait up. We'd like to talk to you."

The women increased their pace, almost running away.

Lu started after them.

178

Rona reached out and placed a hand on her arm. "I don't think they're interested in talking to us."

"Too forward?" Lu asked.

"Perhaps. They need time to get used to us," Rona said. "Once they realize we're no threat ..."

But Lu wasn't listening. She pulled on Rona's arm. "Look," she whispered.

"What?" Rona asked.

A short distance from where they were standing, a small, green-gloved hand appeared through the branches of a nearby bush. It picked a bright pink flower and then disappeared.

Lu was already moving toward the small hand.

Curious, Rona crept up to Lu and peered through the bushes. A woman sat on a lava path with five children, all of whom sat on their fur jackets. The woman drew something on a handheld blackboard made of flat slate. The children gathered around so they could see.

Lu had found a teacher and her students. They wore fur pants and green socks. Their boots were lined up in a row at the edge of the path. All of them wore the same green, sateen-like blouses, as the women they'd just seen. Every one of them wore matching thin green gloves.

"What a great way to introduce ourselves," Lu whispered.

If Lu doesn't rush things, we might gain the teacher's trust, Rona thought. Even though she felt as excited as a schoolgirl herself, Rona thought it best to leave the class alone and make contact with the teacher at another time. She hoped a teacher would be more curious than the others and more open to making contact.

The child with the flower sat to the side of the group, observing. Perhaps she was some sort of assistant. She seemed a

179

few years older than the others and was considerably larger. The other children were thin, but this one was almost as wide as she was tall. Yet her face showed no signs of being over weight.

She saw Rona and Lu watching them and stared back at them. Her eyes were hazy yellow, with green flecks, and black pupils. Her skin was a dark raw sienna, as though the color had been freshly squeezed from a tube of paint. Her snow-white hair just reached her shoulders.

"Except for the white-haired child, the others all have coal-black hair," Lu whispered.

Every person they'd met so far had black hair and black eyes. Why was this girl different? Was she an anomaly or were there others like her? Her eyes were unlike anything Rona had ever seen before.

"They're all wearing green gloves. I wonder what that's about." Lu continued to speak softly.

Like birds all in a row, one by one, the children turned to see what the white-haired girl was looking at. Except for the girl with the yellow eyes, all the children looked sickly.

Their pale, dull red skin was covered with gray blotches, some more than others. Their black hair lacked luster. One scrawny child in particular looked as if he was about to collapse. His eyes were watery and cloudy. He tilted his head to one side and squinted to better focus.

Rona's heart sank. She'd not expected to find sick children. Like a mother hen, she wanted to gather them up in her arms and protect them from all harm. She wanted to tell them it was all right. She'd do everything in her power to help heal them. If the colony's doctor didn't have a cure, she'd find one. She and Lu had the most advanced technology; technology these people didn't have because of their isolation.

The flowered bush prevented Lu from taking a clear reading. She moved the HMS around looking for an area free of foliage. She tried to push it through the bush without disturbing the leaves.

The teacher turned to see what had captured the children's attention.

"Hi," Lu happily chirped, as she stepped from behind the bush. She inconspicuously held the HMS at her side.

Rona wished she hadn't done that. They should have quietly slipped away. So far no one had welcomed them. What made Lu think this time would be any different?

The teacher let out a mouse-like squeak, and quickly picked up her blackboard, fur jacket, and boots. "Hurry," she said to the children. One might have thought Rona and Lu had come to steal the children.

When she stood, she appeared to be the same size and height as the three women they'd just encountered as if all of them had been cut from the same cloth.

The children hurriedly picked up their things. One child grabbed the sickly boy's jacket and boots. Another girl picked up the white-haired girl's things while the white-haired girl placed her hands under the boy's arms and pulled him to his feet.

He leaned heavily against her as they trailed behind the others. His legs were weak and his feet dragged, but the girl patiently encouraged him along. She didn't look back to see if Rona and Lu were following. Instead, she gave her full attention to the boy.

"Evidently, we don't make any better of a first impression than Jessica," Lu said, disappointed.

"At least Adumie didn't run at the sight of her as if she were lionesses come to eat them," Rona said.

Lu sighed, then said, "They're sick. That boy is dying."

"Did you get anything?" Rona asked pointing to the HMS.

181

Lu checked the readings and shook her head. "Didn't have a clear view or enough time to hone in on just one child. I've got nothing conclusive."

Rona wasn't surprised. Even though she was less than a meter away, at that distance the device would have picked up several people, which would have produced a false reading.

"We should speak to their doctor and find out what's wrong with them, and see if we can help." But even as she said it, Rona had no idea how to find a doctor since no one would talk to them in the first place, and she doubted anyone would let them in the main buildings to look for a doctor's office. "Why bother? If everyone distrusts us, do you honestly think a doctor would be any different? They avoid us like we're flesh eating bacteria."

Lu thought a moment. "We'll have to examine them ourselves."

"We can't examine them if we can't get near them, Lu."

"And if we don't, we'll never know what's wrong with the children."

"And we won't be able to help them," Rona finished with a disappointed sigh.

"Exactly," Lu said. "Have you noticed how everyone wears thin green gloves? I wonder what that's all about."

Another mystery. We'd have plenty to keep us occupied, if only we could get started, Rona thought.

As they turned to leave, their way was blocked. A woman, as solid as a stone wall, stepped in front of them. "You are not wanted," she said, none too kindly. "You must leave."

"We just want to help," Rona said.

"Your help is unwanted," the woman said. "You were told to stay in your area. You do not speak to our life-givers. You will stay away from our children. You will leave all of us alone." She loomed closer. "It is best for you to return to Earth."

"But your children are sick ..." Rona said.

The woman interrupted her. "I am Mercener," she shouted. "You will do as I am saying."

Mercener raised an oversized hand. Fearing she might strike them, Rona and Lu involuntarily cringed. Instead, she snapped her fingers and five angry dogs appeared on the path at her side.

"These will be helping you back to your living area," the woman said.

The dogs dropped their heads, their eyes locked on Rona and Lu. Low menacing growls rose from their throats. Slowly, they began to advance.

Rona and Lu turned and ran.

The dogs gave chase. Above their yelping and howling, Rona heard the woman's harsh cackle of a laugh.

CAPTAIN'S LOG

Akiane Colony
Captain Faris Assetti
Second year, day 35

We have returned—32 days out. It was only to take one week, seven days. It seems like a lifetime.

It took us a week to find the fish. They had migrated to a red line one-third kilometer wide and many, many kilometers long. The line meandered across the ocean much like a river. We didn't follow it to see how long it was or where it originated, though our oceanographer Adryel wanted to.

We should have been able to gather the fish and return to the colony that same day.

We saw the storm clouds on the horizon, but thought we had time. Once finished, we planned to fly over the storm. But the storm was too fast and we were too slow.

The success of this mission was important. It was my decision, but all were in agreement. I was a fool. We all were. We had no idea of the swiftness or the severity of an alien weather system.

Sensing the approaching storm, the fish scattered. The waves weren't too bad at first. Several of us were standing on the shuttle wings concentrating on pulling in the last of our nets when the first big wave hit. It swept five of my crew away. I would have been one of them, but by the grace of Allah, the priest was there. He saved me.

The rest of us had just managed to get inside the shuttle and secure the fish in freezers when another, larger wave, hit us. We were unable to start the engine before a third wave over came us. The combination of waves waterlogged the engine.

We had no choice but to strap in and ride out the waves that battered the shuttle. We were tossed and rolled over and under the water. At the worst of the storm, a half-day into it, we thought we were going to die, but the shuttle was tougher than the storm.

The engine took four days to completely dry out. I hadn't planned on engine problems, nor that our communications and life support might go out. I had not thought to bring an engineer.

There was little land so we worked while floating on water, keeping a wary eye out for more storms.

Our oceanographer, Adryel, has recorded his report on Akiane's waters and storm in his logs.

185

We managed to fix the engine enough to limp home, but we could not fix communications or life support. Flying low, we could leave the door open for fresh air, which meant we had to fly just above the surface of the water at a frustratingly slow speed, delaying our return by weeks.

Adryel's hobby is Scandinavian myths. He has named this storm after a war god called Wuodan, *who causes much trouble. He says from such trials and tribulations, one becomes a mighty warrior able to withstand any adversary. He says we have become stronger.*

I tend to agree with him. Together, we have survived Wuodan, *grieved the loss of our comrades, worked to fix the shuttle, encouraged, and entertained one another on a long tedious and claustrophobic trip home. We have grown closer, know each other better, and are more able to trust one another.*

Personal Log

Despite the hardship, it has proved to be a worthwhile trip. The best part of the trip was the two people with whom I hope will become close friends, Adryel and Father Joseph. The trip back allowed us long talks about life, our likes and dislikes, and spiritual matters.

We honor the same great men in the history of our respective beliefs, though we know them by different names. We read our Holy Books and faithfully pray each day.

I have often missed such discussions with friends at my Mosque.

Most importantly, my new friends ease the loneliness for home.

Personal Log three weeks later

Father Joseph is proving to be more than a good friend. He is becoming one whom I can trust with my thoughts. He listens without interruption and without judgment. Then he offers words to unscramble my confusion. Getting my thoughts out in the open has helped me to overcome the doubts of my faith. He is truly a gift from Allah.

But it is Adryel who continually lingers in my mind. He drifts into my dreams and is there when I wake. My heart races when he is near. I miss him when we are apart.

I am his superior officer. It is not proper for us to be together. I have spoken to Father Joseph. He reminds me that we are on a new world where the rules are different.

Yet I am still a captain in WSC Space Force. I am torn by my affections for Adryel.

Chapter 20

Difficulty Sleeping
Morning of Day Five

RONA HAD SPENT her whole life pursuing her dream of becoming a researcher. She pushed herself; she had to. She stayed up late reading and studying. She'd risen early to be the first in the lab, and was usually the last to leave. It worked. Now she was team leader for the Akiane Genome Project.

On the ship, she'd finally learned to relax. There was little to do and few responsibilities. She still studied, read, and wrote papers for publication. She and Lu completed their PhDs in microbiology. But the stress of deadlines evaporated. The next phase of her goal would not start until she reached the colony. Rona ran on the half-kilometer track, did power yoga, and entered virtual reality role-playing tournaments, which was something she'd always wanted to do, but never had the time.

Since the on-board games were localized to the ship and did not communicate back to Earth, some of the technicians rewrote the game's code to make the game more interesting. The gamers, military and civilians, were highly competitive. The games became challenging and addictive, but not physically harmful.

It had been a fun and relaxing trip, like a six-year vacation. Now she was here at the colony and ready to get started, but all her plans of research and dreams of Nobel Prizes were quickly trickling away. The colonists had made it plain that they didn't want her, or the others, on their planet. Without personal contact, the Akiane Genome Project was on hold. Rona needed a plan.

First thing in the morning, after a good night's sleep, while her head was clear, Rona enjoyed lying in bed, thinking and processing. She wanted to plan her next move and decide how to study the colonists without their cooperation, and how to develop a cure for their children. But it was impossible to think when sharing a room with thirty-four women.

The dorm room was full of voices and activities, as women got ready for the new day. A good part of the morning's discussion was going on right over her head.

"All these dogs appear to be female." Lu sat on the side of her bed brushing her hair.

"How do you know they're all female?" Jess stood by her bed towel drying her hair.

That was another thing Rona missed. Though there was plenty of electricity, there were no electrical outlets. No hair driers. Hair had to air dry.

Lu asked *Britannia's* technicians for help, but they'd said they didn't have the time. Rona wasn't sure they wanted to take the time; they saw nothing wrong with a few whiny scientists roughing it. Even if the women were not interested in the latest hair fashions, why did they have to start each morning with a wet head of hair?

"I checked," Lu said.

"Why were you checking dogs? What were you looking for?" Jess asked.

Their beds were on either side of Rona. She wanted peace and quiet so she could think. Rona pulled her sheet over her head. They didn't get the hint.

"Why not check, Jessica?" Lu let out a silly little laugh.

Jess joined in. "If that doesn't sound like a scientist, I don't know what does."

Today, she was in a good mood, Rona thought unhappily. Usually Jess was somber and quiet, but not today. No, today she was talkative.

In frustration, Rona slapped the sheet back down. She was beginning to understand Jess' bad moods. Rona was feeling one coming on.

Lu stopped brushing her hair and rested her hands in her lap. "I guess it does." She smiled proudly.

"So I guess it's not out of character for you to lift doggy tails," Jess said.

"I guess not," Lu said. That giggle of hers was becoming annoying. "Every dog I've checked so far is female. I haven't found one single male."

"How many dogs have you checked?" Olivia plopped on the end of Rona's bed, without an invitation.

At least she had the decency to have her bathrobe securely wrapped around her. Lu sat in her lacy pink undies. Jess stood in her military-issued underwear, no lace on them.

There was no such thing as privacy when one shared a room with thirty-four women. With a sigh, Rona moved her feet out of Olivia's way.

"Twenty-two so far," Lu said.

"Wait until they start mating, Lu, then you'll find males," Jess said, with a laugh.

"This is serious, Jessica," Lu said with genuine earnest.

"Why?" Jess asked. She pulled on a pair of dark blue military pants.

"Because," Lu said, "how do they reproduce if they're all female?"

"They're dogs," Jess said, "not worms. There must be males somewhere. You just haven't found them yet."

All this talking. Rona wanted to wake up slowly, let her mind drift into a solution mode, but she needed to pee. She threw her sheet and blanket to one side and sat up.

A dog, her five puppies trailing, wandered throughout the dorm. The mother dog sniffed at beds as she passed through the room. So many dogs. They were everywhere. All of the time.

Rona was on the verge of disliking dogs as much as Jess did.

"Lu, have you checked the puppies?" Oliver asked.

"No, just adult dogs," Lu said. "The pups are so squirmy it's it too difficult to tell."

"You need someone to hold the pups for you," Jess said.

"You volunteering?" Lu asked hopefully.

Jess shook her head. She pulled her Space Force blue tee over her head and tucked it and zipped her pants.

"Want to help me check puppies, Rona?" Lu asked. She was now excited at the prospect of having a partner to help her.

Rona looked over her shoulder at the wall where the latrine drains sat. She hated squatting. At least *Britannia* had sent curtains. She stood and stretched.

"Where are you going?" Lu asked.

"Lu, I'm not even awake yet." Rona ran her fingers through her hair. "Give me time to dress and have breakfast."

191

"I'm going for breakfast now," Jess said.

"Give me time to finish dressing and I'll join you," Olivia said.

"If you must," Jess said under her breath.

Those two were like oil and water, Rona thought not for the first time. She couldn't blame Jess. Olivia seemed to thrive on continual bickering.

Olivia was pretty when she smiled, which she rarely did. Her face was usually set in a frown with the ends of her mouth turned down. Her husky voice sounded as if she were growling.

Rona noticed Lu looking at her expectantly.

Oh, yes. Puppies. The idea was uninteresting.

"I didn't come to collect information on puppies, Lu." Rona stood.

"I was thinking we'd do it around our original research," Lu said, with her usual child-like enthusiasm.

"Lu, we haven't even started our original research."

"Well, then, we could do this in the meantime ..."

"We're not going to create a relationship of trust with the colonists by examining their dogs, Lu," Rona said. *Do I sound as surly as I feel? Yes.* She didn't care. "Give it up, Lu. I'm not studying dogs. Instead of checking the sex of dogs, you should be trying to befriend colonists. Then maybe we could start our project and get some serious work done. Like find a cure for their children."

Lu dropped her head. "It was a b-bad i-d-dea." Her shoulders sagged in disappointment. "I'm sorry."

Sometimes she could be such a child. It was time for her to grow up and deal with grownup research.

"Why is the floor damp?" Jess asked. She was near the door examining the floor.

"People are taking showers," Olivia said.

"No, it's wet here by the exit. It's coming from the other side."

"Olivia," a man's voice called from the work area.

"What?" she bellowed.

"Come out here." It sounded like one of her teammates, Adriane.

"I'm not dressed," she answered, pulling her pants up and zipping them.

"Better come now." That was Jorg.

Olivia growled, loudly. She quickly pulled a tee over her head and ran out … and screamed.

Those already dress ran out to see what had happened.

Rona forgot about peeing. She and Lu quickly dressed so they could see what the commotion was about.

Olivia was cussing not only in English, but in her native Dutch language as well.

Those who understood her blushed.

Someone had drilled holes near the bottom of her three aquaria tanks. Water was everywhere.

Since there weren't enough desks and chairs for everyone, several people had set up their equipment on the now-flooded floor, like Rona and Lu.

They ran to recover their equipment and shook the water out of their computer headphones, wrist units, and neck carriers.

"You know, a couple of centuries ago, all this would be ruined," Lu said. "Back then, water was a killer of anything electronic."

"Who would do such a thing?" Olivia cried. She'd calmed down enough to return to English, but not enough to lower her voice. "I'll kill them. I'll string them up and dangle them over one of their godforsaken volcanoes."

"Don't blame the volcano," Spago said, trying for humor to calm the chaos.

"Oh, shut up," Olivia growled.

"Well, at least we didn't have any marine life in it yet," Adrienne said.

That positive statement didn't seem to help either. Olivia stomped and kicked at the water.

"What are we going to do about all this water?" someone asked.

"Who do you think did this?" Rona softly asked to Lu.

"I think it's our fault," Lu said.

"What? Our fault? As in you and me?" Rona asked incredulously.

"Yes."

"Why, Lu? I don't understand."

"If we hadn't been out in the habitat trying to talk to people and scaring them." Lu was now teary eyed. "Mercener wouldn't have done this. We got her angry and she retaliated."

"Lu, you don't really think it was her do you?"

Lu solemnly shook her head yes.

"I wouldn't put it past Mercener," Rona said. "Still it's not our fault that she's vindictive."

"But she wouldn't be if we had just stayed here where we belong."

"Lu, it's not our job to stay in the bay area. We're supposed to be out there meeting people. This isn't our fault and we're not even sure it was Mercener."

But during the commotion, Rona had thought she'd heard Mercener's cackle of a laugh just outside the door.

Chapter 21

Community Meeting
Fifth Morning of Intruders

"WHY DOES World Space Coalition come now?" a voice loudly asked.

Everyone had gathered for this morning's meal, which had been dried tupilak soaked in blubber then slowly baked overnight in stone ovens. Fresh bowls of yellow figs and orange tomatoes had lined the tables. They'd eaten quickly in silence, each thinking of the upcoming meeting.

The meeting had been delayed by one day because of laying the dead to rest.

Tables were barely cleared before the meeting began, without Adumie calling order. Many voices were speaking, demanding answers. In other meetings there had been wonder and speculation, but now many were offended and divided.

It took only five days for the Invaders to offend most of the community. Very few, like Cameron, still wanted to beg their help.

"World Space Coalition demands that Akiane is theirs. They come to claim us as their property," Mercener loudly declared.

When they were healthy, the community had grown to over 2,000. They became too many to gather altogether all at one time. The Community Room had been expanded to take up most of the first floor of *Falcon*. Soon many adults had to stand because there were not enough chairs. If they had continued to grow, the Community Room would have been expanded again. Unfortunately, their numbers began to shrink.

There were now only 244 people, fewer than when Akiane was first settled.

What was left of the community gathered together in one section of the room, leaving most of the chairs and tables empty.

"We are unwilling to be owned," a priest said angrily.

Everyone agreed, sharing the disgruntled attitude.

They had built Endurance without help or interference. Perhaps those of Earth thought to come and claim a prosperous community of people and resources. Or perhaps they came because they knew those of Akiane were dying and wanted to claim what was left behind.

"How do we stop them?" another shouted.

How indeed? Adumie wondered.

"Those from Earth may know of a cure for this illness that brings devastating death to our people." Cameron always spoke of hope. All listened. Some believed. Others wanted to believe. Still others, like Adumie, knew without doubt there was no cure. No hope.

If not for Cameron, everyone would have agreed to banish the Invaders. His misguided opinion only added confusion and brought far too much discussion. This was the fifth meeting upon learning Intruders were coming and they still could not come to a consensus to trust or banish them.

"We should be asking for help before it is too late," Qorow Low said. Few things about her disappointed Adumie; her siding with Cameron was one of them.

Mercener stood. Her loud stern voice said, "They come not to help, but to steal. If we are going to them for help, they will only hasten our deaths."

"What if God has sent them to help us?" Qorow Low asked. Her voice quivered with anticipation.

"Would God send those who abandoned us?" Mercener sneered as she spoke.

"It could be a test to see if we fully trust God instead of relying on strangers," a priest suggested.

And so it continued, each person offering a different opinion, bringing more disagreement. They fought among themselves like chovis over fish.

The final decision should have been left to Adumie. He was high priest, but when he tried, Cameron always objected. An agreement was not forthcoming.

Jecidia stood. He had been the leader until the slow illness made him weak and frail. Still, his voice was listened to and considered. The community silenced.

Here it comes. The real reason Jecidia walked at my heels and insisted upon this meeting. Adumie fumed.

"This is too large of a decision to be made without God's wisdom," Jecidia said.

"We have prayed," a voice said.

"How much more prayer are you requiring of us?"

Evidently, Adumie was not the only one dissatisfied with unanswered prayer.

"We should Woden," Jecidia said and sat down.

The room fell into stunned silence. Adumie sat back in his chair and stared at him. He never imagined Jecidia would suggest such a thing — declare death.

Woden was a dangerous sacred walk across Akiane in winter to see who was stronger, the one making Woden or Akiane's sub-zero weather and blizzards that could last for days.

One either died and was forgotten, or survived and became legendary. The only two who had successfully accomplished Woden were those who had first attempted it, Captain Faris Assetti and the Jesuit Priest Striken. They explored the new land soon after they landed, found the caldera and the place where Endurance now stood.

Not long after that, the colonists were also overcome with unexplained deaths. The captain and priest left again to explore the new world, hoping to find a way to survive. They returned with "that which brought life" that stopped unnatural deaths.

Assetti and Striken left during winter and had been gone for months. The ocean melted. It was thought they would never return, but they unexpectedly returned victorious.

Assetti's famous words, *"We have endured much, but we have persevered,"* were repeated throughout the generations.

Because of those two, the colonists survived and their descendants became the People of Akiane.

Now Jecidia suggested the same treacherous trip across Akiane.

"Woden?" Qorow Low asked, unsure she had heard correctly.

"No one makes Woden and lives," Mercener said. Even she was shocked.

Jecidia started the discussion. Now he remained silent and allowed his previously spoken words to cause new disagreement.

"Yes, let God decide."

"It is too dangerous."

"Do you not trust God?"

"Will you go? Will you trust God?"

Adumie hated division. It only caused anger, accusations, and bruised feelings.

He stood. He was now leader. It was his right to finalize decisions. Only his words were not as readily listened to as was Jecidia's.

Voices quieted.

"What would Woden prove?" he asked. "There have already been too many deaths, yet you propose to send more people outside at a time when they are assured of nothing but death."

All eyes returned to Jecidia, who spoke without standing, "One would allow God to decide. There will be no more need to argue. The matter will be out of our hands and firmly put in God's hand."

Let God decide? Adumie wanted to shout, *We have prayed. God has already decided. We are dying.*

All attention turned back to Adumie. Since this illness had begun, seven different times a small group of people hoped to retrace Assetti and Striken's steps to find "that which brought life." None were ever heard from again.

Each team had set out during the winter years. Each had said God was directing them. None would wait until the summer years; they were too impatient to be heroes.

Adumie had not believed God was directing any of them. If he had, at least one of the teams would have succeeded, but none ever did. Adumie objected to their going, but each time he had been overruled. Now the same thing was happening again. He would object, he would be overruled, and again more would die.

"I wholeheartedly reject Woden. It is too dangerous. The one who attempts such a trip will not return. How can I condemn someone, anyone, to death?" Adumie declared in frustration. He was grieved to his soul that this subject was once again in discussion. "I will not do it. I will not approve this."

Unfortunately, Jecidia would not make this easy. "If they survive, then we will ask for help. If those on Woden do not return, then we will banish the Intruders," he said.

There was a murmur of agreement.

Now the community was of one accord, Adumie thought with disappointment. But need he even worry? *No rational person will volunteer.*

Cameron stood. "I will go."

"I will not allow it," Adumie declared. It didn't matter how much he disliked Cameron, he would not send him to his death.

"You will not allow it?" Even now, when Woden would put his life in danger, Cameron still questioned Adumie's authority.

Perhaps he should let Cameron go. When he did not return, God would have decided and there would be no more discussion, no more dissention.

"Too dangerous?" Cameron demanded. "Why, because you do not trust God? Or because you would let our people die to protect your pride?"

"You insult me in the hopes it will change my mind?" Adumie yelled. "Or would you throw your life away just to defy me?"

"I would sacrifice my life so that others may live." Cameron spoke with the passion of his misguided beliefs.

"I will not agree to Woden." Adumie dismissed the idea with the wave of his hand. "It is too dangerous. There must be another way."

A hush came over the room as all listened.

Cameron remained defiant and would not sit down. He stood waiting for Adumie's permission.

"You are a fool, Cameron," Adumie bellowed.

"We shall see who the fool is when I return. I tell you, we will not die," Cameron said in arrogant assurance.

"How can you be so sure," Qorow Low asked, this from the one who stood most closely with Cameron's opinion. Even she knew Woden was wrong.

"God has assured me if we Woden, we will be victorious," Cameron said confidently.

To say that God was on your side gave any disagreement an unfair advantage. But in this case, Adumie challenged Cameron's relationship with God.

"I have not been given the same assurance." Adumie smoldered with frustration.

Before a rebuttal could be given, Adumie spoke to Nu Venia, "It seems that Cameron wishes to Woden. What do you say?"

"I do not speak for Nu Venia. She …," Cameron started.

Jecidia lifted a hand. Cameron became silent. "Let her speak."

At Jecidia's encouragement, Nu Venia said, in a small voice, "No. I do not want to go." Clearly, the idea frightened her. She understood the dangers.

"I am well within my right to refuse Nu Venia to Woden," Adumie said to Cameron. "One should agree to let you go just to be free of you." But he knew, everyone knew, if Cameron went, Nu Venia would not stay behind. She would reluctantly follow.

No matter how much he disliked Cameron, and disapproved of Nu Venia, Adumie would never have sent them on Woden. Yet he could not stop Cameron, nor could he prevent Nu Venia from following him.

"If that one goes, God will surely curse Woden," a voice said in reference to Nu Venia.

And that was the real reason she would follow. Cameron was the only one who approved of Nu Venia. He did not see her for the disgrace that she was.

"I will bring Nu Venia to prove God's blessings on Woden and on her life," Cameron declared to all in the room.

The community muttered their disbelief. Good. Few agreed with Cameron. If they did not agree, Cameron would not go. It was the way of things. This matter would soon be settled and the conversation would move on.

But Cameron refused to sit. As long as he stood, the discussion would continue.

Tears sprang to Nu Venia's yellow eyes. "I do not wish to go." She sounded small and vulnerable.

Cameron did not seem to notice or perhaps he did not care. *Was he so caught in his own delusion of God's favor that he had no regard for another's life?*

Jecidia sat with his head held high. Was that a slight grin on his lips? Had he planned all this? Was he so devious?

Adumie shook his head. He felt old. Why was Cameron so insistent? "Even if we abide by Woden, what will your deaths mean to the Intruders?" he asked.

"The Earth priest will go with us as witness," Cameron said. "By traveling together, we will come to understanding. From understanding comes friendship. Friendship brings Community."

Nu Venia sucked in her breath from the shock of his words. Clearly he had not consulted her of his plans to form Community with those of Earth.

The mood of the people changed. No one had thought to include the Earth priest, or to be in Community with the off-worlders. *They will never agree to this,* Adumie knew.

"Every ship travels with a priest," Cameron said defending his case. "Since the priest Striken was on the first Woden, it is only right that this ship's priest should also make this Woden."

"What if the Earth priest is not as foolhardy as you and refuses to go?" Adumie asked.

"Then all is lost and there would be no reason to Woden," Cameron said. "But I trust God to move on that one's heart. When we survive, the priest will have the right to speak on behalf of World Space Coalition." Cameron looked directly at Adumie. "And we will listen. Then you will understand that those of Earth do not come to harm us, but to live among us and bring a cure for this illness."

Adumie made no comment. Woden was a waste of lives. He was sure the priest would not be so foolhardy.

"Where will you go?" Qorow Low asked softly. There was disbelief in her voice and in the expression on her face. She didn't believe. "How long will you be gone?"

"We will travel until we and the priest have understanding," Cameron said.

No one objected. They spoke quietly among themselves. Heads nodded. Was the community was beginning to accept the idea? Adumie bowed his head and closed his eyes. He sat down and dropped his head in his hands.

It sounded simple. If the priest did not except the invitation, there would be no need for Woden. The matter would be settled.

Something will go wrong, Adumie knew. Deep within his very being, he knew that Cameron, Nu Venia, and the priest would Woden. *But why?* He didn't understand.

"Who will speak to their priest about Woden?" Halmahera asked.

Without hesitation, Cameron said, "Nu Venia."

Adumie's head jerked up, his eyes focused on Nu Venia.

She sat like a small child, head lowered, not in submission but in misgivings. Her dark skin paled. She was not worthy to be chosen for such a task. Everyone knew, even Nu Venia.

Only Cameron did not see, but believed in her destiny. More than once he had declared that she should be leader. But only priests were leaders, not a life-giver and certainly not Nu Venia. No one would follow one such as her.

Many loudly objected.

"Woden is doomed," Adumie said quietly to himself, but the matter was out of his hands. The discussion would settle itself.

"No," Cameron yelled above the hostile voices. "Nu Venia will once and for all prove God's favor."

"God will once and for all prove Nu Venia's shame," a voice retorted.

Jecidia stood. The room quieted.

"Cameron will go. Nu Venia will go. The priest from Earth will go. God will decide victory or failure." Jecidia sat down.

The meeting was over. They would gather again once the priest had been summoned.

This was Jecidia's plan all along, to override Adumie's authority. It was settled and there was nothing Adumie could say or do to sway the community. *Had Cameron and he conspired together?*

At times like this, Adumie wondered why he was even leader since he seemed to have no authority and his word was rarely heeded.

CAPTAIN'S LOG

Akiane Colony
Captain Faris Assetti
Second year, day 42

All told 852 died from the virus. Dr. Beasley has determined the source of our illness is the fish. They carry a virus. As of yet, he knows of no cure. His findings are in the medical log.

Our first thought was to dump all the fish, but the good doctor said no, that was not necessary. He assures us that cooking fish will kill the virus, but those who handle the fish must wear gloves when catching them, cleaning and preparing them for a meal. No one is to touch them barehanded.

It is good that we have found a new food source so we don't have to eat fish if we don't want to.

The red line was made up of some kind of plant, or rather leaves of a plant. The leaf is pointed at one end, blooms out at the middle then narrows to a rounded end. It has ridges in the wide part along a thick middle. The cook has

*done amazing things with it. His recipes are in his kitchen
logs.*

*Even Harrie likes it she can't seem to stop eating the
plant, along with the fish.*

Captain's Log one month later...

*For the most part, we have stopped eating fish. Now the
only one who eats fish is Harrie. The soft bones don't seem
to bother her. Fishermen are finding other chores to do and
take turns fishing for my dog.*

*People have been dividing up into the kind of work they
prefer; cultivating the hydroponics, cooking and cleaning
up afterwards, tending the native gardens, fishing and the
such.*

*There have been no new illnesses. Those who were sick
have recovered. We now number 453 from the 2,038
colonists that began this journey. It has been a rough
beginning.*

*Beasley doesn't know for sure if the virus had been fully
eliminated. He's not a researcher, but he is an excellent
doctor. All his reports are in the medical logs.*

Personal Log

There are times when I grow weary of this place and long for the conveniences of Earth. There are no vacations here. No restaurants. No holidays.

I often wonder what new musical is on Broadway. I wonder how my twin sister is doing. She had just married four and a half weeks before I left. They moved the date up by months so I could be the bride's maid. Do they have children?

Father Joseph says I must let go of Earth and all it represents if I am to bond with this world, which would mean I will never see Earth again. I will never take another pilgrimage to Mecca. I will never meet my sister's children, her grandchildren, or her great-grandchildren.

I am undecided. What is there for me here when I have left so much behind back on Earth? All of it is progressing without me. Here there has been so much death and disappointment.

Chapter 22

Lieutenant Jessica Hewitt
Kitchen Detail

IN ALL, it had been a good couple of days' work. We'd set up the men's and women's dorm areas, we'd installed the walls for the couples' room, and set up a dining area with tables and chairs.

I even managed to stop Olivia from constructing all six of her large aquaria. Good thing. The three that were sabotaged were ruined. She had three more she could set up. Her research was not ruined.

But did I get a thank you? Of course not. So I left her to do her own clean up.

I've been here five days. I've avoided my mission long enough. It was time I saw to it before it was too late and I got stuck here. The ship was scheduled to leave in two days. It was time to face my fears and seek out Adumie. I'd thought and fretted on it long enough. It was time to take action, but first, one cannot move mountains on an empty stomach.

I stuck my head into the kitchen hoping for something to munch on.

The kitchen was a mess. Boxes had been hastily pulled into the room. There were pots and pans, dishes and utensils scattered all over, opened crates, floor, tables, and shelves. What had they been doing all this time? I'd envisioned a well-ordered kitchen. They'd had days to set it up. The rest of us had organized the living and work areas. What had these guys been doing?

To my surprise, four tupilak hung on the kitchen walls, each as large as a bull. There was enough meat here to feed us for years.

The two doctors, Mathieu and Lesley, were dressed in scrubs for surgery with caps, masks, and gloves. Even their shoes were covered.

"What are you two doing here?" I asked the docs.

"We're helping butcher meat," Lesley said.

"Lots of meat," Mathieu said.

He threw several fair-sized chunks of meat onto the table where Zhoa stood. With a cleaver in each hand, Zhoa expertly chopped a piece of meat into thin slivers. I was amazed, first at his precision and secondly that Zhoa didn't slice a finger off.

Vong pulled a pan of dried meat out of the oven, then returned to preparing breakfast.

The brothers were as different as night and day. Zhoa was tall, wiry, and well-read. He enjoyed feisty intellectual conversations with the scientists. Vong was of average height and a bit heftier. I'd not been to the shipboard martial arts tournaments, but according to rumor, under his loose-fitting shirt, Vong was solid muscle.

He was the kick-ass martial arts champion. Even the big guys couldn't bring him down. It became the military's goal to defeat him. No one did.

Pointing over his shoulder with a cleaver, Zhoa said, "I've got more tupilak in the smoker and in the freezer. Two have been cut up into steaks."

"What's going on?" I asked. "Why all the meat?"

Sounding a bit frazzled, Zhoa answered, "The colonists keep bringing them." He stopped chopping and pushed the meat slices to the side. He placed one cleaver down and wiped his forehead with the back of his wrist, then clumsily reached for his cleaver. "Ouch!"

"You okay?" Vong asked. The brothers may have been different, but they were closer than most brothers I'd known. Vong was immediately at his big brother's side examining his hand.

"Yeah, I just nicked my thumb."

"Want me to look at that, Zhoa?" Lesley asked through his surgical mask.

"No, Lesley, I'm fine. It's not the first time I've cut myself."

Zhoa washed his hands. Vong sprayed a protective bandaid over his brother's thumb and palm.

I again asked, "What's going on? Why all the meat? We can't possibly eat all of this."

"It seems we're preparing for a long warm summer," Mathieu said.

"I don't get it," I said.

Vong explained, "These people are gathering fish and tupilak in the same manner farmers used to gather their harvest for winter."

"Like how farmers harvest in the fall and save everything they can for a long hard winter," Zhoa said. "Well, summer is on its way and these people are preparing as if a famine is coming."

"Doesn't make sense, does it?" Lesley said.

"It must to them," I said. "Did you ask them?"

"I tried," Zhoa said. He returned to his table and carefully retrieved his cleaver. "All they said was summer is coming. Does that explain all this?" he said, waving his cleaver.

"It doesn't," I said.

"No," Vong agreed. "Not unless tupilak migrate to another part of the planet during the years of summer."

"What are you going to do with all this meat?" I asked.

Zhoa pushed one chunk of meat to the side. "Dry it or smoke it." He nodded to the room behind him and nodded at the industrial oven next to Vong. "So that's what we're doing." He proceeded to slice the remaining pieces of meat.

"Vong and I are afraid to go to sleep for fear they'll bring meat and it'll spoil before we get to it," Zhoa said.

"Is that why Lesley and Mathieu are helping you?" I asked.

"Yes," Zhoa said. A big grin spread across his face. "We recruited them. Being surgeons, they already knew how to handle knives. We figured they'd be the easiest to train."

In unison, the doctors stood at attention, proudly lifted their large butcher knives, and saluted me.

"You two don't exactly look like butchers," I said. They were dressed like surgeons.

"They're not!" Vong said. "Look how clean they are."

The doctors were covered with spots of splattered and smeared blood. Their skin might be clean, but their clothing was not.

Zhoa had blood on his hands and forearms, as well as his apron.

Vong was preparing breakfast. His was the only one who was truly clean of the bloody mess.

"Hey, I don't like blood," Mathieu declared, seriously.

"You're surgeons," Zhoa reminded him.

"Doesn't mean we have to like blood!" Lesley laughed.

211

"See what we have to put up with," Vong said.

"As long as they get the job done," I said, "don't knock the help."

Zhoa shook his head. "I just don't know. It doesn't seem right." He winked at me.

"You four deserve each other." I took a bite of jerky and said, "Mmm. Tasty."

"Excellent!" Zhoa said.

"I have to go," I said. "I was just looking for something to eat."

Vong handed me a bowl with several slices of fruit that almost looked like nothing I'd ever seen before, and something shaped like a star. The flavors were also different, but delicious. After I finished, he gave me several pieces of jerky to take with me. They too were good, but they were also freshly made. Eating dried meat for the next two years wasn't an appealing thought.

As I headed for the door, Zhoa said, "Jess, think you could find out how many more of these tupilak we'll be receiving?"

"I can try." But I didn't think I'd get any better answers than he had.

Chapter 23

Lieutenant Jessica Hewitt
Success Comes in Stages

I LEFT those four to their work and walked thought the habitat, looking for a way to find Adumie. I turned to walk the path I hadn't walked before. I was looking for a way to the main buildings. I could see them over the trees, but there didn't seem to be a direct route to them.

I came to a massive entanglement of trees and vines on both sides of the path. *Was this another neglected area?* I wondered.

Green leaves ranged from the size of my palm to the size of a man's hand.

The thinnest vines were greenish while the medium vines were a deeper purple. The thickest vines were the size of small tree trunks and were blood red. The veins on the largest leaves were also blood red.

Multiple colors and shades of green, red, and purple peeked through leaves and vines, creating an abstract painting like atmosphere.

I'd never seen anything in nature like it before.

My gut told me this place was important. Akianeans hadn't allowed it to become overgrown out of neglect. I should take the path around it, but my curiosity pulled me in.

My instincts told me to turn back. These were private people. If I was caught, Adumie would not be happy, but then, I didn't think he'd like anything I did.

I pushed leaves out of my way and stepped into a dark, warm, humid vined jungle. There was a strange muffled noise, so soft I thought I'd imagined it. I stood perfectly still and listened. For a long time, there was nothing. Then just as I was about to move on, I heard it again.

The first time I heard it, the sound came from my right, then it came from my left, as if it echoed off the leaves.

My interest was stronger than my common sense. I didn't plan to linger. One quick look and I'd be on my way.

Stepping off the path, I pushed through the undergrowth and followed the noise. Frequently, I stopped to listen. The sound seemed to move, but I didn't hear the foliage rustle with movement.

Was that a growl? It was too muffled to tell.

The noise was jumping around, to my right, now behind me. Who was stalking whom?

Was the creature dangerous? It didn't sound big enough to be threatening.

Then the noise came from right next to me, just through a thick clump of vines. Gently, I moved the leaves to one side and peeked in.

To my surprise, I found a meter-high nest perched on the top of intertwined blood red stalks. As the stalks thinned, they turned purple then green. The vines were interwoven to make a basket a half-meter in diameter. The vines' leaves covered the basket.

Next to the basket was an iron lamp stand made of long thin iron strands braided together. The top the strands opened up to loosely form a nest similar to the one made of the vines. In the iron nest was a softly glowing light.

The canopy of vines was too thick for Kahair's light to shine through. The lamp was the only illumination.

The noise came from under the leaf covering. I pulled several large leaves back to get a better look and froze.

It wasn't a basket, but a nest and resting in the nest was a cocoon. Not a tiny butterfly cocoon, but one large enough to hold a small dog.

The cocoon looked like moist cheesecloth. I couldn't see what was inside, only moving shadows. The membrane didn't fold in, but held its shape even when the creature inside pushed or kicked. What was inside?

I wasn't about to tear open the membrane to see, even though I wanted to. This was one curiosity I would *have* to resist. But I did want to touch it, just to see what it felt like. Just a touch, I wasn't going to handle it or pick it up.

As I reached out, someone behind me screeched, "Nooooo!"

I tumbled over a thick vine growing along the ground and started to fall. Two sets of hands roughly clutched my arms and forcibly dragged me off. They didn't take the time to gently push vines, leaves, or branches out of the way. They bulldozed me through, not caring what slapped me in the face.

They were too strong for me to struggle free so I went limp and ducked my head hoping to protect my face from scratches. Thin branches entangled my hair and pulled strands out as I shook to my head free.

Clearly, I'd done something wrong. "I'm sorry," I tried to explain. "I didn't mean …"

One of the women began to cry.

"I'm sorry," I said again. "I didn't touch anything. I was just curious." That probably wasn't the right thing to say. "I won't do it again. I promise."

When we reached the path, the crying woman could walk no further. Her steps faltered. She looked over her shoulder several times. Her face was etched with fear and worry.

"I have need for returning," she said between sobs.

"I will see to this one. You go," the other woman said.

What did that mean? What sort of disciplinary action was I in for?

Her grasp on my arm tightened, and seemed strong enough to snap my arm. My fingers tingled for lack of blood flow.

"Please," I grunted. "You're hurting me."

"I will hurt you more," she snarled. "You have your own area. You have no right to impose where you are not wanted. Why do you not stay where you belong? I have told others."

"I didn't know. I'm sorry." And I truly was, not just for her and her friend's sake, but for mine as well.

"Why have you come? What are you wanting?"

"I was looking for Adumie."

"Adumie is not found here."

"Do you know where he is? I need to talk to him."

She didn't answer, but continued to drag me along the path, out of the vined area into the clearing. She snapped her fingers.

Five large, snarling dogs appeared from the overgrowth, their eyes fixed on me. Ominous yellow teeth leveled next to my unprotected stomach.

She left me with the dogs and moved to one side to watch.

My first thought was to stand my ground. But I was outnumbered. From the look in their eyes, they intended to have me for dinner. Saliva dripped from their jaws.

I did not run.

I did not challenge.

This was it. I was about to be torn to bits and eaten.

Sweat threatened to soak my shirt. I felt it dripping down my spine.

A white dog, smaller than the five, with one red ear, leaped in front of me, snarling. Two more all white dogs joined him.

The woman cackled.

The dogs yelped and snarled, but didn't attack. She didn't encourage or stop them. She turned and walked back into the vines, leaving me alone with my fate.

I closed my eyes and braced for the inevitable.

Log of Father Joseph Striken

I think Faris is not doing well. I have tried to assist her when possible, but she takes on too much. She is encouraging to the others and rarely speaks a negative word, but when she is disturbed she's short with people and seems to bark all her commands.

Harrie had a litter of puppies, all of which died. Faris will not speak of them. She speaks little these days. I doubt she has mentioned them in her log.

I think she longs for Earth and fears she will never return.

There has been so much disappointment. Many people have died since we first arrived. Many regret coming and longed for the next ship to arrive, but Earth seems to have forgotten about us. Some could not wait and would not be consoled. They took their lives. Then the strange virus attacked.

I fear Harrie's puppies are the final straw. Faris may be headed into depression.

218

Now Harrie is acting strangely.

But I will start at the beginning.

Two months ago, Harrie the Spitz had seven puppies, which should have been impossible. Harrie was spayed before we left Earth and was genetically altered to live beyond the round trip to here and back to Earth. But more importantly, Harrie was the only dog on the planet; she didn't have a male partner.

Harrie was pregnant for only a few weeks. The puppies came out wrapped in a membrane, which looked like cocoons. Harrie fretted over them.

Faris called Beasley and me to her room to help with the puppies. Beasley tore one of the membranes open, but the puppy immediately died. Not knowing what else to do, he suggested we leave the puppies alone and let Harrie care for them.

She licked each pup then turned it over and licked the other side. She did this repeatedly to each pup. Harrie didn't eat, relieve herself, or sleep for two days. Each membrane shriveled and the puppies died.

We took them outside and buried them. Harrie watched. Once we finished, she went to the area where she relieves herself, then returned to Faris' room to eat and sleep.

On this day, I saw Harrie sniffing the ground. I thought she had forgotten where her pups were buried and was

219

looking for them, but when I tried to redirect her, she was not interested.

Eventually, she found an area where some tiny vines were growing. She proceeded to scratch at the ground around them. She was loosening the soil to help the plants grow.

It makes me wonder if she too is heading for depression. How does one minister to a dog? Faris thinks as leader, she must stand-alone. Harrie is Faris' best friend. If something happens to the dog, what will happen to Faris?

Chapter 24

Rona Montgomery
The Project

FINALLY SOMETHING to settle the gnawing in the pit of Rona's stomach. Thanks to Olivia and her trauma, breakfast was over two hours late. The floor wasn't dry, but most of the water had been soaked up and everyone's equipment was off the floor and stacked on the crate wall.

After breakfast, Olivia and her teammates would break the ruined aquaria down and build the new ones. This time, everyone would watch to make sure she built them against the wall out of the way. It seemed when everyone else was happy Olivia was even more sour.

"Coffee." Rona sat at the table and immediately reached for the pot and poured herself a large cup. That first drink was like sunshine in her belly.

Supposedly there were enough coffee beans to last until the next transport arrived with supplies. Rona certainly hoped so. She couldn't imagine a morning without it.

Gino sat at the next table. He leaned over to say something to Jorg who sat at his right.

Spago sat across from them and peeked around Gino. He appeared to be looking at Lu.

Rona tried to inconspicuously steal a glance at Lu sitting next to her.

Her cheeks were a little rosier than her natural blush.

Spago had difficulty concealing a flirty grin.

Rona was shocked. Was something going on between those two? And how long had it been going on? Lu had never said anything. She wanted to ask Lu about the juicy details, but not in front of Olivia. One critical comment could crush a budding relationship.

Gino straightened. He and Jorg were laughing about something. Spago disappeared from view.

Lu picked up her coffee cup and buried her face in it. Rona guessed her thoughts were off somewhere with Spago.

Rona took a sip of her coffee. "Well, this is strong enough to wake up a dead horse."

Like a rabbit hiding in the brush, Lu jumped as if startled. She almost looked at Rona, but quietly diverted her eyes instead. What was bothering her? She reached for the spoon in what looked like roasted potatoes and dropped a serving onto her plate.

They didn't exactly tasted like potatoes. Rona hadn't decided what they did taste like, but she liked them, even if they were purplish.

Olivia sat across the table from Rona and Lu. She was whistling as if she were happy, something rare for her.

"You're unusually chipper," Rona said.

Lu took small delicate bites of her food.

"You mean, considering my mishap?" Olivia asked with a little chuckle.

"Now that you mention it, yes," Rona said.

Olivia's smile broadened. "Well, I guess it could have been worse."

Rona had never known Olivia to see the glass as half full.

"Guess I'll have to express my gratitude to Miss Lieutenant Jessica." Olivia reached for the plate of roasted potatoes.

There was stunned silence. Rona and Lu almost dropped their forks. Olivia thankful for anything?

Olivia replaced the plate and looked up at their bewildered faces and laughed. "Think about it. If she hadn't stopped me, I would have assembled all six of my aquaria, but because of her I only lost three and I still have three left."

"You're as grateful as a cat in a tuna factory," Rona said. "What's wrong with you?"

Her smile eased as Olivia's eyes scanned the area where her aquaria were. "At least they weren't full of marine life. I had a few rocks and coral," she said thoughtfully. "I'm sorry for the coral. I ... We were testing the water for temperature and acidity. We planned to add a little marine life at a time, but we didn't get the chance." She turned back to them. "But thanks to Jessica, we will finish our project."

"Olivia, I'm impressed over your reaction to the day's events," Rona said with genuine awe.

"Rona, one can't mope over what one can't fix," Olivia said. She reached for a plate of tupilak and served herself. "Not like the two of you are doing."

She was just raising her fork to her mouth when Lu stopped and stared at Olivia.

Rona was in mid sip of her coffee when she stopped and asked, "What are you talking about?"

Looking directly at her, Olivia admonished, "Rona, you are all out of sorts because you can't do the project you want."

It took a moment for Rona to realize where Olivia was headed. *She's giving* me *advice on* my *attitude?*

"And you…" Olivia rested her elbow on the table, bent her wrist, and pointed her fork at Lu. "… are moping just because little Miss Princess here won't join you on your doggy project."

"You have no right," Rona started, but Olivia cut her off.

"Personally I think a dog study is a brilliant idea."

"You do?" Lu asked surprised.

"You can tell a lot about a society by how they treat their livestock and pets. But in this case, they seem only to have pets. I wonder why," Olivia said. "I mean why have so many? What else are they good for? Are they also used for some sort of labor? Do they eat them?"

"Oh I hope not," Lu said.

Holding a sizable piece of meat with her fingers, Olivia continued, "Tupilak is good, but I can't imagine eating only this forever. A little variety would be nice." She popped the meat into her mouth. "A little chicken, beef, fish, bacon even. For the colonists, dog seems logical."

Lu frowned. She pushed the tupilak in her plate around with her fork as if examining it.

Olivia looked at each of them in turn then her eyes scanned the room, plotting, no doubt. "Notice how the dogs never beg for food. They leave the dining area every time we eat."

Dogs again, even at breakfast. Was there no getting away from this conversation? Rona cringed. *Well, at least we aren't talking about projects anymore.*

It had taken a great deal of effort to keep the dogs out of the work area. Once a few of them understood, suddenly every other dog understood, almost as if they'd passed the information telepathically. No one had taught them to stay out of the area during a meal. They automatically left when the food arrived. They lay quietly, resting on the path between the work and eating areas.

"Maybe the colonists trained them." Rona started in on her plate. "I'm famished." She dug in.

Lu ate in silence. *Was she that lost in thoughts over Spago?* Rona wondered?

"They don't just leave when the food comes, they leave when the meat arrives," Olivia said. "Watch this."

She threw a chunk of potato over the heads of two women sitting at the far end of the table. They ducked just in time. "Hey," one complained.

"Sorry," Olivia said, but by her tone, she wasn't.

The potatoes landed right in front of one dog's nose. She quickly ate it and licked the floor clean.

"Now watch this." She picked a chunk of meat off her plate. "Incoming," she said, to the same two women.

"Do you have to?" one asked.

"Conducting an experiment," Olivia said.

Begrudgingly, they agreed and dropped their heads.

Olivia threw the meat high over them.

"Thanks," she said.

The women shrugged.

"All for science," one said without cheer.

The meat landed near a group of dogs. They scattered as if Olivia had thrown a stink-ball at them.

"Interesting," Rona said.

Olivia said, "I think you should add that to your studies."

"What studies?" Lu asked.

"Your dog study," Olivia said.

"Oh, we're not going to do that, remember?" Lu said sourly.

Rona dropped her fork in her plate. "Is that why you're sulking?"

"I'm not sulking, Rona."

"It looks like it to me, Lu."

"Looks like there's trouble in paradise," Olivia taunted. She was more than willing to stir up other people's problems all the while ignoring her shortcomings.

"Oh shut up, Olivia." Rona pushed her plate away.

She didn't. "Why not have a dog project?"

"Because I didn't come here to study dogs. I came to study humans," Rona exclaimed.

"And how's that study coming along," Olivia asked in mock sweetness.

"They won't even talk to us," Lu said.

"So you're doing nothing?" Olivia asked.

There was a good comeback, one that would explain Rona's point of view, but she couldn't think of it. "We're looking for a volunteer," she said weakly.

Olivia screwed up her nose. "And you, Lu. Just because Rona is willing to sit around doing nothing, is that a reason for you to do nothing?"

"What do you mean?" Lu asked.

"I mean … if you want to study dogs, then study dogs. You don't need Rona's permission."

"Thanks, Olivia," Rona said sarcastically. "I wasn't trying to stop Lu. I just don't want to participate."

226

"No, you'd rather sit and stare into space instead of doing something productive," Olivia scolded.

Rona stood. Suddenly, she wasn't hungry any more. "Lu can do whatever she wants. Just like I can do whatever I want." She left them and her breakfast.

Chapter 25

Rona Montgomery
The Project

IT WAS like the pot calling the kettle black. Could Olivia truly not see her own faults? Who gave her the right point a finger?

Rona hadn't traveled twenty-seven light-years to study dogs. She'd come to study human beings.

But what had she expected … that these people would welcome her with open arms? Yes. It never occurred to her that she'd be rejected. How was she supposed to examine people if she never met any of them?

Rona stomped through the gardens at such a fast pace she didn't notice that she had crossed the bridge spanning the little creek. Ignoring the beauty of the garden, Rona plopped on a rock overlooking the pond. She had not seen the pond either. She was too distracted to enjoy the vibrant colors before her.

In five days, she'd accomplished exactly nothing, and if things continued in the same manner, she never would.

And then there was Olivia.

A red dog with a white chest and belly came up to her and tried to nuzzle her hand.

"No," Rona said. She pushed the dog away. The dog took the hint and moved on. Ah but there was another eyeing her.

There were so many of them. They were everywhere in the dorm rooms, in the work area, throughout the entire habitat. Some seemed to have attached themselves to people as if they'd become pets and became their shadows following their new masters everywhere they went. Rona wanted nothing to do with any of them. And she didn't appreciate having them forced on her.

"Olivia is good at passing out advice, like a mother hen teaching her chicks to peck," Rona said to no one. "Who does she think she is, talking to me like that? I'm not a child. I'm fully capable of conducting my own life and making my own decisions."

For Rona, the Akiane Project had been a lifetime opportunity, which she had almost missed. Her mother had cried and feared she'd never see her eldest daughter again. Rona almost resigned from the team. She was her way to do just that when she'd run into Olivia.

"You can't let your family run your life," Olivia had said.

Following her advice, Rona stayed in the project. Leaving her mother was the most difficult thing she'd ever done. Rona's only consolation was that she had three sisters. Two of which had already provided grandchildren. Remembering her mother's tearful face made Rona homesick and guilty that she'd left at all.

Mathieu interrupted her thoughts when he sat on the rock next to her.

"What do you want?" She spoke with more hostility than she'd intended.

"Come like so many others to watch the lake," he answered. "Why are you here?"

She didn't respond. Rona had gone for a walk with no destination in mind. It was only then that she realized where she was, but it didn't surprise her. There were few places to walk in the habitat.

Mathieu shifted his weight. He pulled his right leg up and rested his right ankle on his left knee. His foot politely faced away from her. "You don't look well," he observed.

"Don't feel well." She crossed her legs with her left leg facing away from him. She even turned her body slightly away. He didn't take the hint.

"What's the matter?" he asked.

"Things … life … this place is not turning out the way I'd hoped," she said.

"Ah, disillusionment." He resettled himself, rested his arms on the lower half of his leg, and looked out at the pond. "That can be a bit disruptive to one's life," he said, as if he understood.

"Any solutions, Doc?"

He gave no notice of her sarcasm.

"Well, if I had to make a quick diagnosis, I'd say you are a scientist with nothing to do…my prescription…find a project."

"Project," Rona said, without enthusiasm. "I came here with a project in mind. I had visions of flying with the eagles. Instead I'm walking with …" She stopped.

"Turkeys," he finished.

"I didn't mean that you were…," Rona was suddenly embarrassed. "That anyone is…It's just that…" She kept her back to him and lowered her head.

He laughed. "Forget it. I know what you meant. But considering what you've accomplished so far, you learn anything yet?" he asked.

"No Matt, of course not," she said. She didn't even feel as grand as a turkey. She felt more like Olivia's chicken pecking at empty ground. "It's difficult to examine someone who won't even speak to me." She raised her hands and swept them over the scene before them. "People don't even seem to exist. I come here every day. I've not seen anyone here but us. It's almost as if they're a figment of my imagination." She paused. "And when I venture into other parts of the habitat to meet someone, they run off as though I have a flesh-eating disease, or they chase me away as if I'm some demon."

"I think they're elves," he said conspiratorially.

She uncrossed here legs and twisted around to look at him through narrowed, suspicious eyes.

He leaned in and softly said, "They come while we sleep and bring us meat and take our trash. They also care for this lake and the surrounding foliage."

"How do you know?" Rona asked.

"Know what?"

"That they take of care of this place?"

Overacting, Mathieu raised a hand to his eyes and scanned the area. He dropped his leg and lifted his feet one at a time to look under them. "Well, there are no weeds for one."

"How do you know weeds even grow here?" she asked.

"Well, I don't, but there are weeds everywhere on Earth, so why not here?"

"This is an alien planet," Rona said. "There might not be any weeds."

231

Mathieu laughed. "There's a project for you. Discover the truth about alien weeds."

"Humph," Rona grunted.

"You're bored, Rona, you have nothing to do," he said.

"Aren't you bored?" she asked.

"Haven't had the time," he said. "When I'm not being a doctor or counseling out-of-sorts scientists, Zhoa and Vong have me butchering meat."

"Who have you been doctoring?" Rona asked.

"At the moment, you," he said.

She didn't want to be his patient. What business was it of his, anyway?

"You've forgotten what fun science is," he continued. "That's why you became a genealogist in the first place. You like studying genes, experimenting on them, and unraveling the mysteries they create," he said. "And like every other scientist in the world, or in this case, the universe, you need a project to keep yourself occupied, keep your mind busy, and something to have fun with."

"This is not a vacation, Mathieu. I came to work," she said, fully annoyed. She had responsibilities; people to report to. It was important that she succeed. Everything she'd worked for all her life depended on it. "Science is messy. It's a lot of good hard work. You spend years doing research. You come to a conclusion, then someone challenges and tries to disprove everything. So you have to defend your work or start over," she said.

"If you wanted an easy path, maybe you should have stayed on Earth and been an information technologist."

She gave him a look of disgust.

"I didn't want to be sexist and say 'barefoot and pregnant.'" He shrugged and smiled sweetly.

Rona burst out laughing. "Yeah, that would be a so much easier life, giving birth, raising children, staying up all night, and let's not forget the endless diapers."

"So you'd rather be an information technologist?"

Rona let out a heavy snort. "OK, I'd rather be here. But I'm not having fun."

"That's because you're feeling sorry for yourself, Rona."

"Oh, why don't you sugarcoat it for me, Mathieu?"

""It's only been five days, Rona. What did you expect, to have completed your first project by now?" When she didn't answer, he said, "You're being narrow sighted."

That was it! Rona jumped to her feet and looked down at him. "You're no better than Olivia. I've worked hard to get here. What was am I supposed to do now?"

"Stand around and do nothing?" he said innocently.

Was he mocking her?

"Lu wants to study the dogs," she said scornfully. "I didn't spend my time and money training, throughout my childhood, my entire adult life so I could study the mating habits of dogs." Now she was yelling her frustrations at him. She knew it wasn't his fault. But she'd kept in for so long. And since he wanted to evolve himself, well here it was.

Mathieu remained calm.

What did he care? His life isn't in shambles.

"And I was going to have fun, with genes," Rona said, a bit more calmly. "My whole career is set on that study. The entire reason for my coming here was to study the colonists' DNA. I waited my whole life for this."

Her mind flashed back to when her mother bought her a velvety red dress for her eight birthday. She'd wanted a microscope. Her mother didn't understand. Rona was broken hearted. That same feeling was threatening to overcome her now.

Then she'd pouted and cried the whole day. Was she still the eight-year-old girl? She was supposed to be thirty years old. She didn't feel like it. She felt like crying.

"You do know how old you are?" Mathieu asked with a smirk. "Your life is not over. If not this project, there will be others."

She could feel her anger rising again. Rona was goal-oriented and whenever she found herself without a goal, she became disoriented. That's how she felt now, disoriented. She hated that feeling. Hated that no one understood. She turned her back on him.

"You're a type A personality," he said.

She didn't answer.

"Remember, Rona, it's only been five days," he continued. "That's not enough time to be a failure, not when you have at least two years before the next transport, plenty enough time to get started. Something will happen."

She didn't want to listen any more. She started to walk away.

But he was another one who would not give up. "Where are you going?" he asked.

"I need some air," she said.

"The best air is outside," he said, "but you'll need to dress a bit warmer."

She stopped and turned to glower at him. "My life is one big joke to you, isn't it?"

"No but you're acting like a teenager whose life is over because you took home an excellent instead of a perfect report."

"Mathieu ..." She shook her finger at him.

He stood and grabbed her finger. "I'm telling you, Rona, it won't get any better, no matter how much you declare foul." He took her fisted hand and kissed the top of it. "Relax. I'm not the bad guy. I'm not out to get you. I just want to help. You are out-of-sorts because you have nothing to do. It's in all of our natures. That's how we off-worlder scientists are built, and why we were picked for this mission. We're driven to succeed."

She tugged her hand out of his.

"It will only get worse," he continued. "Find something to do before you become angry and your friends find you unpleasant."

Rona sat heavily back on the rock, like a deflated balloon.

Mathieu was right. She needed a project. Something fun. Studying humans was fun. She watched the pond.

"Lu wants to study dogs," she said in a docile voice.

"Why?" Mathieu re-sat himself next to her.

"She can't find a male dog."

"They have to be somewhere. Just wait until they start mating." When he chucked, his whole body joined in. "You'll be able to find them then."

"Jess said the same thing." Rona scrunched her face.

"So what's the problem?" Mathieu asked.

"They don't seem to be mating," she said.

He put an arm around her shoulder and squeezed. She knew he was trying to help, but she didn't respond. His arm fell away. She didn't want to give in. She didn't want him to be right.

She wanted to work on her intended project.

But Mathieu *was* right and she knew it. It was time to let go of what she couldn't have and accept what was available to her.

Gino and Spago, with their respective teams, walked along the path toward the pond. They had plenty to do. They carried bags and cases full of equipment and were dressed for the cold. Just outside the habitat a small hovercraft land rover waited to carry them and their equipment to the mountains.

Rocks and mountains don't reject their researchers, Rona thought bitterly.

Lu walked with Spago. She didn't look happy either.

That's my fault, Rona knew. *I've not only deflated my balloon, but I pen pricked Lu's as well.*

"Why would I want to study dogs?" she asked.

"How many human discoveries have been made from studying animals?" Mathieu asked. "I'm just saying …" He shrugged when she looked at him. "Animals are very similar to humans. We're all mammals. What you learn from dogs could be the beginning of something you might learn about the colonists."

"Like what?" Rona shifted her body so she could face him.

He narrowed his eyes and in a serious tone said, "These dogs are not native to this planet any more than the colonists are. Both were imported from Earth. Both seem to have adapted to their new environment. How?"

Rona puckered her face.

"Maybe there is a survival reason as to why there are more female dogs than male dogs. Does that same survival reason transfer to humans?" Mathieu asked.

Her frown disappeared as she contemplated Mathieu's question.

"You know, officially only one dog made the trip to this planet," he said. "There are no records of another dog other than the captain's Spitz. And yet, there are dogs everywhere. Where'd they all come from?" He paused. "There's Lu now. I think it's time you two made up."

"How did you know?" Rona asked a little shocked.

"With such a small number of people, there are few secrets. Besides, like so many others, I was just having breakfast," he said. "And this place is too small to successfully avoid one other. As your doctor, my prescription is to study dogs until you can make friends with the colonists. Show them you're no threat and they will come around."

"You make good arguments," Rona said, as she stood. "Was debating part of your curriculum?"

"Actually, I began in drama and would still be there if I hadn't taken biology as an elective." Mathieu shrugged when Rona gave him a questioning look.

"I would have never guessed," she said.

"We came that close to never meeting. Tell you all about it sometime … if you'd like," he said.

"I'd like." She meant it. What little she knew about him she liked. They hadn't taken the time to get to know each other on the ship, but maybe it was time they did.

His face brightened.

For some reason that warmed Rona's heart. "Thanks for the advice, Doc. Maybe I'll soar yet."

She went to meet Lu. As soon as she saw Rona coming toward her, Lu left Spago's side.

"I'm sorry," they said at the same time.

"No, Lu, it's my fault."

"I'm to blame, Rona. I shouldn't expect you to be interested in something just because I am."

"We're teammates, Lu. I should be more willing to listen. So let's start over."

Relieved, Lu smiled. "Teammates."

"Teammates," Rona confirmed.

"Want to walk?" Rona asked.

Lu stole a quick glance at Spago.

He nodded. "I'll see you later for dinner."

Rona and Lu walked back over the bridge toward their work area.

"I haven't been my chirpy self lately, have I?" Rona asked.

Lu shook her head. "It's because you have nothing to do. I know what it's like. It drives me crazy when I have nothing to do. That's why I thought I'd study the dogs. It's not what I really want to do, but it's better than sitting around."

"Mathieu mentioned how studying animals has helped in breakthrough cures for humans," Rona said.

"You think studying dogs might cure the children?" Lu asked in surprise.

Rona shrugged. "Who knows? Found a male dog yet?"

"Not yet."

"How many dogs have you checked?"

"Sixty-five," Lu said.

"And what have you learned about the puppies?"

Lu shifted her shoulders in frustration. "That they don't like being handled. They're too squirmy for me to get a good look."

The dogs still didn't tickle Rona's interest, but working with Lu was better than being self-absorbed and moody.

"Want a squirm holder?" Rona asked.

Lu's wide-eyed excitement clinched Rona's resolve.

"We'll take blood samples and photos, and catalogue each animal we check. We'll turn this into a real project," Rona said. "Who knows, we might get that Nobel Prize yet." What did a little white lie hurt if it made Lu happy? And who knew, they just might anyway.

Lu did a little bounce of an excited dance. "Definitely," she said, in between wind-chime giggles.

Log of Father Joseph Striken

Harrie's Story
Second year, day 132

Harrie has come every day and has marked close to one-meter square with her scratching.

I got a hand-held rake to help. I knelt, sat on my legs, leaned forward, and braced myself with my left hand. With my right hand I loosened dirt several centimeters deep.

Harrie came and sat next to me on my left side. She leaned against my leg and stuck her head between my left arm and chest. No matter how many times I pushed her away, she came back. So I let her stay.

Gardening

"What are the two of you doing?" Faris asked.

Joe sat back on his heels.

Harrie pulled away from him. She looked up at Faris with a wide doggy grin, her tongue hanging out and her tail happily thumbing the ground.

"We're gardening," Joe said.

"Why? We have hydroponics inside. I thought we were leaving the land outside for native plants," Faris said. She folded her arms over her chest and cocked one hip. She was annoyed.

"I think we are cultivating a native plant," he said.

"Which one?"

"I have no idea."

"Then why bother?"

Joe shook his head. "It seems to be important to Harrie."

Faris stood for a long while. "Have you deserted me for the priest?" she asked Harrie.

Harrie barked once.

"I think that is a no," Joe said.

"I've always heard that one bark meant yes and two meant no."

He didn't know the captain well, though he'd tried, she remained aloof. Joe didn't know if she was joking or serious. "I'm sure it's just a temporary situation. She's still loyal to you. I'm just helping out."

"If you are looking for work, Father, I have plenty of suggestions." She wasn't joking.

Now he wasn't sure what to do. She was captain and had the right to order him to stop.

"I...ah...It seems important to Harrie." He knew it sounded strange; it was strange to him. He couldn't really explain it.

"Mmmm." Faris didn't look pleased. She stood for a seemingly long moment before she shifted her weight. Finally, she said. "Carry on then."

To his surprise, Faris hadn't ordered him to stop. Instead she stood and watched as if she approved.

Joe leaned forward, braced himself with his left hand, and raked at the ground. Harrie slipped back into her place.

No one spoke, but Joe had a strong feeling that God was pleased, which made no sense. There were more important things to do like help with building the habitat.

Why? Joe silently asked God. *A garden for a dog? Why does this please you? What inspired Harrie to do this in the first place?*

But what surprised Joe the most was the fact that *he* was the one doing the gardening. He hated gardening. He'd much rather read and study.

And yet, he could not shake the feeling that this was more important than reading his Bible.

It didn't make sense.

Harrie's Story, Continued

Second year, day 153

> *Harrie continues to come to her garden every day. She comes to the community cafeteria with Faris, but she sits at my feet. As soon as I'm finished eating, she herds me outside.*

> *Faris says nothing. Sometimes she comes to the garden to watch, but she never helps. She doesn't understand why I'm encouraging her dog. I can't explain it myself.*

> *Now that the ground is loosened, all kinds of native plants are coming up.*

> *Harrie digs up or bites off all the plants she doesn't want in her garden. Once I knew what she was after, I helped. Now we're weeding.*

241

Faris no long watches us. She says she has a wall to build. I should be helping with that, not gardening with a dog. She says she not, but I think she's aggravated with me for wasting my time when there is so much work to do.

Yet, she does not order me to stop.

Two Weeks Later

Second year, day 167, 5 months

Harrie has given birth to another litter of five puppies. Once again, the puppies were born in some sort of cocoon, but this time she gave birth in her garden.

Preparing

Harrie delicately took a vine in her teeth and pulled the vine over one of her puppies. Droplets of a white milk-like substance dripped over the cocoon. The cocoon absorbed the liquid as if it were a dried plant soaking up water. She moved the vine back and forth until the membrane was totally moist. Then she released the vine, rolled the pup over, and did the same thing on the other side before starting on another cocoon.

Joe sat next to Harrie. She looked up at him and whined. He picked a cocoon up and very carefully wrapped one of the longer vines around the center of it.

Evidently, when the vine was bent it continually leaked. The membrane soaked up everything, but the substance only covered the middle of the cocoon. The rest of it remained dried. Joe wrapped two more vines, one on either end without pulling the vine out of the ground.

The entire membrane became moist and slightly transparent. They could see the shadow of a puppy moving inside.

Harrie barked her approval.

Joe wrapped each cocoon in the same way.

End of Day Log

Faris is no longer depressed. She hums. She has brought a chair out to Harrie's garden nursery. Together they sit, watch, and wait.

Chapter 26

Lieutenant Jessica Hewitt
Commons Area

"ARECHIT!" a male voice calmly said. The dogs became obediently silent.

I let out a slow breath and opened my eyes. I was not to be eaten alive this day.

All the dogs sat, happily panting with their tongues hanging out and their tails wagging as if expecting a pat on the head for a job well done. They moved out of the man's way as he approached. All but the red-eared dog, left the area.

Jecidia stood in front of me. He wasn't as tall as I remembered. He seemed shorter.

"Hi," I said.

He nodded his greeting. "You are in need of saving from chovis."

"Chovis?" I asked.

He pointed to the one dog peacefully sitting at his side.

"The dogs," I said. "You call them chovis."

He gave me one nod.

"Is many chovis or just one chovis?" I felt stupid asking, but it was all I could think to say.

His seemed a bit confused. "Whether many or one, it is chovis. Come with me." He turned and motioned for me to walk with him.

Hesitating, I said, "I was hoping to speak to your leader." Even though I knew the answer, I asked, "Who is your leader?" There was always the possibility I was wrong.

"Adumie," Jecidia said.

Of course. I couldn't be that lucky. All the times I'd been wrong in my life and now when I needed it most, I was right. Adumie was leader.

"Is there someone else I could speak to?" I asked. "He doesn't like me."

"Adumie is not liking Adumie," Jecidia said.

"That's not helpful." I walked at his side. "I got the feeling that I insulted him in some way. Maybe if I apologize, but first I need to know what I did wrong. It would be helpful if you told me."

Jecidia smiled. "You have come to Akiane."

"That's it?"

"That is it."

How was I supposed to beat that?

To my surprise, he didn't walk me back to the bay area. He walked me into one of the main buildings. I looked up in time to see *Falcon* painted across the hull. The ship's gray paint had long lost its luster, but the letters FALCON were bright cobalt blue.

We walked down the hall. Several people were also walking in the same direction as us.

"What's …?" I started to ask.

"Mercener told me where to find you. I sent her to call the others," Jecidia explained.

I wondered why, but I was afraid to ask.

We entered a large commons area that seemed to take up most of the first floor. The room was huge. A couple of thousand tables and chairs filled the room. But except for a group of people gathered into one small area the rest of the room was empty. The people looked lonely and lost.

Then every single pair of eyes of more than 200 hostile people turned toward me. The most hostile were those of Adumie. His stare made my insides wither.

Clearly, I was not welcome. It reminded me of the dream where everyone stares because I've shown up naked. But this was no dream and I was fully dressed. Yet I felt the same shame and embarrassment. It was a little creepy. I looked away and scanned the room. The walls caught my attention.

Someone had painted one continuous mural all around the room. It so fascinated me, I temporarily forgot how uncomfortable I was.

The painting was of three spherical ships trekking across the stars. The next area was of an exploding ship. Parts were flying in all directions. Another ship was on land near the ocean. It was overwhelmed by amazingly large blue-green waves with angry, white foam. On the edge of the caldera were two people waving at the last ship, which made a perfect landing in the caldera near majestic mountains.

It was their history of how they came here and what happened upon arriving.

The mural-story continued with the building of this habitat. There were figures of sad people, happy people, adults surrounded with children and finally paintings of people dying.

Within the mural were holographic images of people's faces. None of them looked like these people, but looked like people from Earth. The images were mostly moving holograms, but some pictures were made of paper copies. I guessed these were the ancestors.

Jecidia pulled on my sleeve and motioned me toward a group of people sitting near the center of the room. They seemed small and forlorn compared to the size of the room.

The chairs were comfortable with stuffed fur cushions. The tabletops were made of clear, tinted green glass filled with dark green fibers like fiberglass. Chair and table frames were made of black metal that swirled and curled into beautiful, ornate designs. No two chairs or tables were the same. *These people had a lot of time on their hands*, I thought.

The room was so silent I might have thought the people before me were an illusion.

In a low voice, I asked Jecidia, "Why is everyone here? I thought you had arranged a quiet conversation between Adumie and me. He is your leader, right? He makes all final decisions. Right? So why is everyone here?"

Jecidia's voice spoke so all could hear. "It is your time to speak."

My heart raced. What did I miss? Now it was my time to speak? What did they want me to say? I was not a public speaker.

Jecidia directed me to a table and chair in the center of the group of people, where everyone could easily see me, and left me there.

I stared back. I didn't try to hide my curiosity about these people.

They were all dressed exactly alike. Even their children, what few were here, wore green sateen pantsuits and green gloves.

247

Variety was not the spice here. It was difficult to tell men from women. All had stout bodies, flat faces, fat cheeks, and straight black, shoulder-length hair. Their skin colors ranged from deep pink to dark raw sienna. Most adults appeared to be exactly the same size. Their heads were level with one another, except for those who were a full head and shoulder taller. They also had heads full of tiny black braids like those of Jecidia, Cameron, and Adumie.

Many people had a few tiny, gray blotches on their skin. Some had large, gray blotches all over their faces and were going gray and/or going bald. The worst of them, their skin seemed transparent; I could see light violet veins. Those adults were smaller than the others. They appeared withered and shriveled with age.

About half looked healthy, with no blotches and coal-black hair.

There were a few children and toddlers, but no babies.

There had to be a good explanation for the missing children. Maybe they were in some sort of school and babies were in a nursery. *Must be it*, I thought.

All those black, unblinking eyes were focused on me were devoid of emotion. I wondered what they were thinking. What did they expect me to say?

I rubbed my sweaty palms against my jacket.

Remain calm, I heard Dad's voice say. *Don't panic. Explain the situation and go from there.*

With all my heart, I wished he was here with me. But if he were still alive, I wouldn't be here. I'd be happily married living in Baja, California. Reality: Dad was dead and I was alone.

I'd never been more alone in my life.

I expected Adumie to say something. He didn't. His eyes kept shifting away from me. He sat with his back rigid, his head held high, and a permanent scowl on his face.

He hated me. I knew it was only because I was from Earth. I knew I shouldn't take it personally, but I did. I felt that I was the one to blame. That it was my fault he hated me.

Cameron walked toward me. Was it his turn to yell at me?

The young girl with the white hair and yellow eyes peeked from behind him. Was she his daughter? Rona had said something about a girl with white hair when she and Lu had found a class of children. I wondered if this was the same girl. No one else had hair or eyes like hers. Why was she so different from the others?

When I first met Cameron, I thought he was nice, but not now, not with that penetrating stare. He seemed to be looking deep inside, analyzing my soul. I shifted uneasily in my chair.

He stepped to one side, and with a slight nudge from his hand, the white-haired girl moved a step closer to me and stopped. Cameron nudged her again. She resisted. Clearly, she didn't want to be here anymore that I did. He pushed a little harder. She sat at the table across from me. He stood behind her as still and cold as a mighty warrior.

I guessed the girl to be about twelve years old, but the seriousness of her expression said she might be older. She was shorter than the adults but slightly taller than the other children present.

She was as Rona had said, almost as round as she was tall. Her legs, her arms, even her fingers were thick, but her face belonged to a thin person. Everything about her was strange. In every way, from the color of her eyes to her size, she was different from the others, except she was dressed in green, just like everyone else.

And now, for whatever reason, this conversation had been surrendered to her. Who was she? And what did she have to say that was so important?

She glanced around as if looking for an escape, but Cameron blocked her way. She scanned the crowd. For what? A friend? Among those angry faces? Finally she looked up at Cameron and sighed, her shoulders slumped. She sat as if the weight of the world were on her. Then, resigned to her fate, she gave me her full attention.

I waited for her to speak.

She placed a hand on her chest. "I am Nu Venia." Pointing to Cameron she said, "He is Cameron. One of our priests."

Priest?

When she said nothing more, I blurted out, "Why do you hate us?"

"You abandoned us." Nu Venia sounded personally offended.

"World Space Coalition thought you were dead," I said.

"Why would you think that?"

"They never received one communication from you. All attempts to make contact failed. They assumed everyone had died."

"Then why send a ship?" she asked. "Just one with no one aboard."

"They sent three robotic ships. They were support ships. WSC didn't want to risk more lives. The first left two years after you did. "

"Only one arrived," she said. "There were no people aboard. You promised to send ships with people to maintain the habitat our people built. Those ships were supposed to take those who wanted to return back to Earth." She spoke as though it had happened yesterday.

The Indians in the village near Oconto, where I grew up, passed their oral history down to the succeeding generation with the same passion. Time seemed not to exist. They spoke of each offense, war, or historical event as if all of it had happened yesterday.

I could only assume that these people passed their history down with the same intensity, which would explain why this twelve-year-old sitting before me would react to a three-hundred-year-old offense as if it had just happened to her.

"There were no people, and the ship was incapable of returning to Earth," she continued. "We were stranded here. Now you return 318 years later. We suffered greatly and barely survived under the harsh conditions of this land. Yet now World Space Coalition claims all we have built as theirs. They call us Colony as though we belong to them. We belong to no one." She emphasized the last words.

I began to understand these people's animosity.

Heads nodded. Soft voices confirmed her speech. According to them, she'd spoken well.

"If we had heard from you ..." I stopped. Trying to vindicate Earth was not going to work. We both needed to know the facts. "What happened after the first people landed?"

"*Hawk* landed first, 3 kilometers from shore. That ship carried the power source for the new colony. There were 900 people aboard that ship.

"Shortly after, a ferocious storm hit. Those who were outside were lost. Waves took them away. The force of the storm was so strong it pulled *Hawk* toward the ocean. The thirty-two people inside the ship were the only ones to survive."

What was she talking about? What storm? I looked at the mural, where the waves were washing over one of the ships. That must have been a horrible day, to have just landed with the hope of a new world and to lose so much so soon.

She continued, "Only the *Falcon,* carrying 1,035 people landed safely."

I remembered our history of those ships. They were named after raptors: *Hawk, Eagle* and *Falcon*, because those birds were greatly admired, could fly far distances, and survived under harsh conditions. The three spacecraft going to Akiane had been similarly admired.

By her silence, I knew it was my turn to speak. "What happened to the *Eagle*?"

"It exploded as it orbited Akiane."

"The *Eagle* was supposed to carry DNA to breed livestock and farming seed," I said.

"All was lost," she said.

"Building a colony twenty-seven light-years away was to be Earth's greatest scientific achievement. But people on Earth didn't agree on how the project should be run. When nothing was heard from Akiane, they took their money away. WSC no longer had the funds to continue the project," I said.

She only stared at me, as did everyone in the room. That feeling of nakedness swept over me again. I placed my arms on the table and leaned close as if to hide my nakedness.

"No one ever planned to abandon you. It was thought, hoped, *believed* that you would survive and send word to Earth about your situation." I stopped to take a breath. I didn't think they believed me. I took a deeper breath and kept speaking. "If they had heard from you, it would have reignited the project. Then it would have been easy to raise the money and rescue you.

"But when no word came, it was assumed all had perished. The hope of colonizing space beyond Earth's solar system also died.

"Three robotic ships were sent, one at a time, years apart just in case there were survivors. The ships carried food and equipment. Each ship also carried new communication equipment. Earth did not receive one transmission from any of them. Each ship was sent here to take survivors back to Earth. You were never abandoned."

Nu Venia looked shocked.

"You lie!" someone yelled. "Only one ship came."

I kept my eyes on the girl. I thought if I pretended it was just the two of us, I could get through this. "I don't know what happened to the other ships," I said. "I wasn't there."

The crowd didn't like my answer. A murmur of objections rose from them.

"All I know is three ships were sent," I tried to speak over the crowd. "I don't know what happened to the others."

"Of the 2,038 that began the journey, only 852 survived." Nu Venia looked so sad, I might have thought her immediate family had died.

"Before we were completely settled, people died of broken hearts from longing for home, and others died of the severe cold. When it was learned we would never return to Earth, more committed suicide because of despair. Then we were overcome by a deadly disease. Officially, 419 of us began this colony you claim as *yours*."

What could I say? Akiane truly was theirs. What claims did WSC have? It had spent billions of dollars to discover the planet, travel here, and build the habitat, but they hadn't died or suffered like these people.

253

"Tell us why you abandoned us," someone demanded.

The crowd agreed with loud shouts.

"We didn't abandon you," I said. "We thought you were dead." Still, there was more to it than that.

Chapter 27

Earth Politics

HOW COULD I explain Earth politics, or how, as one world, we'd outlawed war, moved past intolerance and prejudice? How would I explain nations like China that had existed for centuries, explain what a third-world country was or how they had finally become developed, prosperous countries? How could I explain of national pride or the importance of religious morality?

By the end of the 22nd Century, we had obtained world peace, which gave way to the Golden Space Age.

Instead of each country working on its own space projects, repeating what had already been done, the United Nations created World Space Coalition where nations pooled their resources, including personnel to run the base, scientific data, and scientists, to accomplish the impossible.

WSC was built on the moon so no country could lay claim to the space program. Scientists and civilians ran it and decided that English would be the common language. The only military was the multi-national WSC Space Force, whose work was building and maintaining all aircraft and training astronauts.

The International Space Station became WSC Docking Space Station. The DSS was expanded to the size of a small city, with over 5,000 permanent residents who lived and worked on the station. The station had gravity and was a real city with apartments, schools, playgrounds, stores, restaurants, hospitals, and a university.

Earth colonized Mars, and Saturn's moon, Europa. The next worldwide venture was a galactic colony in the Pegasus Constellation. The entire world was behind the project.

The planet was named Akiane, Russian for ocean. Like Earth, Akiane appeared to be mostly ocean. It was similar in size and gravity and had oxygen to support life. The project was called the Akiane Colony.

In 2132, three ships were built to travel by folded space, and take 2,038 people twelve years to travel twenty-seven light-years to the new planet. Each ship launched one week apart.

The first to launch was *Eagle*, with eighty crew members. The ship's cargo was fabricated building supplies to build homes and an enclosed habitat to protect the colonists from their six long years of winter. The ship also carried DNA for breeding stock and seeds for farming during the five years of spring and summer.

Eagle was to orbit Akiane, send probes to take photos and gather data of the planet and its star. All information collected was to be sent back to WSC. It would not land until the colonists arrived and picked a suitable place to live and build their new home.

Hawk carried the colony's power source along with 111 crew and 789 colonists.

The last ship, *Falcon*, carried 1,053 people.

But Earth politics fell apart.

It didn't matter what year it was or how far the human race had evolved, human nature never seemed to change.

The same elements of human nature continued to prevail like greed, power, and personal ego, but the two that brought the dream of the Akiane Colony down were national pride and religion.

As crew members and colonists were chosen, Brazil and Bolivia complained there were too few of their people from South America allowed to be part of the new colony.

WSC feared that people used to hot weather might have difficulty dealing with the extreme cold. To ease the tension, WSC added more South Americans to *Eagle* and *Hawk's* crew.

China took offense. They declared that they had provided the majority of financing and had supplied the most scientists, there was not one Chinese captain even though there had been Chinese at every phase of the project and many were members of the colony. WSC had appeased South America, but had done nothing to accommodate the Chinese.

China withdrew its scientists, its civilians, and its money from World Space Coalition.

Pakistan and Saudi Arabia became suddenly silent. They questioned the morality of single women being allowed to live in the new colony. WSC said not all women in any city were married. The colony would be like a small city.

In truth, the real issue was Captain Faris Assetti, the unmarried female captain of the *Falcon*. It didn't matter that she was a Muslim and represented the African continent.

Islamic extremists quietly incited other extremists throughout the Muslim world. Then with one loud voice, they made their objections known. They would not support Akiane Colony unless all women were married.

The window of opportunity was closing. There wasn't time to argue. WSC launched, thinking to resolve the issues later.

Extremists loudly objected that their concerns were being ignored. They pulled their money out. Not all of the Islamic nations agreed, but the most influential decided for the rest.

WSC no longer had the funds to continue. Still they hoped to pull the project together once the colonists landed and sent images back of their accomplishments.

Those images never came.

Two years later, even though nothing had been resolved, it was time to the launch the next three ships. WSC did not have the money to hire a crew to operate the ship. At the same time, they didn't want to forsake the colonists. The next three ships were programmed as robotic ships and launched two, four, and twelve years later.

WSC knew the colonists had not yet arrived, but they didn't want the colonists to think they'd been abandoned. So the ships were sent in good faith with the hopes that as soon as Akiane colonists sent back word of their success, the project would again have worldwide support.

Each ship was filled with support supplies. The computers were programmed to return to Earth with any colonists who wanted to return. The ships were never heard from again.

After thirty years, not one word had come from the colonists or the three support ships.

It was thought all had died. The Akiane Project became a tragic reminder that Earth should not colonize outside its own solar system.

෴

In the year 2429, a young technician, David Kress, was testing the newest communication update at WSC. He sent a message to Earth. Arrival time: 30 sec.

He sent a message to Mars. Arrival time: 1 min. 15 sec.

He sent a message to Europa. Arrival time: 3 min.

The report file stated: Success. New communications online.

It was the fastest time for a message to be received by another planet or moon.

As the technician continued to check the systems, he noticed one more colony receiver, Akiane. For the fun of it, he sent a test message.

Twenty minutes later, his communications panel lit up from Akiane: MESSAGE RECEIVED.

He filed the report, but was told the colony didn't exist. He'd received an echo.

꧁꧂

WSC's communication was the newest most improved equipment. It took only twenty minutes for a message from Earth to reach Akiane.

Akiane's communication equipment was over 300 years old. A message from them would take twelve years to reach WSC.

꧁꧂

In the year 2441, a message was received from Akiane: WE ARE HERE. WHERE ARE YOU?

Chapter 28

Jess Hewett
Community Meeting Continued

HOW WAS I to explain earth politics? I didn't have a clue. I couldn't, so I didn't. But I did have to say something to make things right.

"WSC planned that as soon as they heard from you and had proof of your success, they would send a ship with people and you would be relieved and brought home," I said.

"What else happened?" Nu Venia asked.

"Nothing else. They never heard from you. Of the six ships sent here, not one sent a message of success. It was assumed the mission had totally, completely failed. WSC thought everyone had died. They couldn't risk more lives. That's why they didn't send any more people."

I guess maybe they had abandoned these people. If WSC had sent living people instead of robots, they might have known what had happened. Still, what was WSC supposed to do when they never received confirmation of success?

These people had managed to survive without WSC's help. As far as I was concerned, it didn't have the right to claim ownership. If WSC was honorable, it would treat Akiane as a sister world. When was the last time bureaucracy was honorable?

Unfortunately, it was my job to convince these people that Akiane belonged to WSC. If they refused, they would be taken by force. Like any other empire builder, WSC was not about to give up her colony. The best I could do was help make the transition as painless as possible. And the sooner I accomplished my task, the sooner I could go home.

This was day five. *Britannia* would be leaving in two days. Not much time left. But how to start? What would Dad have done? He'd gain their trust.

"What will it take for you to trust World Space Coalition? They won't take your home from you. They only want the right to explore and study Akiane. In exchange, you'll receive whatever provisions you need." I remembered Rona saying something about sick children. "Including medical help."

Many heads turned to Adumie. He stared at nothing. I wasn't even sure he was listening.

Cameron spoke.

"You must gain our trust first by proving yourself worthy." The words seemed to burst out of him as if he could no longer contain them. "Once that trust is obtained, then you will speak for World Space Coalition and we will listen."

My trust? I wanted them to trust WSC, why did they want to trust me?

I wanted this over. If they needed to trust me, fine. I'd establish that trust. It's what Dad would have done.

"What must I do to gain your trust?" I naïvely asked.

Nu Venia hesitated and dropped her head.

261

Cameron placed a hand on her shoulder.

She lifted her head.

Nu Venia had spoken with such authority when she spoke of the history of her people, but now she seemed to have lost her confidence. In a small voice, she said, "You must make Woden."

If I remembered my Scandinavia mythology, Woden was the name of one of their Gods. He lived in Northern Europe. He was the God of Battle, Master of Fury. When he wasn't fighting for a cause, any cause, he was grumpy. Was I supposed to fight someone?

I looked around the commons area. No one was drinking, eating, or speaking. Every eye was on me, waiting for what I would say. They shifted in their seats. They sat on the edge of their seats. They leaned forward not wanting to miss the next word spoken.

What would happen if I said no?

Woden was obviously a rite of passage, a means to prove myself worthy to speak for WSC. Why? Who were these people that I had to subject myself to their primitive ritual? But if I didn't do it, I'd be stuck here, maybe for years. What was more important, my pride or my escape?

How difficult could this be? It's not like they wanted to throw me in a live volcano, swim in a frigid ocean, wrestle a tupilak; or at least I hoped not.

Whatever Woden was, it was serious. It meant gaining their trust, which I would need before we could start negotiations. What choice did I have? I'd have to comply with their customs. My next decision was important. It would affect the policy of interplanetary relationships. But before I made any commitments, I needed to know what Woden was.

I opened my mouth to ask, "What is Woden?" Instead, I blurted, "Okay, let's do it. Let's do Woden."

The crowd gasped. I got the feeling it was too late to take back my "Let's do it." I didn't even know why I'd said it.

Nu Venia looked ready to fall off her chair. She silently mouthed, "No."

I thought she wanted this, so why was she upset? Evidently, she hadn't expected me to agree to Woden. Which begged the question; what had I agreed to?

Adumie's maroon skin paled.

I began to sweat.

I opened my mouth to say, "No, that's not what I meant. Let me explain," but before the words could come, a murmur rippled through the crowd. Instead of fear or anger, they now stared at me in awe.

"Good. When you die, we will send the others back to Earth," an angry voice said.

Die? What had I agreed to?

I thought these people wanted this. Why were they still angry at me? Evidently, nothing I did would satisfy them. Not even Woden.

Nu Venia stood and left.

"We leave at first light," Cameron said.

What? Leave? To where? I wasn't going anywhere. Not outside this habitat anyway.

Then something chilling happened. Something I had not thought possible and I knew I was in trouble.

Cameron smiled.

Log of Father Joseph Striken

Harrie's Story
Second year, day 164

Five puppies came forth today. All are healthy. No one is more amazed and pleased than Faris.

Coming Forth

Faris sent word to Father Joseph and Dr. Beasley to come quickly.

They met as they were exiting the main building and ran together to meet her.

She was almost in tears. "I don't understand," she said. "They were fine, then they changed. All the cocoons have hardened."

Beasley knelt down to check one of the cocoons. He unwrapped the vines around it.

"What are you doing?" Faris demanded.

"I think they're getting ready to hatch," he said.

"Hatch?" Faris said in wonder. "But it's only been a week. Shouldn't it take longer?"

"My dear captain, your Spitz shouldn't even be having puppies, or producing cocoons, but she has. As for what should or shouldn't happen next, I have no idea," he said. "I would never have thought any of this possible." He picked up one of the vines.

Now that it was no longer wrapped around the cocoon, the vine no longer leaked.

"We will have to wait and see," Beasley said and unwrapped the other cocoons.

By now a small crowd was beginning to form around them. No one spoke. They stood in hushed curiosity and watched.

One of the cocoons wobbled from something moving inside.

"Shouldn't we help it?" Faris asked. "Break the shell or something?"

"I think not," the doctor said. "This could be the same as when a bird hatches. If we help, it might die."

"But you don't know." Faris knelt and reached for one of the hardened cocoons.

Father Joseph gently helped her back to her feet. "I think Beasley is right. Be patient and we shall see what happens."

She started to pull away, but stopped. Instead, she unconsciously placed her hand over his and waited.

Adryel came to stand on the other side of her.

Without removing her hand from Father's Joseph's hold. She slipped her arm around Adryel's arm. He stepped closer. She rested her head on his shoulder. It was the first sign of public intimacy between them.

It didn't take long for a paw to come scratching through, then a head appeared. As the puppy broke free, Dr Beasley picked it up and handed it to Faris.

"Now," he said.

Faris picked at the shell as the puppy continued to squirm out.

All five puppies came forth wet, but ready to go with eyes were opened and covered with fur. They were larger than newborn pups and were the size of three month olds. Within a few moments, they were trying to walk, within and hour, the puppies were running and barking.

Beasley proudly announced, "They are all female. I might even suggest they are all clones of your Spitz, though I have no idea how this is possible."

"I think it is by the divine will of Allah." Faris smiled broadly and giggled like a little girl.

End of Harrie's Story Log

I tend to lean toward Faris' hypothesis. These pups are a gift from God, but why I cannot say.

There is the feeling that they are more important than the captain's wellbeing. None of this makes any since. And yet that is what faith is all about. To trust when one does not understand.

So I will trust that one day God will make things clear.

Chapter 29

Rona Montgomery
Zhoa

AT LEAST Rona wasn't on the porch anymore; she was running with the big dogs now. Yea, she'd turned an old southern saying into a pun, but it fit. Instead of feeling sorry for herself, she was finally engaged in an almost real project.

Rona sat cross-legged on the floor. There weren't enough tables and chairs to go around, because the dining area took top priority and most of the chairs. *Britannia* didn't have the time to provide the scientists with everything they needed. Many people used the dining tables as work space. But they had to pick up and move before each meal. She wished Lu hadn't volunteered them to sit on the floor.

Lu sat hunched over. She snapped her thin plastic computer to her wrist and raised her wrist to her mouth. She said, "On." Her wrist lit up. "Screen."

A holographic screen appeared in front of them.

She turned to Rona. "How large?"

Rona considered. "Large enough for both of us to see."

Lu nodded. "Fifty-four centimeter screen."

The screen disappeared and in less than a second reappeared as a fifty-four centimeter screen.

Rona preferred headgear. She slipped her computer on her head and touched the mouthpiece. "On." A second screen appeared in front of her. "Synchronize with Chow Lu."

Rona's screen hesitated.

Lu repeated the same command to her computer.

The two screens disappeared and reappeared as one.

"What should we call the project?" Lu asked.

Rona shook her head as she shrugged her shoulders. She had no idea. "Dog Project?"

"I was hoping for something more exotic, more alien," Lu said.

"Canine Project?" She grinned.

Lu shook her head. "OK, we'll think of a better name later." She turned to the screen. "Computer, the project is called ..." she shot a quick glance at Rona. "Canini Project."

Canini was Latin for dog.

"You're more clever than a mouse stealing cheese out of an ancient mouse trap."

"They make a better mouse traps these days," Lu said.

Rona smiled and said, "Computer, synchronize with Canini Project."

Now any information added to the project, whether from both of them at the same time or one at a time, would be updated on both computers.

As Lu read the identification number on each sample of blood out loud, the screen recorded the information. She placed the sample in the Regenerator. It took ten years to map the first DNA.

It eventually took only thirteen weeks. Today the Regenerator could process the data and have it ready to analyze in 30 minutes.

Once programmed, the Regenerator would process thirty blood samples at a time. It would read the blood count and check for foreign viruses and bacteria. Every mammal carried viruses and bacteria that are natural to them. A human carries two kilograms of bacteria.

The Regenerator also separated the plasma, mapped the DNA, and entered all information into the appropriate file on their computers.

Rona loaded the appropriate digital dog picture with the matching ID number Lu had just read. The HMS took realism digital holographic images. The 3D image was so life-like Rona could see individual strands of fur. 4D showed the interior organs of the dogs, their muscular and skeleton structure, veins and vital organs. 5D showed a detailed image of each organ.

But blood samples still held the most answers.

To her surprise, Rona was enjoying herself. A good project was the best remedy for most ailments. She'd known that, but had forgotten. She pleaded temporary insanity. It was good to be back on track.

The dogs seemed to like the attention. After they'd had their heads scratched and their tummies rubbed, they'd shown their affection by licking faces and hands. Then the dogs were willing to have the HMS analyze them, take pictures, and have their blood drawn.

Rona and Lu decided to start with every adult dog that frequented the scientists' quarters, and accumulated images and blood samples from 72 dogs. Twenty-eight had adopted a person and rarely left their side. The others visited often and liked to hang around.

They planned to begin with 120 adult dogs. Then they'd start with puppies.

There were certainly enough of them. Puppies were everywhere. On any given day, there could be as many as fifty puppies in their quarters.

Zhoa walked over and sat between Rona and Lu. People had the habit of dropping in to see how a project was progressing. But they'd just started the Canini Project and didn't have anything to report.

Rona's first thought was to ask Zhoa to come back later. She and Lu were too busy to entertain visitors, but when she opened her mouth to speak, she closed it.

Zhoa's face was etched with worry. He held his left hand as if it had been injured.

She signaled to Lu. "Save," Lu said. The screen obeyed. "Sleep." The screen disappeared.

"Would you take a look at this?" Zhoa extended his hand for her and Lu to examine. "I can't find doctors Mathieu or Lesley. I probably wouldn't have noticed, but it itches. So I took the sprayed bandage off and found this."

Tiny, barely noticeable red bumps covered the inside of his thumb to the middle of his palm.

She ran her fingers over the area. She didn't think it was serious. Still, it was smart of him to check and make sure. She noticed a thin scab at the base of his thumb. "It looks like you cut yourself."

"Yes, yesterday, while I was butchering meat," he said.

"It looks like you may have a little infection under the skin because of the cut," Rona said.

"I washed my hands right away. Vong sprayed a bandage on it."

"Once the skin is cut, Zhoa, any number of bacteria can get in. Looks like a rash," Lu said.

"I'm not usually allergic to anything," Zhoa said.

"It happens. Most people are allergic to something, even if they don't know it. It's normal," Rona said. "We're on an alien planet. No telling what any of us might pick up, or have brought with us."

"That's why we were so thoroughly decontaminated when we arrived," Lu said. "We shouldn't have brought any new diseases, but no matter how careful we are, there is always something."

WSC had provided a number of medicines to cover emergencies. This didn't look that dangerous. It looked like a simple itchy rash.

"I guess." Zhoa didn't sound convinced.

"We have some cream," Lu said.

"Will that help?" Zhoa asked.

"It's simple, but it should help. You'll know soon enough. Mathieu and Lesley will reappear and they'll have something stronger," she said. "It's best to let the doctors treat you."

Lu pulled a small white tube out of her medical kit. She squeezed ointment onto his thumb. Zhoa rubbed it over his rash. Rona sprayed a bandage over the area.

"There, right as rain. It's old tech, but sometimes the old methods are best," Rona said. "Check with the doctors when you find them. You should be okay until then."

"Thanks. It feels better already." Zhoa wiggled his thumb checking Rona's handiwork.

AKIANE LOG

Faris Assetti
Year 4, day 52

I am no longer captain.

This day, we are no longer an Earth colony.

From this day forth, we are "Endurance" for we have endured much and have survived. We will continue to prosper without help from any other, but ourselves, and Allah.

A Ship Comes

Faris, along with many others, stared up through the glass dome ceiling in wonder and could hardly believe her eyes. A ship was passing overhead.

Like so many others, she ran outside to witness this monumental event.

A ship from Earth was here. A wave of relief swept over Faris. They had not been forgotten after all. At the same time a sick feeling rose up from her stomach.

272

Did this mean she would have to leave? She was a captain in the World Space Coalition Space Force. If she was ordered to return, she'd have to obey, but did she want to obey?

The ship landed half a kilometer away.

All hurried to welcome those who disembarked.

The drawbridge slowly descended, but no one came out.

They waited. No one appeared in the doorway.

Father Joe left the crowd and walked up the drawbridge and into the ship.

Faris knew she should go with him, but her feet would not move. She held her breath in anticipation.

After fifteen minutes, Joe reappeared. He stood for a moment, then said, "I checked the logs. There are no crewmembers. The logs say Earth thinks we have all died, but just in case they were wrong, they set this ship full of supplies."

"What kind of supplies?" Faris asked.

"Frozen food. Blankets…"

"Blankets?" Faris demanded.

"Building material …"

"Anything important?" Faris asked.

"Seeds for farming. DNA for livestock," Joe said.

"Is that all?" someone asked.

"There's no one on the entire ship? How is that possible?"

"It's robotic," Faris said. "They set it on autopilot and launched her."

"But why? What did that prove?"

"It proves that no one is coming for us," Faris said. She realized she was glad that there was no one to order her back to Earth but, at the same time, she knew this empty ship was not a good sign.

"It proves," she continued, "that we are on our own."

"No reinforcements from Earth?" someone asked.

"We are masters of our own fate. We no longer belong to anyone." Her voice rose so all could hear. "We are no longer a colony. This day we declare our independence from WSC, for no one provides for us, but Allah."

It took only seconds for the crowd to rally behind Faris' words.

"The ship is programmed to take anyone who wishes to, to return to Earth," Joe said.

The crowd behind Faris became suddenly silent. Even the smallest of them knew something was wrong and quieted to a whisper.

"Does anyone wish to return to Earth?" Faris asked.

Two years ago, there would have been plenty who would have said yes. But that was then. They'd been through so much together. They'd accomplished so much.

They'd become a community that had survived together against the odds.

No one spoke.

"Can I take you're silence as a sign that all stay?" Faris asked.

She received a resounding, "Yes."

Last entry of the day

A WSC ship arrived today, two years late. No one was aboard. It was programmed to take us back to Earth as if we were failures.

We are unsure as to what WSC meant by not sending personnel reinforcements and only offering to take us back as if we are failures.

WE ARE NOT FAILURES!

There is much pride in being the first humans to leave the Solar System and become residents of a different star system.

We have accomplished much in four years. Only the strongest of us have survived after a devastating beginning and under harsh conditions.

We will not return with our tail between our legs.

We will stay and prosper. In a thousand years we will have built several major cities full of Akiane natives.

We will see who is the failure then.

Today, we celebrated our independence and all we have accomplished.

Chapter 30

Lieutenant Jessica Hewitt
VS
Admiral Grossman

"YOU'LL BE a hero."

If I'm dead, who'll care?

Admiral Grossman was agreeing to Woden. He was ordering me out of the habitat on an expedition across a frozen planet. "When you return, you'll be able to have any job you want, anywhere on Earth."

A hero? Any job? What had gone wrong? How had this happened?

As soon as I finished talking with Cameron and Nu Venia, I was quickly escorted back to the bay area, without going near the Blood Vines. Four short hours later Admiral Grossman requested my presence on the *WSC Britannia* for a conference call. Unfortunately Cameron had the privilege of talking to the admiral before I did.

I suddenly wished the *Britannia* had already left so I wouldn't be having this conversation, but it wasn't scheduled to leave for two more days.

"But, Sir ..." I was trying to object to my new orders without dissolving into hysteria.

The Admiral's holographic head and shoulders and the back of his chair hovered over the table in front of me. His colorless face and that counterfeit smile safely sat in his World Space Coalition office. He didn't wait for the communication time delay for my reply. He kept talking.

With only a layman's understanding about quantum gravity, quarks, subatomic particles, or how space folds, all I knew was that some mathematical physicist performed the right calculations and the admiral and I could speak. And even though we were light-years apart, there was only a twenty-minute time delay as our words reached across space to the other.

As Cameron escorted me back to my friends, he explained Woden to me. *Falcon's* Captain Assetti and the first mate Father Striken mounted an expedition to explore the planet. They had packed their gear and walked out of camp alone, just the two of them. They were gone for so long, everyone thought they'd died. When they did return, they brought back something that saved the crew from certain death and helped them thrive. Cameron called it "life" but he insisted he didn't know what it was. I was sure he was lying. I just couldn't prove it.

Conversation with the admiral was slow and almost endurable.

My father's voice tried to calm me, but my fear was beyond his reach of reason. I didn't care about anyone's point of view but mine. I did not want to go outside. This was not a day trip to the mountains. Woden was a voyage in unbelievable and uninhabitable cold!

We were headed to the North Pole where temps would drop far below zero. My entire body would become one solid icicle. I could die.

I wasn't ready to die.

Finally, the admiral stopped speaking.

His image would remain frozen until the arrival of my words reactivated his image or he started speaking again.

The streaming image could continue, but it was disconcerting. His image was not responsive to me, but he could be doing almost anything: like paperwork or having a different conversation with another person while waiting for my response. The admiral could go to the bathroom and return in time for my words to reach him.

"Sir, the ocean is melting," I quickly said, hoping I didn't sound as if I was whining—even though I was. "Summer is coming. The expedition will be traveling over melting ice. I don't understand why this is necessary." In my head I screamed, *I don't want to go.*

I waited for his response, hoping he'd understand the danger. He didn't.

"Cameron assures me you'll cross the ocean to the permanently frozen ice before the ocean melts. There's no real danger," he said.

One conversation with Cameron and the admiral thought he knew him. If only I had spoken to the admiral first.

I watched his plastic smile as he waited for my response. How I wished I could reach into the monitor and swipe that irritating smile of his face.

"Religious fanatics rarely realize the danger they're putting themselves and others into, Sir," I said, before I could stop myself.

When Assetti and Striken returned, their accomplishments brought new respect, which I was sure it had grown into reverence over the years. I had no way of knowing what had really happened or how much of the story was true or how much was exaggerated and had become legend.

Cameron wanted to bring the same unity to his people who were undecided about trusting Earth. No one since Assetti and Striken had succeeded in surviving the same trip.

It was unclear why Nu Venia was going. I guessed by her expression that she didn't want to go any more that I did. I feared this was a political move and Cameron was willing to risk Nu Venia's and my life for his ambitions.

On our walk back to the bay area, Cameron told me about his people's two opposing thoughts about off-worlders. He wanted to reunite with Earth. Adumie wanted to remain isolated. As leader, Adumie had the right to make the final decision.

Hoping to override his decision, Cameron volunteered to make Woden to prove his worth. If he survived, he would earn the right not only to speak to the people, but to force Adumie to listen to those of Earth. Cameron adamantly believed our successful return would bring harmony. He also had the mistaken impression that I would personally save his people from some illness that was slowly killing them.

I was equally sure we would die out there. Somehow I had to convince the admiral this was a bad idea, that Cameron was wrong, and I was the one to listen to.

"What are you talking about?" Admiral Grossman asked. I'd waited forty minutes for this?

"Permission to speak freely, Sir?" Now I'd have to wait forty minutes for his permission. Twenty minutes for my words to reach him and twenty minutes for his words to reach me.

This was going to be a long conversation.

There was a pad and pen on the desk just in case someone wanted to take notes during a conference call. To settle my nerves, I doodled.

"Permission granted."

The room was so quiet by the time he answered I jumped at his words.

"Cameron has an agenda. I think he's crazy," I all but shouted.

The admiral's next words continued over my outburst. "Cameron mentioned someone named Nu Venia. Who is she?" he asked.

"Nu Venia? I'm not sure who she is to him, his daughter maybe. I know she's loyal to him, to the point that she'll follow him anywhere. I think she does whatever Cameron says," I said. "Though, I'm pretty sure she doesn't want to go on this expedition. She hasn't exactly said anything; not to me anyway. But I can tell by her body language and the expression on her face that she doesn't want to go." I tried to say as much as possible to help my case. "Sir, I truly do not want to go. There are civilians who would love to make this trip and might be more helpful to your cause to open a dialogue with these people."

I was fighting for my life. I didn't want to die out there traipsing across a winter wasteland on some stupid quest I didn't understand. With all my heart I wanted the admiral to believe me. I waited for my words to reach him and have him order me *not* to go on Woden.

I was too nervous to continue drawing. I paced.

"Lieutenant," his commanding voice came in loud and clear.

I whipped around to face his holographic image.

"I've talked to Cameron. He seems of sound mind to me." The admiral didn't sound pleased with my objections.

He was also a man of few words who seemed content to drag this conversation on. Evidently, he had all the time in the universe and didn't mind wasting it.

I was ready to pull my hair out.

"Sir, it's more than 2,000 kilometers to Akiane's North Pole!" I pleaded. "When the star sets here, it's total darkness. The cold is extreme. The temperatures drop well below zero, blizzards that last for days. We could die. Forget them. *I* could die!!!" What more could I say to convince him? "It will take at least two years to make this trip. I'll miss the transport back to Earth." I was running out of arguments.

Forty minutes later: "I'm sure that won't happen." My heart sank. His pasty face smiled at me. "Cameron is native to Akiane and is used to the extreme weather. He knows how to survive. He'll take good care of you. You won't die.

"There will be another transport. You won't be permanently stuck there." Again that fake smile hanging under uncaring eyes. "This mission could secure you a prominent position anywhere you want when you return to Earth," he repeated.

The words were similar, the tone more ominous; the meaning had changed. If I didn't make the trip I would not have a job or be able to get one once I returned to Earth.

"By the time I return to Earth, I'll retire from Space Force. With the money I'm making for coming to Akiane, I can take a permanent vacation when I get back."

Meaning: *Admiral, you can shove your job.*

The expression on his face told me he understood. His fake smile had faded. "It is my understanding that you had already agreed to make this journey."

"Not really. I was tricked." It would take time for my outburst to reach him.

Admiral Grossman was in a nonstop dialogue. "You're under orders, Lieutenant Hewett. If you don't make the expedition, you'll not only have failed to fulfill your contract, you'll be court-martialed for disobeying an order. You'll be an embarrassment to the space program, America, and the world. Not only will you be dishonorably discharged, but you'll forfeit all your pay, and you will be thrown in the brig as soon as you return — for no less than twenty years! I will see to it."

I slumped back in my chair, the anger that had fed hope seeped out of me. If I didn't go with Cameron, I'd lose everything and spend the best part of my life in a cell. If I went with Cameron, I could die. To go or not to go, what was the difference? Either way, my life was over.

"Do we have to walk, Sir?" I asked, resigned to my fate, but a shuttle or a hovercraft, it would make the trip more durable, if not faster. Olivia had one, why couldn't I. Ah but, I knew the answer. Nothing else I'd begged for had been granted. Why would this?

My mind flashed back to the time I had been lost in one of the worst blizzards to hit Northern Minnesota. I almost died of hypothermia.

School had been cancelled because of the blizzard, which was unusual. School was rarely cancelled, even when it snowed. But Dad said this blizzard was exceptionally dangerous.

I was thirteen and had been reading a book about a girl on an adventure to save her father from criminals. I suddenly realized my cat was no longer sitting on my lap. I couldn't remember when she'd moved.

I searched the house; she was nowhere to be found.

If the cat wasn't inside, she had to be outside in the blizzard.

I stood in the opened door and called her name. She didn't answer. The snow was so thick I couldn't see the edge of our yard. She'd never be able to find her way back. I went out to find her.

I'd gone no more than a few feet when I realized my mistake. I wasn't wearing my snowsuit and boots. When I turned around I couldn't see our house. I tried to find it, but was disoriented. I couldn't even tell if I was heading in the right direction or into the village. I was lost in my front yard.

"Daddy, Daddy, DADDY," I screamed, but he didn't answer.

The snow swallowed up my voice. Frantically I tried to find the house.

My toes and fingers became like ice. I shivered from the cold.

I lay down and burrowed into the snow. The snow quickly piled on top of me. Soon I was snuggled in and warm, and about to fall a sleep when I heard Dad's voice calling from far off.

I'd left the front door wide open. Dad guessed I was outside. He dressed properly in his snowsuit and boots then he tied a rope around his waist and tied the other to the house so he wouldn't get lost. He methodically searched the yard until he found the mound of snow with me in it.

He carried me into the house, bundled me up in front of the fireplace and filled me with hot chicken soup.

The cat had been sleeping under my bed.

Hate wasn't strong enough word about how I felt about blizzards. I was outright terrified of below-zero cold, eighty KPH winds, and whiteout snowstorms. Unfortunately, telling the admiral about a bad childhood experience wouldn't get me out of this expedition.

The admiral ignored my last outburst. He only answered my last question. "I offered Cameron a shuttle when he asked for supplies, but he said you have to walk, something about woods. Do you know what he meant?"

"It's Woden, Sir. Wodan, Wotan, he goes by many names. I don't know exactly what it means to Cameron. It's part of a Scandinavian Myth. Woden is a war god who empowers and encourages his followers to defeat their enemies. I don't know what the myth means to these people, or what it has to do with this trip, or why we have to walk. The walking might have something to do with the fact that the captain of the lead ship and her first mate explored Akiane on foot when they first landed there." And before he asked the obvious question of, "How do you know?" that so many ask when I know things like this, I told him, "My father studied northern cultures. He liked to tell me about them. I guess I listened."

"Whatever." Whatever? I didn't think admirals knew those kinds of words.

"The point is you're going. Not just because it's your job, or because of your orders, but for the expedition. We need to gain these people's trust. And if that means you have to go outside for a while, you will go outside." He made it sound as if I was only going out for a couple hours, not two years. At least he said his little speech without that fake smile of his.

"Lieutenant, you have until the next transport arrives. If the colonists are not in agreement to their fate, a military convoy will be launched."

Visions of Marine boots trampling flowers, and axes hacking at trees loomed before me. I had a sick feeling there'd be bloodshed over the Blood Vines.

"Those people must accept the reality that they are an Earth colony," he finished.

Admiral Grossman had won.

Then it dawned on me ... I sat straight up.

"Sir, why is the Admiral speaking with me?"

I kept an eye on the clock, and leaned into the screen when I knew my words would reach him and return to me. I watched closely for any signs of surprise. He covered it well; his eyes widened then quickly narrowed. Grossman shifted slightly before he spoke, "This is such an important mission. Of course *I should* be the one speaking to you." He settled back in his admiral's chair as if his words were enough and I'd submissively salute him and be on my way.

Instead, I asked, "If this mission is so important, Sir, why send me? Why not send someone with more authority or a civilian who wants to go? Perhaps a scientist who could study the ice, snow and astronomy?" Jorg wanted to come along. Gino or Spago would gladly take my place.

Then I had a revelation. One that was so obvious I almost cussed at myself for being so stupid. "You wanted someone you could order and who would have to obey you. If I was a civilian and refused, whatever you're planning would fail."

Again the shift. I guess he thought I'd be a nice little sailor who'd do as I was told. He hadn't planned on my questioning or thinking.

Admiral Grossman's resolve returned. His whole body language changed. If possible, he became more rigid. Fire blazed in his eyes. "Are you alone?" he asked.

Forty minutes and that's all he had to say?

I looked around the *WCS Britannia* conference room as if looking for someone. There was an oval table that comfortably sat fifteen people. Instead of a large overhead projection of him, where the admiral could prove his dominating presence, I had chosen the smaller life-size hologram so I could look him directly in the eye as if we were equals. But in fact, as he was proving to me, I was his subordinate.

He'd asked to speak to me in a secure room. Yes, I was alone.

This time, not waiting for the time-delay reply, he leaned in closer to me and lowered his voice, "You are on a top secret mission."

So top secret that he forgot to tell me?

"It's not possible for the first crew to have survived. Humans can't survive sub-zero temperatures like that. They must have had help," he said.

If they couldn't survive the temperatures, why send them here in the first place?

And who did the admiral think was out there besides us Earthlings?

"It's possible there are other beings living on Akiane," he continued.

This idiot was my superior? I couldn't help it, I burst out laughing before I knew it was coming; I laughed so hard I missed the Admiral's next words. I immediately gained control, but it was too late. The transmission of my laugh was already on its way.

Nevertheless, I said, "Admiral, you can't seriously believe there are aliens living on Akiane. It's impossible for life to exist outside the habitat. These people only survive because of the habitat they've built."

When I saw the return image, his face looked as if it had turned to stone. I was in grave trouble.

"We thought it was impossible for the colonists to survive for 318 years without our help, but somehow they managed," he said in his strict admiral voice. "It is your mission to find out if there is indigenous life on Akiane or if some other alien life came there from another planet."

Other alien life?

"If there is intelligence on your side of the galaxy, we need to know their intentions."

Intentions? Was he serious?

"Are they hostile? And if they are, we need to prepare ourselves for possible attack," he finished.

"Sir, if they're hostile why would they stop on Akiane, then leave everyone behind? Wouldn't they abduct everyone for questioning?"

"That's what we want you to find out!" He spoke with such authority that I knew my freedom of speech had ended and that I was expected to obey orders.

I was the point person on a mission to learn about hostile aliens. Why me? There were plenty of Space Force men and women on the transport. What made me so special? I didn't even believe in aliens.

What a waste of money.

What a waste of time. My time and life.

The fake smile returned. Grossman said, "Bring back specimens for the scientists of whatever you find while crossing Akiane."

Just what did he expect me to find besides aliens?

AKIANE LOG

Faris Assetti
Nearing the end of the fifth year

Winter is coming. Each morning there is frost on the plants outside. They are beginning to wilt. To the north of us, thin sheets of ice are forming on the ocean.

The fish are returning and with them a new creature we have not seen before. They, like the fish, must have left for open waters. The creatures were not here when we first arrived. Now that the ocean is beginning to freeze they are returning to the only land available near the equator and what will soon be the only open water.

The creatures are fierce and as large as polar bears. The monsters explode out of the ocean, attack and carry their victims into the water to devour them.

We have named them tupilak after an Inuit mythical monster that lives under the ice.

Guards now watch over the fishermen. After they have filled their nets and return to Endurance, the guards become hunters of these creatures. We now have out first kill and have experimented in cooking it.

Tupilak is good meat, but the dogs won't eat it. They only eat fish. It's good that the fish have also returned. Now we don't have to fly to the red line any more. But that also means no more of the plant that makes up the red line. We shall have to wait until spring before we can head back.

First Taste of Tupilak

Faris smiled when she saw Fatimah standing at attention as if she were still in the Space Force. She held her blaster across her chest with both hands, the barrel pointing upward.

"I hear you killed a sea creature," Faris said. It was the first to be killed since the creatures' arrival.

"Yes, Mum," Fatimah said.

How many times had Faris reminded her troops that they were no longer in the military space program? Still some were not able to let the training go. So she'd stopped reminding them.

Fatimah made an excellent sergeant, but she made an even better friend.

World Space Coalition had trained Faris to stand aloof from those she commanded. She was not to become friendly or take a lover from her crew, but things were different here.

On Earth, even on WSC Moon Base, Faris had the opportunity to make friends with those who were not under her command, but here on an alien planet, everyone was under her command. Was she to obey orders and remain isolated?

It didn't feel right. They were a community and were no longer apart of the Space Force.

When she consulted Father Joe, he encouraged her to follow her heart. Allah teaches love and trust not isolation. Faris decided it was to her emotional well-being, and the betterment of her command, if she made friends.

When off duty, Fatimah had become her best friend. They had each been in the other's wedding. But when on duty, Fatimah was still a sergeant.

"It jumped out of the water as easily as a cat jumps onto a table. What do we do with it, Mum?" Fatimah asked.

"I say we eat it," Adryel said as he came alongside.

Faris passed her hand over her full belly and smiled up at her beloved.

"How do we cook it?" she asked Adryel. "That thing is at least 400 kilograms."

"We build a smoker," Joe said, joining them. "We have the materials."

"We should build a room," Adryel said.

"A room?" Fairs asked. "You are joking."

Adryel smiled. "No, I'm not."

"Why a whole room?" she asked.

"If the meat is good, we'll want to smoke more of them or grill them or make a stew or steaks," Adryel said. "We'll need place to store the meat after we've gutted and cleaned it."

"How do we distribute it?" Joe asked.

"An Inuit Indian tribe would hang the meat and people would come to take what they want," Adryel said.

"So we build a room to store the meat," Faris said. "People will come and take what they want for their personal needs."

"Yeah," Adryel said, "but we'll roast this one."

Faris eyed him.

"Might as well cook this one to see if we even like it before we build a whole room," Adryel said. "We'll celebrate and all will eat."

"Do you know how to roast it?" Faris asked.

Adryel laughed.

"He's from Texas," Joe said, also laughing. "He grew up smoking meat and barbecuing."

"Fatimah, what do you say? It's your kill," Fairs asked.

She grinned from ear to ear.

"Well, gentlemen," Faris said, "there's your answer. Have at it."

"We'll need more than one to feed all of us," Fatimah said with a twinkle in her eye.

"Then you'd best go hunting," Faris said with a shake of her head and a light laugh.

Fatimah's smile of pride changed into the smile of a huntress. "At your command, Mum."

Dinner of the next Afternoon

Adryel nervously hovered over Faris as she cut into the first piece of meat. She didn't bother to wave him away. She didn't dare. He needed an answer.

"Tender cut," Faris said admiringly. "That's a good sign."

Adryel's chest swelled with pride.

She sniffed. "Smells divine."

Great satisfaction lit up Adryel's face.

Faris brought her fork to her mouth, and without hesitation, bit into the meat. "OH!" She closed her eyes, dropped her head slightly to one side. "Mmmm!" This was better that she could have hoped for.

He continually surprised her. She knew he could cook, but she would never have guessed he could roast an alien creature like this.

"There's your approval people," Adryel loudly declared. "Come and get it." He bent down and lightly kissed Faris.

She reached up, placed her hand on the back of his neck and held him there for a few seconds longer.

Chapter 31

Lieutenant Jessica Hewitt
Day Six
The Expedition

IT ALL happened too fast. One minute I was inside a perfect warm habitat where I could comfortably roam for hours. At first light the following morning after my conversation with the admiral, I was outside getting ready to trek across Akiane's frozen forlorn tundra.

Tomorrow will be *Britannia's* seventh day and her departure for Earth.

Instead of being on that ship, I'll be camping in the snow and ice. Don't tell me life's fair.

On this insane trip, I'll be traveling with strangers to the other side of this world in hopes of finding *something*. That's what Captain Assetti and the priest Striken had done.

For some reason, my military-issued winter suit, with its miracle fabric, which would have kept me very warm, wasn't deemed good enough. I was issued an Akiane red and white fur suit with fur boots, suspendered pants, fur jacket, and gloves.

The boots were turned inside out, fur inside, with the top turned down to make a white cuff. Gloves were the same. The fur on the coat and pants were turned outward.

The front of the coat was secured with several leather fasteners from just under my neck to past a leather belt. Just below the fasteners, the coats hung down to my knees and opened up, giving me room to move.

Underneath, I wore three pair of wool socks, two pairs of long johns, liner gloves, fur gloves and, under my hood, a knitted cap. Stuffed in my jacket pocket was a plastic breathable visor that snapped onto my hood to protect my face from extreme night cold, and a pair of sunglasses to protect my eyes from sun glares off a white world of snow and ice.

My fur hood, with its white cuff, cut off all peripheral vision. I hated not being able to see what was going on around me. I had visions of being attacked and eaten alive before I saw which animal the teeth belonged to.

I was advised to write a farewell letter to my family, just in case I didn't make it back. I didn't write it. I couldn't. There wasn't anyone to write to. Dad was dead. I didn't know where Mom was and didn't care. I couldn't write a letter to any of my relatives. I'd have had to begin by telling why I left Earth in the first place, which was to get away from them. They'd been too "supportive" after Dad died. I desperately wanted space to grieve. Well, I'd certainly been given space now.

Two sleds and all the supplies and food we'd need for the trip. How could we carry enough food for the three of us and all those dogs? What were we going to do when we ran out of food? Cameron said I was not to worry. We would not starve. Right.

Cameron separated the gear into two piles. It took awhile, but after rearranging the piles three or four times, he finally satisfied. Large leather bags of dried meat, vegetables and fruit, blubber for heating and cooking, dried fish for the dogs, cooking utensils, and our personal belongings were piled next to one sled. The tent, sleeping blankets, one Space Force issued orange plastic boat for the return trip over open water, and all other miscellaneous equipment would be on the other sled.

Lu tried to comfort me by reminding me that there were no wild animals on Akiane. Jorg said there wasn't any plant life. Olivia said it would be difficult to fish. The Admiral assured me Cameron knew what he was doing. Nothing anyone said was very encouraging. All I knew for sure was that my life was in Cameron's hands and I didn't trust him.

Seven priests stood to one side, their faces hidden by their fur hoods. They were supposed to be Cameron's brothers of the cloth, but not one of them offered to help. They just watched as he heaved and hauled gear to its proper place. They stood so motionless, I couldn't tell if they were praying or were frozen in place.

Some forty fishermen prepared for their day of fishing. Their hoods were pulled back with their jackets open and their heavy fur gloves stuffed in their pockets as they mended nets and sharpened spears. All of them wore green gloves. What was that about anyway?

A pair of puppies chasing each other got tangled in a net that had been carefully laid out. A patient fisherman spoke softly to calm the confused pups as he freed them.

The net was again laid out for another careful inspection to make sure there were no tears or tangles. Once he was satisfied that all was as it should be, he and a friend folded it so they could carry it to the fishing waters.

Another dog playfully tugged at the blunt end of a spear. A fisherman tugged back. They seemed to enjoy their game.

Close to 100 dogs, and puppies were underfoot, yet no one seemed to mind. Those people were incredibly tolerant of their pets.

From the dogs and puppies milling around, Nu Venia decided which would pull the sleds. She'd already harnessed one team in place and was starting on the other. We were taking thirty-three dogs, two teams of sixteen, one for each sled, and one dog that calmly sat at Cameron's side.

Nu Venia fur suit was too large for her. The sleeves and pant legs were bunched up. Why not wear a suit that fit? Did she expect to grow up while on this quest? That would take more than a couple of years. Just how long did they expect this quest to last?

Her jacket was open and hung down below just scraping the snow, her hood rested on her shoulders, and at this moment she wasn't wearing fur gloves nor her green ones. She needed the dexterity of her fingers to hitch the dogs to their harnesses. This cold weather was only a mild discomfort for her. I wished it was only a mild discomfort for me. Just the thought made me miserably cold. How long before my blood did turn to ice? Twenty years in a warm Earth prison was sounding pretty darn good.

Nu Venia checked one animal's body and hips and decided it was not right for the job. She examined another, which was strong and sturdy. She placed him with another larger, forty-five-kilo dog she'd just chosen. Dad called them wheel dogs, the largest and most powerful dogs on the team. They were always placed directly in front of the sled.

The dogs in the middle were called the turn dogs. The two in the front of the team were the lead dogs, or point dogs. One of them was the alpha dog, the leader of the pack, the one the rest of the team would follow. That one was usually the most aggressive and would keep the others in line.

Inside the habitat, against the black lava rock floor, the dogs appeared white, but against the pristine snow, they looked dingy. Their light apricot tufts made their white coats look stained, as if they'd been rolling around in red mud and a good washing had not completely gotten it all out. There were few dogs that were truly white.

Cameron's fur hood also rested on his shoulders, but his jacket was fastened closed. He used his belt to help keep the ends of his jacket out of his way while he knelt in the snow. He only wore his thin green gloves.

He didn't like the way the first sled was packed. So he unpacked it. He was almost halfway through reloading when he stopped and unloaded again and started over. Evidently it was important to the mission that everything was in the exact right place.

A dog sniffed at a bag of blubber on the sled. Delicately, it tried to undo the tie with its teeth.

The red dog, with a white belly and three white paws that sat next to Cameron, softly growled.

Cameron had finally finished packing the sled and was getting ready to place a tarp covering over it and tie it down. He turned to see what was happening, "Ai!" he yelled at the blubber sniffing dog.

It ignored him.

Cameron moved toward it, but the dog was too fast for him and scampered off.

"Stay away," he yelled at it.

The dog complained with short whining noises at being denied a treat. Cameron pulled the tarp over the packed sled and blubber bag, and tied it down. Once the dog realized the treat was lost, it moved on.

With a fisherman's help, Cameron placed the folded, orange plastic boat on the bottom of the second sled.

I kept hoping, praying, begging that I would wake up. I tried to convince myself I was really in my bed, back on Earth, not light-years away about to trek on some insane quest across a thawing ocean.

I watched the habitat entrance for some last minute reprieve, for someone, anyone, to run out of the habitat and relieve me of duty. No one came.

It didn't matter how many times I told myself this was not real, that it was not happening, this insane nightmare kept progressing.

Chapter 32

Lieutenant Jessica Hewitt
My Friends

"ARE YOU sure about this?" Olivia asked for the millionth time. One might have thought we were best friends by the way she carried on. What did she care? She didn't even like me. I'd have thought she'd be glad to be rid of me. I certainly wasn't going to miss her.

"No," I said, "but orders are orders." I must not have been feeling myself, for I was uncharacteristically tolerant of her.

"Makes you sound brave." Rona was having difficulty holding back tears.

"Hardly," I assured her.

Jorg stood silently at my side, staring at the snow and his orange snow boots. He was unusually quiet as if he were contemplating something important.

I should have been nicer to these people. They were the closest I had to family. Olivia had given me more attention than my mother, who didn't care enough to even say good-bye when she left. Jorg, Rona and Olivia were the only friends standing with me, in the cold, to see me off.

Gino and Spago had been by earlier, but they'd left with their teams in the hovercraft, heading for the mountains. Research must continue. Gino, at least, gave me a hug and a wave good-bye.

"Don't worry, you'll make it back." Jorg didn't sound or look any more convinced than I felt. "And if you don't, I'll make sure these people build a monument in your honor." He attempted a smile.

"Thanks," I said. Somehow his humor was lost on me right then.

Our eyes locked.

Oh how I wanted to get lost in those blue eyes. If only he'd take me into his arms and ... and ... and what? Well, at least he was here with me. My friends had given me the courage to walk outside. I'm not sure I could have done it by myself.

How will I survive without them? Who will give me the courage to endure? I looked at Olivia. *She'd encourage me by yelling at me when things become intolerable. It was her way of making me angry enough to succeed. Maybe I would miss her — a little.*

Tears of resentment, mixed with fear, threatened to swell up and undo what little resolve I had left.

I turned around to see how Nu Venia and Cameron were proceeding.

Cameron. I hated that man. He'd lied to the admiral. He promised I would be safe. He was a delusional man who believed his own lies. He believed we would return alive and well.

I couldn't help wondering what was his agenda? Why was this trip so important to him? When I asked, his answers were always evasive, something about Nu Venia's honor, my destiny and the community's survival. I didn't understand how his community, Nu Venia and I fit together. He didn't seem to be able to explain it to me other than he had a feeling.

None of it made any sense.

Why was Nu Venia going? She hated the idea. Yet, she seemed resigned to Cameron's will. Did she ever stand up to him? Did she always follow him like a puppy? Or was her resentment smoldering, waiting for the right moment to blow?

"All the fish are female," Olivia said.

I was caught off-guard.

"What?" I asked, turning back to my small group of friends.

Olivia had a habit of starting a conversation about something that had nothing to do with the present situation. Sometimes she did it to kick start a dull moment, but today she did it because she didn't know what to say. None of us did.

"Lu thinks there's something strange about the dogs," Rona said. When I looked at her, she blushed at the foolishness of her statement and fell silent.

"Algae seems normal," Jorge said absently.

"What are the three of you talking about?" I asked.

"We can't find one male fish," Olivia said, as if I cared. "Yesterday afternoon, we started collecting fish. I have no idea how they reproduce.

"On Earth, there's a blue female fish. When two meet, one turns orange and becomes male. After they mate, they change sexes and colors and mate again. When they part, they're both blue, female, and both pregnant." She sighed heavily before she continued. "On Earth there are some 52 different kinds of fish that can change sexes. We think Akiane fish can also change sexes." She paused.

She must have known no one cared. Yet she kept going. "When a female changes to a male, it's called protogyny."

I'd had enough. If I didn't stop her, she wouldn't stop until she'd told us everything she knew about fish. Was she trying to start an argument during my last moments here? It was just like her.

"Who cares?" I said a little too loudly.

"Olivia, now's not the time," Rona said.

"I'm sorry," Olivia said, but with emotion. "I just don't know what to say."

Jorg looked around as if he'd just awakened and wasn't sure where he was.

"I'm leaving," I harshly reminded her. "Have you forgotten? I'm going to freeze to death. Can't you talk about fish after I'm gone?"

"I'm sorry, Jessica," Olivia said. She gave the impression of being genuinely sorry. She looked as sad as I felt.

My friends dropped their heads and shuffled their feet. I looked at each one in turn.

Rona was still on the verge of tears.

Jorg looked as if his best friend had died.

When Olivia first heard I was leaving, she'd thrown her arms around my neck and held on as if I was her sister. Tears trickled down her cheeks. How could she have so many tears? Why did she care? I thought she disliked me—immensely. I certainly didn't like her. At least I didn't used to. But her reaction made me stop and think. Maybe she wasn't so bad after all. She'd been so irritating on the ship.

I just couldn't bring myself to read the reports Captain Norris had ordered me to read on Akiane.

Olivia would often sit with Rona and me at lunch and ask me questions about the planet. I could tell by her questions that she knew the answers. She just wanted to show me how stupid I was. One day I got so fed up and angry with her that I read every report and memorized the information.

The next time she sat with us and preceded to interrogate me, I had the answers.

She smirked. At least, at the time, I thought she'd smirked. I had wanted to slap that smile off her face.

But now, thinking back on it, it might have been a smile of pride that I finally had the answers. I'd read the reports because of her.

Olivia was not the type to pamper or sympathize with anyone. Instead she aggravated people to the point of doing something about whatever the problem was.

I realized, to my utter surprise, I was going to miss our bickering. I was going to miss a lot of things. Rona and I had spent hours talking about our lives back on Earth and our future plans. Then there was Jorg. Tears threatened.

At least fish wouldn't make me cry.

"So all the fish are female," I said.

Olivia's head bobbed. "Yes," she said, snuffling.

"And the dogs, Rona? Find any males yet?" I asked.

"Not so far, but Lu is determined." She pulled her hand out of her glove and wiped tears. She attempted a smile.

"Maybe, by the time I get back, you'll both have something to show me." I tried to sound encouraging.

"Jessie," Jorg said. He looked self-conscious, as if he was about to say something embarrassing.

"What?" I asked. I was going to miss the sound of his voice, his smile, his jokes—him.

303

I wanted to take a step closer to him, gently press against him and lean my head on his shoulder. I wanted him to wrap his arms around me and hold me close. I wanted him to tell me not to leave, that he'd protect me from Cameron and Admiral Grossman. But what if I did take that step and he took a step away?

I didn't move. Why make a scene now?

The expression on his face changed. He had something to say, but didn't know how to say it. If there was something important to say, now was the time, even if Olivia and Rona were listening.

He looked me in the eye. His head dropped. His shoulders slumped. He seemed smaller. It was just like a man to wait until the last possible moment.

I held my breath. *Was* he going to ... to tell me not to go, that he couldn't live without me? I braced myself for what was coming. I was scared of what he was about to say. I had no idea what I would say or what I was supposed to say. I never thought this moment would come. Did I really want this?

My heart did a happy flip-flop. Yes, I did.

Finally, he stopped fidgeting. His head slowly rose. Resolve appeared in his eyes. He asked, "Will you bring back samples of any algae you might find?"

My heart stopped beating. A sigh escaped my lips. I'd let my imagination run away. Profoundly disappointed, I heard myself say, "Yes. The admiral made sure I have plenty of containers to bring samples back with me."

We stared at each other for what seemed like an eternity. He wasn't going to say it. Why should he? I was leaving and might never come back. Why start something now?

Or maybe it was just my imagination and there was nothing to say after all.

I turned to Olivia. "You want any fish?"

"Only if you find one that's male."
"How about you, Rona? Any requests?" I asked.
"Just you." She burst into tears.

Chapter 33

Lieutenant Jessica Hewitt
Love at First Sight

WE'D COME outside at dawn, but it was midmorning before the sleds were finally packed. The dogs were harnessed in place and were mostly quiet waiting for us to be on our way. Cameron was making his final check. Nu Venia stood to one side and stared at nothing.

One squirrelly white dog with a single red ear hopped in place as if the snow was burning his paws. He seemed anxious to be on his way and unwilling to wait any longer. Out of boredom, he attacked the flopping tail of the dog in front of him. That one, with a half-apricot, half-white face, turned to defend her rear.

Playful dogs make a lot of noise, growling as if angry or whining as if they were the victim. They come at each other with mouths wide open, but seem to gum each other as if they were toothless.

Squirrelly's running mate, a white dog with a red back and one large black spot on the side of his pink nose, joined in, but

Red-back was serious. His muzzle pulled back as he bared his teeth. He snarled and snapped as if he meant to tear into Apricot-face.

Red-ear looked at his running mate in surprise.

Apricot-face hunched her back, preparing for battle.

I didn't actually know which were male or female. I guessed by their mannerisms.

The all-white, lead dog moved as far from the fight as she could. Even Squirrelly backed off.

The harness prevented Red-back and Apricot-face from circling each other. They shifted from left to right, sizing the other up while planning their attack.

Just as they were about to leap at each other, Cameron jumped in between them. He held Red-back by the scuff of his neck in one hand and Apricot-face in the other. He kicked at Squirrelly, but didn't actually hit him. The squirrelly, Red-ear dog jumped out of the way.

"Enough. You will settle or you will stay behind," he said.

The dogs settled down as Cameron placed each in their proper place and returned to the other sled.

Then Squirrelly saw me. That dog actually looked as though he recognized me. In an effort to greet me, he walked toward me. He pulled on the harness. Five of the dogs moved with him. The wheel dogs hitched in front of the sled rolled over on their sides as if they were going to sleep. The two lead dogs got up and moved toward the other team. Three dogs from that sled came over to greet them. They nuzzled noses as if they were old friends who hadn't seen each other for quite awhile.

Squirrelly's partner, Red-back, snapped at one of the other lead dogs. That dog jumped him. Now they rolled entangling themselves in their harnesses. Cameron grabbed each of the fighting dogs.

They yelped in pain.

"Arechit, Addle!" he yelled at Red-back, "Or I'll leave you here! This is your last warning." The dog whined as if he understood.

Nu Venia ran to untangle their straps. Cameron held onto the dogs until she was finished.

"And you, Essal!"

Squirrelly dropped his head as if ashamed of the trouble he'd caused.

"Return," Cameron yelled at him.

Red-eared Essal crawled back to his place and lay down.

Cameron dropped the dogs he was holding in their places. "Stay, Addle!" he yelled, at the red-backed dog.

"Huth, you know better," he said to the all-white lead dog.

"One must stand here," he said to Nu Venia.

Immediately, she obeyed. She would watch over the other team and keep them from fighting and tangling the harnesses.

"One must stand here," he said to me, pointing to Essal's team.

Essal's head popped up. I swear that dog looked as if he were smiling. I wasn't going near him.

Who did Cameron think he was, anyway, ordering me around like that? Just because he's a priest, did he expect the world to obey him? I had no intentions of helping him or obeying him. It didn't matter to me if the dogs got tangled and delayed our departure.

"No," I said.

"I do not understand," Cameron said. I guess he wasn't used to anyone defying him.

Too bad. He wasn't my commander.

"I don't like dogs," I said. "I'm not standing by them."

"To keep untangling them will delay our leaving," he said.

And the problem with that was ...?

Essal's tail wagged excitedly. It was all he could do to lie there. Again, he moved to get up.

"Essal," Cameron warned him. He dropped back down, but his tail kept wagging while he watched me. "If you stand with Essal, he will be better able to keep in place," Cameron told me.

Nu Venia was standing between the lead dogs from the other team. Each rested its head against one of her thighs while she scratched their ears. They seemed content and wouldn't be any more trouble.

"Cameron," Nu Venia said, "I will watch over all of them."

Ignoring her, he said to me, "It is best to keep the teams separated."

She said, "I am able to keep both teams calm."

She was an appeaser.

I noticed the priests made no move to help.

A fisherman came to Cameron. "I will do as you request."

With a disciplinary look at me, Cameron handed the team over to the fisherman as he did his final check of the sleds. He pulled on straps to see if they were secured and pushed on the packed to make sure it wouldn't shift position.

Essal's eyes were bright with expectation that I would give him attention.

"Not on your life," I told him.

Disappointed, he dropped his head on his paws and stayed put.

And then it was time, just like that.

"We go," Cameron announced. He and the dog at his side started the journey. There were no last good-byes, last hugs or the shake of the hand. He turned and walked off as if he and his dog were going by themselves.

My stomach lurched. This was it. I couldn't look at my friends. If I did, I'd never be able to leave them.

Nu Venia turned from the lead dogs she'd been watching and followed Cameron. The team immediately followed her.

The fisherman stepped to the side of the team he'd been watching. That team fell in line.

All of them—Cameron, Nu Venia, and the two dog teams traveled in one long straight line.

I hesitated. How long before Cameron knew I wasn't with them? I could go back inside and hide, like a coward. My feet began to move, stepping in behind the second sled. With head down, my spirit crushed, one slow step after another, I followed.

As I reached the first small rise, I stopped before I crested it and turned to see if anyone was still watching.

Two shadowed figures stood at the edge of the habitat's roof. I couldn't see who they were, but I knew one of them was Adumie. Why did he hate me? What had I ever done to him? *I should survive just to spite him.*

I hadn't turned around looking for spite. I was looking for that last memory to take with me, someone who might miss me and remember me while I was gone. I wanted that last look that would comfort me.

The priests were already gone. The fishermen were headed south to open water, surrounded by their dogs. You'd think we were going for a casual walk and would be back in time for dinner. I watched as Jorg and Rona walked away. He draped a consoling arm around her shoulders. She rested her head on his shoulder as they re-entered the habitat.

It wouldn't take long for him to forget me. It wasn't as if we were committed. Rona was beautiful. Raven black hair, large dark doe-like eyes, beautifully full lips, and skin the color of polished bronze.

She was brilliant, easy to talk to with those cute little southern saying of hers.

Jorge would be a fool not to fall madly in love with her.

Uncontrollable tears sprang up. I wasn't good enough for him anyway. Not like Rona was.

She'd have him all to herself. It wouldn't take long for him to realize that she was perfect for him. We had never walked with his arm around me like that. We'd never even kissed. Now we never would.

Only Olivia stood watching. She was the last person I would see. She waved. I gave her a half-hearted wave back.

A sick feeling swept over me as I realized the real reason I'd resigned to my fait. I deserved this. It was my Karma for being such a horrible person, friend and daughter, not just to Mom, but also to Dad. I deserved every bit of what I was about to get.

I turned from Olivia.

With a complete sense of isolation, I descended the little hill and began my journey over snow-covered land toward a melting ice-covered ocean, to the North Pole of this planet where there were no answers, no hope, no destiny—just nothing.

LAST LOG ENTRY

Endurance
Faris Assetti
Eleven Years

Akiane tried to beat us, but we have persevered.

We have survived another gravitational storm. The dome stands. There is a volcano in the mountains. It appears to be dormant until the gas planet returns, but it is far from it.

Poisonous gas flowed down the mountain like fog. Those outside didn't make it back inside. The gas seeped into Endurance through the tunnels. Those in the gardens barely made it to the main buildings and safety.

After the gravitational storm was over, it only took hours for the winds to clear the air outside. But it took weeks for the air in our habitat to clear. Now we will install movable doors over the tunnel entrances to keep the poisonous gas outside.

The giant gas planet will come every 11 years. I doubt any of us will ever get used to it. Unfortunately it is something we will have to endure. We will call the event The Storm. Someone has named the gas planet after a Scandinavian God Loki, who brings devastation. The Storm brought much devastation to the land.

This world shook as if it might come apart. It literally changed the landscape. Some mountains are taller while others crumbled. The hot springs moved by several meters.

This is my last entry

In all this time, there have been no communications from Earth. Besides the one robotic ship, no other ships have come. We are on our own.

Of the 2,038 that began this journey only 852 survive the landing, more died afterwards. 453 people officially began the colony. As of this morning, with the two new births, we are now 511. We are growing.

This is my last entry. I am resigning my post. I'm not sure what I will do with myself. I can't go to the beach, put my feet up, and soak in the sun.

It will no longer be my responsibility to fix problems regarding the building complex. I will no longer arbitrate between disagreeing individuals. My days will be spent wandering the native gardens in the habitat and caring for my children.

I can't complain; it was my idea to retire and let another lead. It is the right thing to do. I have accomplished for more than I would have ever thought possible. Not only have I been a part of the start of a new world, I have gained friends who are closer than any I knew back on Earth. I have married the most wonderful and loving man in our entire galaxy. My greatest accomplishments have been to give birth to two magnificent girls and a son, and another is soon to arrive.

Life on Earth would never have been so sweet.

New Beginnings

She felt his presence before he spoke.

"I like your braids," Joe said.

Faris passed a hand over her hair. Cornrows ran from her forehead to the back of her head then dangled freely down her back. "Fatimah did it."

"I approve," he said with good-humor.

"So glad you do." Faris saved her last entry. "I'm ready." She sighed. She'd been captain for twelve years and leader of Endurance for eleven years. She had accomplished far more than she ever could if she'd remained as captain of *Falcon*.

"Now tell me. What has been decided?"

"Everything is ready, Captain," he said in a more serious tone.

"I'm no longer captain, Joe, I haven't been for a long time."

"About that," he said.

Faris swiveled in her hair to face him. "Father?"

314

He smirked. "You haven't called me that in a long time."

"Well if you're going to be formal, I thought I would too." They both laughed.

Faris would never have thought she and a Catholic Jesuit priest could be such good friends. *It's funny how life turns out*, she mused.

"We have decided," Joe said.

Faris had stayed in her office and had not attended the community meeting to choose a new leader. She didn't want her presence to influence the outcome.

"I don't think you should step down," he said.

"What?" She was shocked. "I don't understand." She pushed herself up from the chair. Joe lent her a helping hand. "Of course I should. If things had gone as originally planned, I'd be arriving back at WSC just about now and I'd be retiring, anyway."

"Well things have not gone as planned, have they?"

"No they have not," she agreed. "And you know what?"

"What?"

"I'm not the least bit sad."

"Good. Then you won't mind not retiring," Joe said.

"You've never been a tease before, Joe. Why start now?" Faris asked.

"No joke. It seems you are well loved," Joe said. "The community will not follow another."

Pride swelled deep inside Faris' heart. It spread up over her face. A little laugh followed. "I never expected."

Joe smiled at her reaction.

Then Faris sobered. "What do you think? Should I accept?"

"Of course you should, what else will you do with your time?" he asked.

She shrugged and turned from him as she considered the offer. She turned back to face him. "I'll do it under one condition."

He sighed. "Must there always be a condition with you? What will it be this time?"

"That we co-lead."

"Now you're the jokester?"

"My offer is as serious as yours," she said. "I may not be military, but I do represent authority. You represent the softer side of leadership."

"Softer side?"

"You're like a father to all of us."

"I'm a Jesuit Priest."

"I don't mean like that. You advise us with compassion and reason. You care for us with love," she said. "Spiritually, you care for us as though we are your children."

He bobbed his head from side to side and up and down as he thought about it.

"You've always had the job. Now it will be official," she said, hoping to convince him. "We both have our strengths."

"And we both make up for the other's faults," he said.

"Ah yes, our faults." Faris grimaced. "I'm afraid we have spent far too much time together, Joe."

"Complaints?"

"None." She reached her hand out. He took it. "You have been a good adviser to me and a good friend."

"And you to me," he agreed.

"Together we will lead Endurance and continue to bring people together into a community," she said.

They left her office. She slipped her arm through his. He placed his free hand over hers. They walked together into the gardens and joined the celebration.

"That robotic ship still sits outside," he said. "What should we do with the bags of seed and livestock DNA?"

"We can use the seeds, but do you really want herds of cattle or flocks of sheep roaming in our gardens?" she asked.

Joe shook his head. "Not really."

"It was a brilliant idea to create a native garden. It relieves the harness of winter. We should spend the next winter developing the garden," Faris said.

"We could build a separate dome for the livestock," Joe suggested.

"You ready to start another building project?" Faris asked.

"I guess not. I really don't think anyone is quite ready for another dome just yet," he said.

"I think we can wait on livestock. Save the DNA until we decide what to do with it," Faris said.

"What do you want us to do with the ship?"

"We should take it apart and use it for components and raw materials," she said.

"That will be a good five year summer project," he said.

"Just so. We wouldn't want to become too complacent."

Personal Log Continued

For a long time I was torn between my desire to return to Earth or stay on Akiane. I am glad I stayed. I cannot imagine my life on Earth being better than the one I have here. I look forward to the continual prosperity of our community.

I have always held to the belief that our true future and success lies in the next generation. And since I cannot ask another to do what I am unwilling to do, I married Adryel.

Our relationship started on a fishing trip, though at the time, I did my best to deny it. I held to the believe that as leader I should stand alone, but Joe, my very good friend, convinced me one leads best when one is at peace with their heart. I found my heart could only be at peace with Adryel.

Our fourth child comes in a few days. I can barely contain my joy at meeting this new little person.

If I were any more blessed, I would melt from pure joy.

People of Akiane
Book Two

Storm's Coming

By Phyllis Moore

Odds don't look good …

Lt. Jessica Hewitt is working her way across a frozen planet for no good reason. She's angry with WSC Space Force, which sent her to negotiate with an alien Earth colony. Now, for the sake of public relations, she's been ordered on this expedition.

She can barely tolerate her two native companions, who travel with their own agenda. She has an extreme dislike for dogs, but is traveling with thirty-three of them, all of whom want affection.

The planet Akiane is warming, whiteouts and blizzards are coming, as is a planet-shaking storm.

And things are only going to get worse.

If Jess wants to survive, she must cooperate with her companions, but first, she face down her old life.

***

To be notified of when *Storm's Coming* is published, sign up at MythRiderPublisher.com/ MooresMyths, where pre-sell, signed copies will be available.